Daisy May

Trevor L Evans

ADALA
Publishing

A self published title designed and produced by Adala Publishing
www.adalapublishing.com.au

 A catalogue record for this
book is available from the
National Library of Australia

ISBN 978-0-6485272-8-2 (Print)
ISBN 978-0-6485272-9-9 (eBook)

ACKNOWLEDGEMENTS

In this fictional novel I have used names of friends and colleagues I travelled with through time.

Special thanks though go to the following people: Captain William Farquhar (Bill) (deceased). Bill was the youngest man to obtain his Master's Ticket. I worked for him on his fishing trawler and he taught me about the sea and stars. Also to his wife Lesley (deceased) a true and dear friend.

Walter H. Wright (deceased) for having faith in me.

Jack Fox – a work colleague, he always used to say *In one stubby there are as many calories as in a T-Bone Steak.*

I would like to thank author Terry Barca for all his encouragement in getting me to actually write this novel.

My wife Jackie, for all her help, and understanding.

Also, special thanks go to Sonya Murphy of Adala Publishing.

London, England

The man stood in front of the tall windows. He was of average height, shoulders bent slightly forward. He had black hair that was going grey and balding on his forehead.

Blue smoke from his cigar curled up around his shoulders. From where he stood he could see Big Ben, the Houses of Parliament, the River Thames and the Tower of London. He could see people hurriedly walking up and down the street, the children trying to keep up with their parents and the double-decker buses, with their stairs curling up at the rear.

He watched as men were stacking sandbags in doorways, while others taped up windows, blacking them out so that light could not penetrate to the outside. This city of London was his England; England that he loved and cherished so much. When he closed his eyes, he could still see it. What was about to happen to his people, to England?

There was a knock at the door, and with his deep throaty voice he said, 'Come in!'

A tall, thin man entered the room. It was his secretary. 'Have you signed those papers yet, Winston?'

Winston turned around and looked at the man; took another deep draw on his cigar, and blew out the smoke. He walked over to his desk, placed his cigar in the ashtray and sat down in his chair. He picked up his whisky glass and took a sip. Still holding the glass in his hand, he looked down at the two documents and read the name on the first report 'The Castle'. The name of the captain, Jack Fox, below it. There was a lot of information about the old tramp steamer, and the history of its captain, Jack Fox. Winston read further down the document. He read that Jack Fox had started his life at sea as a cabin boy on a four-masted low sided clipper. When this clipper was decommissioned, Jack started crewing on a three-masted high sided Braque Sailing Clipper that carried part cargo and part paying passengers. Jack eventually obtained his Master's Ticket and was given a commission on a Tramp Steamer, of which he is still the captain today. There were glowing references from the Steamer's owners; Captain Fox was one of their most prized Captains, one hundred percent reliable. He did not bother reading any more but looked at the captain's name, and the vessel's name 'Castle'. Winston took another sip of his whisky and put the glass down. He picked up his fountain pen, unscrewed the top and wrote his signature next to the other.

He then looked at the other document, 'Daisy May'. She was a barque clipper; the name of her captain was William Farquhar. His mind went racing back to when he had been a passenger on this vessel many years ago. The memory had stayed in his mind, for Winston had a deep passion and love of the sea and the white sails; to him, it was the pure joy of being free. He looked at the name again. 'Daisy May', Captain William Farquhar. The memory of her was fresh in his mind. The Braque rose up and over the waves, she had high sides to keep the spray off of the decks. Her forecastle was forward, behind which was the lifeboat that was tied down. On the inside, she had a comfortable saloon, where you could play cards, read a book or relax. Everyone had a good view of the bow. Adjoining the lounge was the ship's galley, from which the cook would make yummy meals and delicacies. The captain's quarters were above the kitchen. Winston sighed good memories, pleasant memories. He looked again at the Captain's name, William Farquhar.

Further, Farquhar had joined Daisy when he was only fifteen years old and had been her skipper for thirty years, another Captain highly praised by their owners. But what impressed him most was that they talked about his *honesty and integrity, Captain William Farquhar would never bend from his principles. He did not touch alcohol, nor would he allow any on his ships. Winston's eyebrows rose, and he chuckled to himself as he finished his whisky. He then signed the document.*

He looked at both captains' names. 'God, help you, gentlemen. England needs you so desperately.'

Winston put the top back on his pen; placed it neatly on his desk, picked up his whisky glass, and drank the remains. He picked up his cigar and walked back to the window. As he drew once again on his cigar, he placed his two hands behind his back and said aloud, 'When my job is done, then I shall be free.' There was a knock at the door; a woman opened it and walked in.

She spoke in a soft, gentle voice, 'Pug, are you ready?'

'Yes, Clementine, I'm ready.'

He turned and walked back towards her. She held his overcoat out, he slipped his arms into it, and she pulled it up over his shoulders. He turned around and looked back at the desk, then reached out and took her hand.

'God help those men Clementine. God help them.'

'Yes, Winnie, yes, Winnie.'

They both turned, walked out the door and it closed behind them.

CHAPTER 1

The sun was setting to the port side. I watched it as it started to descend below the horizon, its golden rays touching every part of the vessel. I had a deep sadness within me. I had been on this old barque for over forty years. My Aboriginal mate, Jacko and I had come to Melbourne looking for work when we were both fifteen years of age. I was born on the Diamantina River in Queensland and my mother brought Jacko and me to Lakes Entrance in Victoria. Jacko had always been my best mate. He was the helmsman, and he loved the responsibility. In his way, Jacko was highly intelligent. He had an in-depth knowledge of everything that surrounded him; everything that was in his world. Jacko would say things to me but they wouldn't make sense. However, the next hour, the next day, it all made sense, and we needed to be prepared for whatever may occur.

Colin was the coxswain. He'd been on the *Daisy May* longer than me and now he was an old man with a rough cough that was deep in his lungs. Although Colin had stopped smoking that stinking pipe, most of the time he still had it in his mouth. Then there was Ted, the First Mate; he'd also been on the *Daisy May* longer than I had. Ted was a dependable man. Then there was Michael, a top man, who could repair almost anything. Michael was a sailmaker by trade and the sails on this vessel were his; no-one interfered with them. Old Les was the Cook. He had a round face with sparkling eyes and a Roman nose. Les made excellent coffee, soup and biscuits whenever we wanted them. The rest of the crew was an odd assortment of men. The only home they ever had was the sea; it was their life. And their reasons for being at sea? I never asked.

However, the *Daisy May* had become tired, the barnacles and the growth of weed on her hull were holding her back. There was too much drag, and her sails were patched and had been repaired too many times. Her ropes, rigging, her blocks and sheaves were worn and loose. The owners would not spend money on her. She would just be tied up, stripped of her masts, and used as a coal barge or worse, broken up for what money they could get for her. This voyage would be her last. The deep pain of loss, despair and frustration bit deep into me, but it wasn't just for *Daisy May*, it was for her crew. She had become a part of us. *Daisy May* was our mother protector from the hardships of the world on land. We all moved as one; carrying out tasks with our family. What was going to happen to our family, to our mother, the *Daisy May?*

CHAPTER 2

I was still watching the golden rays of the sun on her masts, sails and rigging when I turned my head to my left. There was Cat, sitting on the bench looking out of the window. Cat seemed to be watching the golden rays, as I was. He was a big tomcat, white with grey patches and highly intelligent. Jacko and Cat would stare into each other's eyes as though their minds were locked together; a depth of communication which I could not fathom. It was beyond me. I never knew where Cat came from, some far distant port; he just appeared from nowhere. Every time we were in port, he would be first off the gangplank, swaggering with his testicles swinging between his back legs, his tail twitching back and forth; his ears swept back. At the bottom of the gangplank he would look around with what seemed to be a grin on his face. When we were about to leave, he would be the last on board. With large pieces of fur missing and a lot thinner, he would swagger to the galley where Les would feed him. Then he would be back on the bench in the wheelhouse as if it was rightfully his. Cat belonged to Colin, who was the only person who could touch him. I would often see Cat on his lap. Colin would be talking about days long gone; memories good and not so good.

He would laugh or take a deep breath and sigh, and Cat would look up and seem to know what he was saying. They were the best of mates; they were companions.

One day I reached out to touch Cat and as quick as lightning, that paw, with those sharp claws, struck my hand. I snapped my hand back and licked the scratches. Cat just stared at me for a moment then turned to watch the last rays of the sun.

Les appeared alongside me with a bowl of soup, a cup of coffee and fresh bread rolls. 'This is the last of those supplies, Boss.'

Les could make any food taste good – chicken, beef or pork – and he could make a damn good curry. He put the food down in front of me, and as I turned I saw tears were welling up in his eyes. I put my hand on his shoulder.

'I don't know what's going to happen Les. We can only wait and see.'

Just as I said that Cat sat up, straight tail twitching behind. He stared at both of us. What did Cat know that we didn't? Could he see into the future?

Les's voice broke through my thoughts. 'You best have that soup Skipper. It is going to be a very long night, and you may have many sail changes. The wind is very finicky; it is not the best place to be.' He looked at Cat and said, 'Come on, Cat, I'll feed you.' Cat jumped down off the bench and followed Les out of the wheelhouse.

I thought to myself, *I command every man on this vessel but have no control over that damn Cat!*

CHAPTER 3

We had reached Latitude 45°, just up from the Roaring Forties at Latitude 43°. We were now entering the *Eye of the Needle*. Sailors, through time, had named this stretch of water. For sailing ships it was like threading cotton through the eye of a needle because it was very hard to navigate. On the starboard side was King Island; on the port side was the Australian mainland with its rugged coastline and tall cliffs. So many ships have perished in this treacherous stretch of water; it was a nightmare. Every captain prayed to the gods that wind and tide would be favourable to him. The tides could suck you into the mainland if you didn't have the wind in your sails, or draw you back onto King Island on your starboard side. Rocks and many smaller islands protrude where you least expect. So, as Les said 'A long night ahead and there will be many sail changes.'

I wanted to be at Port Phillip Heads, Queenscliff by 10 am. That would give me high water on the South Channel, it's a narrow channel with sandbanks and mud banks on either side. If I were to get into trouble, I would have more water under my keel. I would need more water since my hull was loaded down with weeds and barnacles. If I could maintain five knots average speed, I would be there on time and the tide would assist me. By now darkness had fallen and I found Jacko at my side. He looked at the chart and my logbook. 'You have planned that good Skipper, but you always do, don't you?'

I just turned, looked him in the face, grinned and winked at him. He gave me that warm smile and shook his head. I thought to myself you have been my friend for so long, no matter what happens, I'll take you with me wherever I go.

'How about some sleep Skipper? I'll call you when I see the lighthouse.'

I stepped aside from the wheel. Jacko's eyes glanced at the compass and barometer as he took over. I picked up my supper and coffee, went into my cabin, and closed the door. I may rest, but I don't think I'm going to sleep, not at the beginning of the Eye of the Needle.

I was half awake and half asleep and my mind went back to years gone by when Jacko and I were on the Diamantina River. We lived on a Cattle station where Mum was the cook. She worked hard for too many hours and with no thanks. One day the foreman of the Cattle station, they used to call him Boss Cocky, walked up to me.

'The Boss wants you. Go up to the big house and see him.'

I was surprised. Usually, you stayed away from the big boss's house, and if you walked past you didn't talk to anyone. I walked up to the big house and stood looking at it. There was a big verandah right around the house where you could sit when it was scorching or keep dry on the odd occasion it might rain. The verandah had bluestones around the base, then weatherboards on the upper structure, with significant imposing steps up to the front door.

I walked up to the steps onto the verandah where there was a young girl about twelve years of age sitting on a swinging chair looking very bored; she was slim with blond hair. She stared at me with a cool look. 'What do you want boy?' she said.

'I've been told to see the boss man.'

'Who are you, boy?'

'I am ME!' I said, rolling my eyes.

The girl slowly stood up and moved slightly from side to side. 'What's your name?'

'Bill Farquhar.' I stood straight and stared right into her face. Somehow she seemed to soften slightly. She grinned, she liked what she saw. The girl moved slightly to one side, one shoulder back toward the wall. I didn't realise it, but she was flirting with me. She brushed her hair back; I felt something deep inside my stomach but didn't understand what it was.

'Wait here, Bill.' She disappeared through the fly screen door; it was impossible to see through the door; it was dark inside.

A big man appeared at the door. 'Who are you?' he bellowed.

'Bill Farquhar boss. Cocky boss sent me over.'

'Come in.'

I opened the flyscreen door and stepped in. Inside there was a long hallway with doors on either side. The girl was leaning against the wall, one leg bent up, her dress tight against her developing chest. She looked at me with a cheeky grin. The boss carrying a canvas satchel stepped out of a room, he looked at his daughter, and then looked at me, and back at his daughter. He didn't like what he saw.

'Lesley get back in the kitchen and help your mother.'

The girl turned and went down the hallway towards a door at the back. She turned and gave me a warm smile, then disappeared into the room. *I must remember her name. Lesley*, I thought.

'You are the cook's boy?' I nodded in acknowledgement. 'I want you to take this satchel to the Post Office in town, I know it's getting a bit late in the day, but I need it there tonight, there tonight,' he repeated. He handed me the satchel, as he pushed the flyscreen door open. I walked down the steps, threw a blanket over the waiting horse and put the satchel over my shoulders, then swung myself up onto the horse. She was a beautiful chestnut mare, a reliable and robust horse. We had an understanding between us. I pushed her into a gallop, then after a while eased her back into a canter. She was so easy to ride. Two and a half hours later we arrived in town, which was just a small pub, five shops and a general store. The post office was part of the general store.

I left the horse tied up to the rail and walked into the post office. A big cheerful woman looked at me as I dropped the satchel onto the counter.

'What's this, boy?'

'The mail from the Johnson station,' I replied.

She opened the satchel and took the letters out. There was an additional envelope which had her name written on it. She opened it and took out some money. She then put stamps on the letters, counted the money and put the change back into the envelope and back into the satchel. She handed it back to me.

I fastened the buckle back up on the satchel as I thanked the lady. She nodded and smiled back at me.

I returned to my horse and led her to the water trough, gently patting her neck while she drank. 'We just made it girl; we just made it. They're closing the store now.'

I swung myself back onto the horse and headed her for home at a gentle canter. The cool evening air was drifting in as the light was starting to fade. The first stars were twinkling against the dark blue of the evening sky. My thoughts went to my horse. *You're tired out, aren't you girl, we'll stop for the night.*

I looked at the riverbank. There was a sheltered spot underneath some bushes and a tree to tie the horse. I led her down to the river so she could drink. After I drank some water we went back up the bank. I tied her loosely to a log. Drovers hobbled their horses for the night to stop them wandering, but I didn't have a hobbling strap. I patted her on the neck, *Thanks for the day, girl; thank you.* I crawled underneath the bush to sleep. It was a windless night, millions of stars now dotted the night sky. A full moon was starting to rise, its silver rays touching the desert. I was warm and comfortable and quickly drifted off into a deep sleep.

I woke suddenly to the horse being disturbed. I knew something was there, but I couldn't see what. The horse pulled back on the loosely tied reins. A cold shiver ran down my spine as I heard what sounded like a small calf caught in a wire fence. The next moment dust-filled air started to swirl around me. I was in a small whirly, whirly of dust. The horse reared up in fright, broke free of the log and galloped off. I knew I couldn't stop it. I hugged the satchel tightly when I heard snorts and groans, something was scratching on the ground. The bushes around me started swaying in the wind. I knew to survive you shouldn't run. I slowly moved backwards squinting into the dark trying to see what was there. Soon I was at the top of the bank, still clutching the satchel as if it gave me strength and support. I slowly turned and then started running as fast as I could toward home.

I was sweating and shaking when I stopped running. I looked back but could only see the full moon. I half chuckled to myself when I realised I'd left the blanket behind. I'm not going back there, but mum will kick my backside for losing the blanket. I continued on towards home. Just as daylight was starting to peer over the desert I saw two horses but only one rider approach, it was Jacko with a fresh horse. I slumped down on the ground, physically and emotionally exhausted.

I heard Jacko's familiar voice boom out, 'Where have you been Bill? The horse came back without you.' He jumped off his horse and handed me a small water bag and some food. 'Mum said this was for you, but I know she wants me to have some too,' and gave one of those small chuckles of his. I told him what had happened during the night.

Jacko said, 'Bill; we never sleep there, that's where the Widgee lives, we never go there, you made him very angry, you lucky he let you go, he must know you're one of us, you are my brother.'

I woke up with a start. I could feel *Daisy May* moving; I knew that the waves were coming from her stern; the wind in her sails was gentle. I looked at the clock on the wall and thought, *I've got more time to rest; Daisy May feels happy.* I drifted back once again to sleep, to have dreams that went back into my past…

Jacko's father passed away a month ago; he was an elder of his people, *The Keeper* they called him, one who takes care of the problems within the lives of his people. Jacko walked up to me one evening, 'Bill; tonight I go with my people; you cannot follow; it is not a place for white folks. We must go back to the time before the time, to our ancestors, I have spoken with mum, she knows as she has sat with the elders.'

I felt lost inside as Jacko and I did most things together. It was another beautiful night with a full moon soon to be rising, and a star-studded sky. I watched Jacko and his people walking off into the desert; soon they were gone. My thoughts went deep, *where have they gone, why are they walking off into the desert, that's where they hold ceremonies, but I've always been with them before.* I watched the full moon start to rise over the horizon, the silver light began to shimmer on the rocks and on the tips of the leaves on the trees. I watched the long shadows formed by the moon. The Cattle didn't move, it was as if they were feeling the magic energy, they were basking in it.

I could not contain myself; I had to know why Jacko had gone without me, where had his people gone? I started to walk in the same direction Jacko and his people had gone, after a short distance he could hear them tapping their nulla nullas* together. It was a rhythm I had often heard before in ceremonies. There was a small rise in the ground, and I carefully walked up it, when I got near to the top I sheltered myself against a small bush and peered over the bank. I could see all the people around a fire, they were stamping on the ground, tapping their sticks together, white paint markings all over their bodies. The elders were sitting in a row behind the dancers, and Jacko was sitting with them. Why was Jacko sitting with the elders?

I felt a cold shiver rush down my spine. The bushes started to sway and bend around me, but there wasn't any wind! Once again that swirling dust cloud began to swirl, I heard scratching on the ground, and the same noise I'd heard once before. I started to panic, I was shivering and despite the temperature I felt cold. The dancers had stopped dancing. They turned and were looking in my direction. Jacko and the elders stood up, and pointed to me.

I panicked, turned and ran straight back home, and into my bedroom. I crawled under the blankets. I couldn't stop shivering. I felt as though something had possessed me. Whatever it was I didn't know, but I thought it was very, very angry.

It was 4:30 am, the time when Mum got up to cook breakfast for the station hands. She was shaking me. 'Wake up, wake up Bill,' she said in an angry voice, 'you could not respect Jacko's wishes could you? You had to go and see for yourself, his people are very angry with you. When it

---

* club for use in hunting and fighting. Often with a knob on one end and a slightly shaped point on the other

is daylight you go back and see the elders, you have broken their laws!'
She turned and walked off.

I couldn't decide what was worse, letting mum down, letting Jacko
down, facing the elders or facing the anger of the widgee? Once daylight came I went to see the elders, who were all sitting around a small
fire, I walked up to them with my head bowed. One of them pointed to
the ground motioning me to sit with them. They didn't say anything for
a while, then one of the elders spoke in this native language.

'Bill, we know you and Jacko will leave this place and will travel to
many other places far, far away, where you will be with water you cannot
drink. You and Jacko are brothers, but you are white, you can be with us,
but you cannot be part of us, we are the dream people. What is going
to happen to us we do not know, and we do not talk about it. Because
Jacko is your brother you want to be with him, we accept this, but now
Jacko has taken his father's place. He is now the Peacemaker, he is an
elder of his people. He now sits at the Billabong where his father had
for many years before, on the stump of the old tree, watching the Eagles,
so that they can give him wisdom and protect him for us, his people. All
the elders reached forward and made the mark of a serpent in the sand.

I stood up and went back to the cattle yards, past the big house, to
the Billabong with the glittering water. There was Jacko sitting on the
old stump, watching the Eagles fly high. I walked up and stood beside
him. Nothing was said for a while, and then Jacko chuckled to himself.

'The Widgee frightened you, didn't he? He was very, very angry, but
I told him once again that you are my brother and you are looking after
me. The Widgee laughed out loud and said "who will be looking after
you both? You are very funny."' Jacko looked up at me.

'Thank you, Jacko. Mum will feed us now.' We both started to run
back to the cookhouse. It was a race to see who got there first.

One day Jacko and I were given some grub in little sacks which we slung over the front of our horses, as we set off just with a rough blanket as a saddle, to find stray cattle. Jacko never seemed to get lost; he always knew where he was. 'No worries,' he would say, 'No worries.' Late the next evening, we found the cattle and decided to camp for the night. We lit a fire and cooked our grub. When we awoke the sun was rising on the horizon, it was shimmering on the red rocks and earth around us. I saw something glinting on an outcrop of rock. I walked over to see that it was a small rock. I picked it up, spat on my fingers and rubbed it. The rock was smooth and full of colours, the like of which I had never seen before.

'Jacko! Bring the water bottle!' I yelled.

I poured some water onto the surrounding rock, and we were both amazed at what we saw. We took our knives out of their sheaves and eased out the glittering rock. Oh, how it sparkled in the sunlight. We grinned at each other.

'These must be worth some money. Let's see how much we can get for them.'

We both had two handfuls each and put them into our sacks. We herded the cattle back to the homestead but never said a word to anyone about what we had found.

The next day we went into the local town. There was a shop there that sold rocks, all sorts of strange little rocks. We went inside and put a couple of bits of our rock on the counter. The man behind the counter looked at us for a moment.

'What do you little urchins want?'

'We found this boss; what do you think?'

The man picked a piece up in his fingers and scoffed.

'It's just bloody shit; useless, worthless rock. Now bugger off and stop wasting my time.'

I grabbed the rocks and we ran out of the shop. On the way back to the cattle station we stopped at a creek and washed the rock and put it back into one of our sacks. It was our treasure, so we told no-one.

A couple of weeks later, we were again sent out to retrieve lost cattle, and we came across some men pushing a lot of dirt around with big machines. What were they doing? We rode up to one of the men and Jacko said, 'What you do, boss?'

The man spun around, surprised. 'Where the hell did you come from?'

'Just roundabout over there.'

The man took his hat off and wiped his forehead. Shaking his head, he looked at both of us. He studied us, confused. A black boy, hair like a loose mop and a white boy, dirty, scruffy, both sitting on horses without saddles. From where did they come? We were miles from anywhere.

'What are you boys doing here?'

'Looking for stray cattle.'

He paused for a few minutes. The next moment we were surrounded by men, one of them said to the others, 'Have you ever seen anything like this in your life before?'

They all shook their heads and laughed. I took some of the rock out of my pocket and held it in the palm of my hand. A tall man, older than the rest, took a piece and examined it.

'How much do you want for this?'

'Whatever you can give us,' I said.

He brought some notes out of his pocket; more money than I had ever seen, and took the rest of what was in my hand and put it in his handkerchief and walked off.

The next moment the other blokes gave us all the money they had for the rest of our stash. Then they fed us with heaps of good tucker, huge steaks, eggs, and big sticky things with jam in the middle of them. We filled our bags up with the food. When we got back to Mum, we told her the story and gave her the money.

She hugged us both and said. 'We're leaving here now; we've got enough money.'

And soon we were in Paradise – Lakes Entrance by the sea in Victoria.

I suddenly woke up with Jacko's hand on my shoulder.

'You are starting to talk a lot in your sleep, Skipper!' He grinned at me and flashed those big white eyes. As he turned to walk out of my cabin, he said, 'They were good days, Skipper, but I don't think those guys were stupid.' I sat up in my bunk and just shook my head and grinned. That's Jacko!

I walked into the wheelhouse. The night was dark, the moon hadn't quite risen. Jacko's eyes flitted to the port side. I saw the flashes of the Cape Otway Lighthouse; the sequence was three flashes fifty seconds, then another three flashes fifty seconds, then a third three flashes fifty seconds. We were right on course.

We were in the Eye of the Needle. I walked out of the wheelhouse and took the bell rope in my hand and pulled. Ted and Colin appeared out of nowhere. 'Put half the crew to rest and get the remainder up on deck and tell them to sharpen up.' I looked at the sea and the wind in *Daisy May*'s sails. I turned to Ted and Colin, but Colin had stepped back and put a piece of rag to his mouth; he coughed a deep cough, there was gagging in his throat. Ted and I saw the pain in his eyes and the blood on the rag. I walked up and put an arm around his shoulders and Ted walked up alongside me.

'Colin, we will take her through the Eye of the Needle one last time, and we will do it together. Give the men a good meal; they are going to need it as tonight is going to be a long one, as will tomorrow.'

I slapped them both on their shoulders and walked back into the wheelhouse. I leaned against Jacko for support. My emotions were in turmoil, but I had to stay in control, now we were going through the Eye of the Needle, the dreaded section of the sea outside of Port Phillip Heads.

CHAPTER 4

I stood in the wheelhouse with Jacko. I was watching him as he stood in front of the wheel. Even though we had been together for so long, sometimes I still found it hard to get close to him. Jacko lived in his world, where he was safe and secure. He didn't sleep in the forecastle with the other men. He had found himself a special place in the *Daisy May* to hang his hammock, his private place.

My mind went racing back to the early days, so long ago. There was no work or money in Lakes Entrance; the fishing had dried up, so Jacko and I decided to look for work in the city. We hitched a ride on a steam train which was carting railway sleepers to the city.

We arrived at the Big Smoke early on a cold, damp, wet morning. We were told if we wanted work to stand outside of Halfords store in Flinders Street, just down from Spencer Street, under the railway bridge. There were about fifty to sixty men crowded to the edge of the footpath, eagerly looking up at gruff man standing in the back of a cart. He held a club in one hand which he used to point at several men who ran forward and climbed into the cart. He looked down at me. I glanced at Jacko. With a deep, gruff voice, he said to us, 'You two, get up on the cart.'

We didn't wait; we climbed in and sat down on our swags. One of the men looked down at us. 'You are a lucky pair!' We didn't realise at the time what he was saying; we didn't understand how many men were looking for work to support and feed their families.

After a short journey we were on the wharf beside a sailing vessel. We were told to go on board. We were going to be working in the hull loading sacks into cargo nets. It was hard work, hot and sticky, with no fresh air. By the end of the day we had finished unloading the vessel.

We climbed out and saw a tall, thin man watching us from above; the other men said that he was Captain Walter Wright. He had a small moustache, and when he removed his hat, we saw that he had lost the hair on top of his head. We saw a bucket of water with a ladle, and though we were very thirsty we drank slowly, we had learned in the outback not to drink water fast.

The Captain walked up to us and in a slow, gentle voice, with the power of command asked, 'Where are you two lads from?'

'From Lakes Entrance, sir.'

'So, you have come to Melbourne looking for work?'

'Yes, sir.'

'I'm looking for two more men for my crew, are you interested?'

I did not hesitate, 'Yes, we are.'

He looked into my eyes as if he could see my very soul and said, 'Put your swags in the galley and get something to eat.' He shouted out 'Colin! These two will do; bed them down.' Colin nodded to him, walked over to us, and stared at us briefly.

'I'm the coxswain on this vessel, do as I say, and never question me. Follow me.'

Over nine years Captain Walter Wright made me study everything about the sea. Ports, harbours, reefs, sandbanks, longitude, latitude, the stars, the position of the sun. He told me to look at the mast and the shadow it forms on the sea. Guess the length of that shadow, and you will know where you are. Keep checking your chart. He told me lighthouses have their unique flashes, all around the world, look at the sequence, look at your map and your books. You will know exactly where you are. The markers in a channel are all the same except for one place in the world, and that was America.

'I was looking for more crew, but I was looking for a certain type of man. When the foreman picked you both up at Halfords Store, it was for a reason.' Captain Walter Wright once told me.

One day we arrived in Sydney Harbour and tied up at a wharf. Captain Walter Wright walked up to me and said in his gruff voice, 'Clean your hair lad and have a good wash. Put on a clean shirt and trousers and clean your shoes. You've got ten minutes!'

Jacko helped me to clean my shoes, and as I stood in a clean shirt and trousers with a sharp crease down the front of both legs, he handed me my box of papers. 'I think you will want these Bill.'

I looked straight into his eyes and knew I should do as he said. I had learned long ago not to argue with him and took the box.

'Follow me, boy,' the Captain said.

We arrived at an office and went up to the secretary. The Captain put a bundle of papers on the desk, and told me to sign them. The young clerk gave me a pen. I dipped it in ink and signed my name on each document, but I did not know why. The young lady took them, blotted the signatures, and put them into a folder. She gave me a warm and friendly smile, glanced at the Captain, and then went through a set of glass panelled doors. We followed her into a large room. Four sea captains were sitting at a long desk. There were models of ships in glass cabinets – sailing vessels, steamers and other fancy ships. I was overwhelmed. All four men stood up and greeted Captain Walter Wright with great respect, shaking his hand, as good friends would do.

One of the men said, 'Please sit down, gentlemen.' The door opened, and a young man and a young lady came in. The young man held a tray in his hand, and the young lady took cups and saucers and placed them in front of each captain. She put a teapot, sugar bowl and milk jug on the table, and then quickly glanced at me. Her eyes were big and bright; she was beautiful. I never see ladies like this at sea, I thought to myself. I quickly snapped back to the moment.

'Captain, is this the young man you've been telling us about?'

'Yes.'

'How old are you, lad?'

'Twenty three sir.' The captains started asking me questions which seemed to go on for hours. Some I had to think about, some I didn't know, so I would reply, 'I don't understand the question, sir.' They looked at each other and grinned.

'Could you please leave us for a moment young man, and wait outside?'

I got up from my chair and did as my mother had told me when I was younger, placed the chair back underneath the table, took three paces backwards, and walked out of the door, closing it behind me. I sat, waiting and waiting. The secretary occasionally glanced up from her work and smiled at me. I could hear the men laughing behind the door. I watched the big clock on the wall and listened to it, tick, tick, tick.

Finally, the door opened, and a warm voice boomed out, 'Come in, William Farquhar.' All four men stepped forward and shook my hand.

Captain Walter Wright stepped forward, he was beaming from ear to ear. He had some papers in his hand, and he handed them to me. I slowly put my hand out and took them; he didn't let go of them for a moment; he just stared into my face.

'Let me be the first to call you Captain William Farquhar!'

I heard the other four men chuckling and laughing to each other; they all said, 'Congratulations, Captain!'

I was shocked and surprised. 'Am I now Captain William Farquhar?'

The Captain stepped forward and put his hand on my shoulder, 'I am an old man and must retire. You are now the captain of the *Daisy May*. I know that you will love her as much as I have. She is now your wife, so love her, and she will love you back. Good luck, young man, good luck!' He turned and looked at the other gentlemen, nodded his head and walked out of the office. I never saw him again.

'Jacko, the wind is strengthening, alter course north two degrees.' I walked out of the wheelhouse and Ted was there waiting for me. 'Stow the fore royal, main royal and gaff topsail,' I told him.

I was worried about how much the rigging could take, but it had been a good night, and the wind had stayed favourable. Daylight had started to rise; the sky was cloudy; just small white caps on the sea. Then we saw it, or rather heard it. The bell bobbing up and down on its buoy. Everybody smiled. This would be the last bell, the Bell of Good Hope. It was at the entrance to Port Phillip Bay.

I shouted out to Jacko, 'Northeast forty-five degrees.'

His voice came bouncing back. 'Northeast, forty-five degrees, Skipper.'

I walked back into the wheelhouse, put my hand on Jacko's shoulder, and said, 'Your boys are home again, Mum. Your boys are home!'

We were entering Port Phillip Heads, heading for a berth in Port Melbourne, but we were not quite back yet. This was one of the most dangerous entrances to a major shipping port in the world, especially if you were under sail and relying on your wits. It was life or death for your vessel and your crew. We were looking for Point Lonsdale Lighthouse overlooking the 'Rip', a narrow channel between two rocky outcrops. It was the only place Port Phillip could discharge its water and receive it. Slack water gave you little time to play with, so we needed to see the lighthouse. It was on the port side when entering the bay. The hazard beam flashed twice every fifteen seconds, but you were looking for the black ball, it told you what the tides were doing, rising up or down depending on the tide.

The light had a range of twelve nautical miles, but if you had a man on your foremast, you could see even further. Today Frank was sitting on the top of the foremast, and he shouted, 'Light ahead.'

I cupped my hand over my mouth and called out, 'How many flashes?'

'I counted twice every fifteen seconds,' Frank yelled back at me.

I raised my thumb into the air. 'Right on course!'

Jacko just grinned at me and shook his head. Then I heard Captain Walter Wright's voice in my head, *Take her in as a lady, fully dressed!* I snapped my head back in total surprise. Jacko was looking at me with a silly grin all over his face.

'You heard him, boss, didn't you?' I just stared at Jacko.

'He's been with us a long time, boss!'

I shook my head and walked out of the wheelhouse. There was Colin, leaning on the rail on the stern, a rag to his mouth and coughing. Ted, hands behind his back, looking forward, waiting for my command. I walked up behind him.

'Ted get the crew together on deck, get Frank down from the topsail, and gather all the lads around.'

I stood at the door to the wheelhouse so Jacko could hear. Les had walked up beside me.

'Well you all know that this will be the last time *Daisy May* will enter her home port. We are going to take her in as a lady, fully dressed, and show them all what a real lady looks like! Some of you will never go to sea again, and you've been on board *Daisy* a long time, and she has been your mother, your home. We are going to give her the love she's given us, sail her in with pride; we are the crew of the *Daisy May*, and we are going to raise every single piece of canvas. We are going to take this lady into Port Phillip heads, jive down the south channel and escort her into Melbourne with the respect she deserves.'

Then I shouted out an order to the crew, 'Snap to it lads.'

Every man ran to his station or climbed the rigging; waiting for Colin's command. He stared at me, tears pouring down his cheeks. I had never seen him cry before. He shook his head, stepped forward, and shouted out at the top of his voice; it boomed out as it had done in the old days, 'Fore- royal, fore topgallant, main topgallant, staysail, main top staysail, gaff topsail.'

The flying jib and the inner jib had already been set. Colin's voice carried to the top of the mast; bright and sharp, the mainsail had been reefed, and he just laughed and said, 'Let her go!'

I saw him take a deep breath and saw the pain in his eyes, but he just nodded, turned, and went back to the stern. I took myself back to my duties; every man had performed his job flawlessly. Ted was still shouting orders, 'Tie this; lash that.'

I watched Michael looking at the sails and rigging; I walked up alongside him, 'Yes, Michael, she hasn't had sail like that on her for a long time.' He didn't turn around, he just slowly walked down the deck, checking, looking at everything. Ted glanced at him and then at me. I saw the worried looks on both their faces. Would the rigging and spas and yard-arms; yokes and shackles take the pressure again? Her hull was sluggish, not sliding through the water, as it should do. They both turned and looked at me. I just raised my eyebrows and hunched my shoulders.

The Point Lonsdale Lighthouse had an observatory where they recorded all shipping entering and leaving Port Phillip Bay; they also had a set of lights. If you were too far to starboard, you would see a red light; if you were in the channel, you would see a green light. The man who designed it was a seaman or a captain of a sailing vessel.

Daisy May had a motor to turn a prop shaft. It was a Gardiner six cylinder 10 PHP direct reversing semi-diesel engine, but it hadn't been running for a long time. In its day, it did a good job, but it had become tired and unreliable, so it was out of the question to use it upon entering Port Phillip Bay.

We could now see the entrance to the Bay. I had to keep my emotions locked away, but it still didn't stop the pain. I could see a vessel starting to come out of the entrance. I picked up my telescope and could see the ship was moving incredibly fast.

Flying the Australian flag on her stern, this was the Pilot boat. We watched it racing towards us. Ted had already opened a small door on the bulwarks and thrown down a rope ladder. The red pilot boat passed us at high speed in a full turn and came alongside, a man standing on her bow, hanging on for dear life. The pilot boat slowed to our pace. The man jumped, caught the rope ladder and clambered on board. He was a Navy lieutenant. I stood facing the doorway, with my hands behind my back. As he stepped on board, he seemed confused and uncomfortable. He glanced up at the sails and the surroundings and looked straight at me.

'Good morning, sir. Lieutenant Fraser, sir. Permission to come on board, sir.'

I stepped forward and put out my hand. 'You have my permission, Mr Fraser. If you'd like to come into the wheelhouse and check the papers.'

He followed me into the wheelhouse, took his notebook out of his pocket and laid it on the bench. He checked my logbook and papers and made a few notes in his book. Les brought in coffee, one for Jacko and me and one for Mr Fraser. He looked up and stared at Jacko for a few moments.

'This Aborigine, he is your helmsman sir?'

'Yes, he is the finest helmsman a man could ever have. He can see over the horizon, no white man I know can do that.' I just looked at him. Jacko put his fist up to his collar, gently rubbing his knuckles up and down his shirt. He took them away and blew on them. Mr Fraser turned to me.

'Captain, I have never taken a sailing ship like this into Melbourne, this is my second day at this job on my own!' I liked this young man; he was not afraid to tell the truth. I put my hand on his shoulders.

'Have your coffee lad and we will take the *Daisy May* into Melbourne together, she won't let us down.'

Now things started to get serious. I was watching the wind, it was just kissing the water, but it was keeping our sails full. I watched seagulls at the entrance, dipping and diving, playing in the wind. They were letting me know the direction and strength of the wind which would help us once we were inside the entrance. I knew Jacko was listening with a grin all over his face.

'Mr Fraser, would you suggest that we hug the port side of the entrance to give us more turning power into the South Channel?'

He looked at me with a worried expression on his face. I glanced at Jacko on the helm and back at Mr Fraser. Mr Fraser knew what I was saying. 'Helmsman three degrees to your port side.'

Jacko's voice boomed out. 'Three degrees to port sir.'

We were starting to enter the rip and I could see the green light on the hill. Mr Fraser nodded to me, I nodded back. That's when I noticed a small fishing boat anchored right on the edge of the channel. He was within his rights as he was anchored directly on the brink of the channel. He must have seen us coming, but he, no doubt, would be a little bit cocky knowing he was within his rights. I walked past Jacko to the other door.

'Get as close as you can Jacko, but keep it legal. Make sure he doesn't forget to stay out of the way of a sailing vessel!' I saw Ted looking at me. He had noticed the small fishing boat as well and was waiting for my command to jive to the starboard. I just nodded at him, and he grinned back at me. He knew what I was up to!

As we entered Port Phillip Bay, the wind was very favourable, gentle on her, keeping our sails full. It would be there in the right quarter, just over our port stern. We got closer to the fishing vessel, I was watching the ship and the beauty of Port Phillip Bay, majestic, tranquil but full of life. The town of Sorrento started to appear on our starboard bow; Queenscliff to our port. You could easily see the old fort and the two guns. Pope's Eye was to our starboard. I could now make out the buoy marks to sandbanks, and the flashing light. Number Two Buoy would be on our port side once we turned at the beginning of the South Channel. But now the little fishing boat was looming up; we were thirty feet away from it, you could see the men on board, very concerned, and apprehensive. They were bringing in their fishing lines. One man was on the bow bringing up the anchor, but it was too late, we were gliding past them. *Daisy May* has a high sided bow, and her hull rose steeply alongside them. The sails made her appear even taller than that. It would be frightening, wouldn't it?

I leaned over to Mr Fraser, and in a quiet voice said, 'Hard to starboard'. Mr Fraser gave the command, but Jacko was already doing it. I leaned over his shoulder again, and now Mr Fraser shouts out, 'Brace the yardarms to starboard'.

Fraser stuttered for a moment, then the command came out loud and clear, but the crew had already heard Ted give the order. *Daisy* gently turned. I watched the Pope's Eye. I knew Jacko had it all under control. I glanced around to see what Colin was doing. He was standing next to Ted, and Michael was just behind them, with his hands on Colin's shoulders as though he was supporting him. Just then I saw a steamer coming up on the other side of the channel; I saw black smoke pouring from its funnel. He was going to make a fast turn around Hovel's marker into the South Channel. Mr Fraser looked at me.

'What does he think he's doing Captain?'

'The captain on that vessel has skippered a sailing ship; he knows to meet on the broad part of the channel, opposite the South Channel fort, on our port side'.

We were passing Chinaman's Hat, and the steamer was now approaching us on our starboard side. The law of the sea is green to green and red to red. Abide by this, and you never go wrong. The steamer's captain had walked out onto the wing, on his starboard side. We slowly started to pass each other. He took his hat off and gave me a salute. I took my hat off and returned it. As he passed me, I realised I knew this man, Captain Jack Fox, an old colleague. I waved back at him with my hand. He placed his hands above his head, clenched his fists together and just moved them up and down; I did the same. As she passed me, I read the name on her stern *The Castle*. I said slowly to myself: Captain Jack Fox, skipper of *The Castle* steamer. I turned sharply to the bow. We were coming up to the other end of the channel. I walked up behind Mr Fraser. The crew was standing by the ready. The wind had increased in strength. It was going to be a tight turn. If anything was going to break, it was now! I could see Michael staring up at the sails, looking for any sign of them tearing loose. Ted was walking back and forth from starboard to port, looking for any trouble.

'Here it comes now.'

I tried to keep my voice calm, 'Mr Fraser, turn the helm to port, jive the spas and yardarms to port, helmsman north two degrees.'

He shouted out commands, and then it all happened all at once. She was turning sharply. The crew were jiving the spas and yardarms; the wind hit her at full force, she lay over slightly. There were no swells to hinder us; just small waves. You could see the people on the beaches; they stopped walking and just looked at her. She must look majestic. Everything was perfect; the crew never missed a beat. Jacko is bouncing up and down on his heels, chanting one of his ancient songs. Mr Fraser stood with his mouth open. *Daisy May* was on her last leg into Melbourne.

You could see people on Safety Beach staring. Other small vessels seemed to come out of nowhere to see her. They went around her in circles or just steamed up behind; taking photos. I walked out of the wheelhouse to the stern, where Colin stood watching the wake behind her. The Cat was in his arms, his head resting on Colin's shoulder. I stopped. I thought leave him alone with his friend. I slowly walked back to the wheelhouse. Ted and Michael walked up to me and stood there for a moment. I knew what they were saying. 'Yes, gentlemen, you're right. Take some canvas off her; whatever you think is appropriate'. I leaned up against the wheelhouse door just watching the canvas come off her.

Mr Fraser walked up alongside me. 'There will be a tug to meet you at Gellibrand dock Williamstown.'

I looked at him, confused. 'I usually tie up at Princess Pier or Station Pier. So what berth do we have?'

'Number Two, Flinders Street.'

'Why Flinders Street?'

'I don't know Captain, but it's the war; nobody knows what's happening. We just follow orders.'

The small tug met us, and the sails were all stowed and lashed tight as we passed the Williamstown dockyard. They seemed to be extremely busy. The Williamstown Ferry moved by us chugging back and forth across the Yarra River, past Victoria Dock, then on to our berth. We tied up in Melbourne, opposite the Seaman's Mission. *Daisy May* had returned to her home port. We lowered the gangplank onto the wharf.

Out of the darkness, two armed soldiers appeared on the dock alongside an officer, they were towards *Daisy*'s stern. One soldier stopped while the other two walked to the bow. The officer spoke to the soldier with him, then walked off. It was war!

The Cat wasn't at his usual spot on the gangplank.

CHAPTER 5

Once we were tied up at the wharf, a slim man of average height with white hair walked up the gangplank. He had notebooks underneath his arm and a big leather bag hanging over his shoulder. I stepped out of the wheelhouse. He stopped at the top of the gangplank with a big grin all over his face. We walked towards each other and shook hands.

'Hello, Bill.'

'Hello, Snowy.'

His correct name was Alan Norwood. He was one of those dependable men you meet and know you can put your life in their hands. Snowy was the wharf's clerk.

'Come into the wheelhouse, Snowy.'

As he entered the wheelhouse, he saw Jacko and shook his hand quite forcefully; he grinned and laughed.

'You still look like a funny kangaroo!'

'And you, Snowy,' Jacko responded, 'you look like an old man. You have changed since I last saw you. I like those puffy cheeks. You're getting a better class about you, a bit of good paintwork, and you've made it!'

We both laughed at each other. I put my papers on the bench, shipping manifest and all the other documents he needed. He opened his ledger book and started copying down the cargo, going through the papers. Les brought in some coffee and biscuits; Snowy looked at him.

'Hello, Les, good to see you again.'

Les put his hand on Snowy's shoulder, nodded and walked out of the wheelhouse. Snowy looked up at me.

'Snowy, they don't know what is going to happen to her, or what is going to happen to them.'

Snowy took a deep breath and sighed.

'Yes, it's the war.'

He finished recording the required information, put his hand out and shook mine.

'You keep being a kangaroo and be free!' he said to Jacko as he turned and left the wheelhouse, walked down the gangplank and disappeared down the wharf. I looked at the gangplank, still no Cat, but a neatly dressed man appeared.

'Captain Farquhar, sir?'

I nodded. He handed me an envelope, turned and walked away. I opened the envelope and read the note:

Captain Farquhar, please report to the Owner's shipping office at a convenient time today.

In my cabin I put on my best jacket and my best skipper's hat and looked at myself in the mirror. I shook my head at what I saw.

'Jacko, get some scissors and trim my hair.'

After Jacko had stopped fussing, I marched down the gangplank, my bag with the papers inside slung over my shoulder. I strode up Flinders Street, turned into Spencer Street, found the building I needed and went up to the big stairs into a foyer. A young lady sitting at a reception desk looked up at me.

'Sir, may I help you?'

'I am Captain William Farquhar. I have an appointment.'

'Yes, Captain, if you go up the lift to the third floor and see the receptionist.'

'Thank you.'

The receptionist on the third floor looked more businesslike.

'Yes, can I help?' she said as she looked up from her desk.

'I am Captain William Farquhar.'

She stood and walked over to a big heavy panelled door; knocked on it and went in, the door closing behind her. She came right back.

'Captain if you would like to come in, they will see you now.'

I hesitated, something wasn't right, this is not how it happens, but the young lady was holding the door open for me, and I went through. Two men were sitting at a desk, businesslike lawyers; these were the owners of the *Daisy May*. They both stood up.

'Good evening, Captain. You have your papers and logbook?'

'Yes, they are all here.'

'Just put them down on the desk and take a seat.'

I didn't like the arrogance of these two men, but they had command.

'Captain, we have another cargo for you to deliver, but it will not be ready for us for another two weeks, so we would like you and some of your crew to return here on the twentieth of this month, September.'

I was shocked, confused, wanting to ask questions, but I knew that I couldn't. I stared at them for a moment.

'I have the purse here, sir, and I have not, as yet, paid the crew off.'

'Captain, we will take care of your crew, you keep the purse in our gratitude for your services to us. You are one of the few captains who could keep vessels safe on the high seas, so enjoy your break, Captain, and we will see you on the 20th.'

I knew that I had been dismissed; I hesitated before getting up from the chair.

'We will take care of everything on the vessel, Captain, thank you!'

I got up from the chair, totally confused, nodded to the two gentlemen, turned and left.

The two gentlemen who were behind the desk walked around to a small bar and made themselves a drink. One of the men's voice boomed out.

'Well, what do you think?'

A man, and a woman in her forties, both dressed in a British Navy uniform of high rank, walked around from behind a screen. The male officer spoke first.

'Well, with his knowledge of the sea and to keep a sailing vessel afloat for thirty years is an outstanding achievement. I also like the way the man handled himself in this situation. He did not argue with you; he just took your commands and accepted what you had in store for him and his vessel, or, should I say our ship.'

The female officer glanced at her senior officer.

'There is something about this man, the way he stands and looks as if he is in total command of himself. Though we know he is confused in his mind; he is no fool. He is aware of the condition of his vessel, but he kept himself totally in control, he analysed every word, every angle, the whole situation that was before him. He can also play politics. I believe he is our man.'

The senior officer stepped forward, showing that he was in command.

'Yes, I agree with you. Can I offer you a whisky?'

'Yes, certainly.'

The female officer said she would decline, but a cup of coffee would be nice. The two men laughed.

'You will get on with him extremely well. He does not allow alcohol anywhere near his vessel, and his principles will never be broken ... he is the

best captain we have ever had, and we would appreciate it if you could give him back to us.'

Commander Lesley Johnson slowly sipped her hot cup of coffee. She had read all the reports on Captain William Farquhar, but seeing this man for the first time was different. She visualised him in her mind again, six foot tall, heavy build, he stands firm but very flexible. You knew he was in command. He had black hair, heavy cheeks, firm jawbone with a black beard. He looked a little Italian, Lesley couldn't see the colour of his eyes, but they had depth to them. He carried his Captains hat under his arm with a sense of pride, and he listened to every word that was said, studying them as if they were pieces on a chessboard. Lesley thought she had better sharpen herself up!

I walked back through the warehouses to the edge of the wharf where the *Daisy May* was berthed. I stopped at the gangplank. There were men on the deck I didn't know. Her cargo was already being unloaded. A man tapped me on the shoulder; I spun around. It was the wharf foreman.

'Hello Johnny Young.'

He nodded at me with that weather-worn face of his, smoke pouring through his fingers as he smoked a cigarette, hand to his mouth.

'Have you been paid yet, Johnny?'

'Yes, I have, but not the sickness fund for our brothers.'

I took some money out of the purse and slipped it into his top pocket. He just turned and walked away. I looked up at the gangplank, and to my surprise, Cat was waiting for me. As I stepped onto the gangplank Cat moved to one side, twitching his tail.

'What's happening?' I asked.

Ted glanced at Jacko. 'I thought you would tell us, Skipper,' Jacko said.

'Come in the wheelhouse lads.'

'Skipper there isn't any room. There are men in there with papers all over the bench.' Jacko told me.

We walked toward the stern instead.

'A man came on board and paid us all our money and told a few of the lads they would not be required anymore.' Ted said.

I turned sharply, full of anger and frustration. They were my crew. They were mine!

'Where are the lads now?' I asked.

'In the Seaman's Mission having a drink together and looking for lodgings for the night.'

I walked back to the Seaman's Mission and went through the doors. There was a big man with the white collar on his neck, wearing his black robe. This gentleman was Padre Oliver. He walked up to me.

'Captain, I have heard the story and will take care of them.'

'Thank you, Padre, thank you. Where are they now?'

'In the other room.' As he turned to walk away, I put my hand on his shoulder briefly.

I walked through the door and the crew turned and looked at me. I just shook my head back and forth.

'It's not your fault, skipper, we understand,' said Johnny.

'You've been my shipmates, my crew, for a long time, you have been the best, and I don't want it to end like this.' I took my seaman's purse that one of the owners had given me out of my pocket and put it on the table.

'This is what the owners gave me. Share it among your lads and good luck; keep the wind in your sails.'

I left the bar and headed back to the *Daisy May*.

A young man walked up to me with his nose in the air and an arrogant tone in his voice. Where have you been? We got lots to discuss. I don't have time to be wasting.'

This was the final straw. My anger boiled up inside me, and I snapped, 'Get your hand out of your pocket and the other hand out of your nose. You will address me as Captain Farquhar. Now go and see my bosun and ask for permission to talk to me. I may consider it tonight. Now snap to it!'

He looked surprised and degraded in front of the other men. I noticed the grins on their faces. He had been arrogant and self-centred in front of the wrong person. I turned and walked to the back of the wheelhouse. Then I heard Ted's voice.

'Excuse me, Captain. There is a young man here who wishes to talk to you.'

I wanted to grin, but I was too angry. I turned around, and I saw the smile in Ted's eyes.

'Very well, Mr Coe.'

Ted turned around and walked away, returning to usher in the young man.

'Captain Farquhar, sir, may I speak with you?'

'Yes, young man, you may.'

'Sir, my name is Jarret. I am the son of one of the owners of *Daisy May*. I wish to know certain things about your vessel. We have some repairs to do on her.'

'Go ahead, young man.'

'The Gardner engine, is it still working, sir?'

'No, it is not.' I replied.

'Do you know why?' the young man asked.

'No, I do not. I am a sea captain, not a motor mechanic.'

The young man asked me many other questions, writing the answers down in his notebook. Darkness had fallen, and when he had finished I was tired and weary. There were lights on board *Daisy May* and the wharf crew was still unloading; all the other men had left for the night.

Michael was putting away his documents regarding her rigging. 'What's all this about Skipper?' he asked.

'I don't know, Michael; I don't know'. I didn't see that Ted and Jacko had walked up alongside us. I turned to glance at them both.

'We've got another cargo. What it is I don't know, but we set sail on the 20th of this month. The destination, I don't know either. I've been told to take a fortnight off, so I should be back on the 18th Jacko, I'm going back to Lakes Entrance to visit my mum's grave. Do you want to come?'

He looked into my eyes for a few moments.

'Don't have to go to a grave; she's here with us all the time. I can talk to her, and I can look after *Daisy May*.'

'Very well, I understand.'

Ted laughed out loud. 'Okay Jacko, then I will stay and look after you. You might not get lost in the bush, or at sea, but in the big city, I'm not so sure.'

Jacko smiled. 'Tell the truth, you'd miss me, and you'd be lonely.'

Just then, Les turned up with the supper.

The next day I arrived at Flinders Street Station, Platform Number One. I boarded my compartment on the train, threw my bag on the top rack above my seat, and sat down in the corner by the window, with an uneasiness deep inside me. This was not my world; it was alien to me. The last time I had been on a train was many years ago when Jacko and I had left Lakes Entrance looking for work. There were soldiers on the platform and women with children. Porters with their trolleys, trying to avoid people. I could hear people shouting, children crying. This was the city; this was the turmoil of people trying to exist.

By this time the compartment was full of people, mostly women and children. A guardsman blew his whistle; then waved a green flag. The carriage that I was sitting in gave a small shudder and shook, then the noise started. I could smell the smoke from the steam engine, as we moved off. We were on our way, the click-clack of the train on the tracks became louder and louder. It became an endless rhythm. This train was the fast train, direct to Bairnsdale.

I studied the rest of the passengers, and I noticed they were examining me. One lady, quite large, with two children, spoke to me sharply, 'Why aren't you in the war? My husband was drafted.'

I stared at her for a moment. I didn't have an answer. In the world that I lived in, I did not know the things that were happening to those on the land.

'I am a sea captain; I live on a sailing ship at sea.'

'You are a sea captain sir?' asked an elderly gentleman sitting alongside me.

'I am,' I replied.

'Do you have a ship, sir?'

'I do.'

'What vessel do you have sir?' he asked with sadness in his eyes.

'I sail a barque sailing clipper, three masts, high-sided.'

He took a deep sigh. 'I was the captain of a four-master.'

I put my hand out. He slowly put his hand out and took mine, placing his other hand on top of mine. I could feel the sadness in that handshake. A smile came over his face and his eyes came alive.

'I have lived a life like no other man; I have lived a life! I am so pleased to have met you, sir, because you understand,' he said.

He sat back in his seat, put his hands on his lap, and closed his eyes. I knew he was reliving the memories of his past life at sea.

I didn't realise that I'd fallen off to sleep. The deep, soothing, hypnotic rhythm of the train on the tracks and the weariness of my mind and body had taken over. Suddenly the noise of the train whistle woke me. We were pulling into Sale railway station. As the train pulled up to the platform, the guard shouted out a twenty five minute break.

I found the platform toilets and chuckled to myself, *You don't get this at sea.* I walked back along the platform and bought myself a coffee, a sandwich, and an apple pie. *What would Les think of this?* I thought as I grinned to myself. I got back onto the train, and before long we were in Bairnsdale, the end of the line.

I boarded the bus for Lakes Entrance, paid my money, and asked the bus driver if he could drop me off at Jimmy's Point, Kalimna. Jimmy's Point was a high point of land that overlooked the entrance to Lakes Entrance.

I walked to the Kalimna Hotel, the man behind the bar looked at me, studied me.

'How can I help you, Skipper'?

'I would like a room for a couple of days,' I replied.

'No worries Skipper, sign the book. That will be one bob in advance.'

I signed the book and paid my bob. He looked at me with a curious look on his face.

'I know you, don't I? You're Mrs Farquhar's son; you're Bill.'

'I am.' He took me by surprise but then I had signed my name and was wearing a skipper's gear.

'My name is Fred; we went to school together.'

I laughed out loud and put my hand out and shook his.

'Your mum missed you and Jacko. How is Jacko doing?' he asked.

'He is doing well. Hasn't changed a bit, always one step in front of you!'

'That's Jacko all right.'

'I've come to visit Mum's grave; I don't know where it is. Could you help me?'

There was sadness in his eyes.

'Yes, I will. I will take you there tomorrow.'

'Thank you; I'd appreciate that. I will be heading back out to sea soon and don't know whether I'll be back again.'

The next day I went to the local church and sat on one of the pews. I was thinking about how much Mum had enjoyed the church. A man's voice startled me. I turned around. There was a man dressed in black wearing a white clerical collar.

'Hello, my name is John. Can I help you in any way?'

'No, I can't think of anything at the moment. I've just come to visit my mother's grave'.

'What was her name?'

'Mrs Farquhar.'

'Oh yes, her photo is in the vestry. Come with me'.

There she was, my mum. I stood staring at the photo. I could hear her voice in my head as if she was talking to me.

'Your mum was an excellent cook; I can still remember the taste of her cheesecakes. She was a wonderful lady.' The priest went to the shelves at the back of the vestry, ran his finger up to the date that he wanted, and brought out a small folder. He handed it to me.

'Your mother asked me to give this to you if you ever returned to Lakes Entrance.'

I opened the folder and found two envelopes inside. One envelope had the name *William Farquhar* scrawled across it; the other had the name, *Jacko Farquhar.* I opened the envelope addressed to me. It was my birth certificate with mother's full name, father's name listed as 'Unknown' and birthplace recorded as Diamantina River. I put the document back into the envelope and opened the second envelope with Jacko's name on it. There was Jacko's birth certificate, his mother's name which I could not pronounce and a note that she had died in childbirth on the banks on the Diamantina River. Jacko's father's name I could not pronounce either. Inside the envelope, there was another document, Jacko's adoption papers. When mum had remarried, she had adopted Jacko officially, all legal.

There was also another document, a title to a small block of land at the back of Lakes Entrance. I handed it to John.

'What is this small block of land?' I asked.

'Oh yes, the gentleman who owned the farm had financial problems. Your mother bought the block to help him out. That was your mum. She had known hard times, so she was always willing to assist those who needed her help.'

I put my hand out and shook his hand.

'Thank you, John. These papers are critical to us.'

Then I went to the cemetery and found her grave. I knelt on my knees and placed both of my hands on her grave.

'Yes, mum, I miss you too. I wanted to hold you to tell you how much Jacko and I loved you. I've carried a photo of you in my pocket always. When your letters stopped, something inside of me stopped also. When I wrote to you and told you that I had become a sea captain, what you said to me in your letters made me so proud that I was your son.'

I got up and walked over to a small seat and sat down. My mind went racing back to the Diamantina River and the Cattle station and her.

I walked down to the Post Office Jetty, looking at the vessels tied up and there she was, the *Pasadena Star*, royal blue hull, wheelhouse forward. Memories came flooding back in my mind. A man is sitting on the deck mending fishing nets; he had broad shoulders and chubby cheeks.

'Good afternoon.' He looked up, surprised.

'Good afternoon,' he replied.

'Fishing good, is it?'

'Could be better; we have had too much wind lately.'

I struck up quite a conversation with this man. We talked about the sea. I told him I once lived in Lakes Entrance. As he spoke, I felt as if I was looking in a mirror; we were so much alike. He told me that he is married with two children, Robyn and Stephen. His pride in his children was evident. 'Robyn is like me,' he said, 'and Stephen is like his mother, but Stephen looks like me, and Robyn looks like her mother.'

I finally said goodbye. I liked this man, he was me, in a different time and different place. Who knows? Who knows?

Time moved on quickly, and I had to leave. I took the bus back to Bairnsdale and soon I was back on the train, black smoke pouring from her chimney stack, heading for Melbourne. There were only two passenger cars, the rest was freight. She was fully loaded, pouring power into a C class locomotive; a powerful source of energy, something you never forget.

In my carriage was a young mother with two very excited children sitting on the seat opposite. I looked at the her and thought of my mother with her two young children in Lakes Entrance. I started talking to her; she seemed a little naive to the ways of the world. There was a sweetness and tenderness in her personality, something I missed at sea. I was enjoying the conversation. No politics, just sweet innocence. She told me that her husband had joined the Navy, and she was now going to Melbourne to stay with her aunt.

The other passenger, a young man of about fifteen, looked frightened and scared as if I had asked him to climb out on the yardarm on his own.

'Hello, my name is Bill.'

'My name is Trevor,' he replied.

'Very pleased to meet you, Trevor, and where are you bound?'

'I don't know sir. I am too young to join the Army. My mum can't feed all of us, so I've got to find work, and Dad's in the Navy.'

I studied him for a while, went over in my mind what he had just said, how he had taken on the responsibility for himself, although he was looking very anxious. Trevor had an enquiring mind, and he showed respect by calling me 'sir'. I listened to the further conversation we had.

My thoughts were always of the sea and its problems and the welfare of my vessel. That was my narrow view, but this young man had a broad range in his mind. I could use someone like this on my *Daisy May*.

'Young man, I am the captain of a sailing vessel. I will be taking her back out to sea in a few days., Would you be interested in coming with me?'

I left the question open to see what he would say. He studied me for a few moments.

'Yes, I would.'

Soon I was back in Melbourne. I had done what I wanted to do. I had visited my mother's grave in Lakes Entrance.

CHAPTER 6

A chauffeur driven car had pulled up outside the Seaman's Mission. The chauffeur got out of the car and opened the back door. A smartly dressed man got out and walked over towards the wharf where Daisy May was tied up. He wanted to see her before she set sail, but he saw a guard wearing a naval uniform standing at the bottom of the gangplank. Anger rose in his mind, he thought with annoyance, 'That secretary of mine is an incompetent idiot.' The man walked over to the telephone box, picked up the receiver and dialled a number. Then he stopped and hung the receiver back; somebody could be listening. He walked back to his car and instructed his driver to go back to the office. He went through the glass doors, passed the clock, passed the sergeant-at-arms, straight on through to his secretary. His secretary stood to attention. 'You are a fool and incompetent! We discussed at the meeting that no attention was to be drawn towards the Daisy May. What did I see? You have put bloody naval guards on the gangplank!'

'No, sir, it was not me; it was the officer of the watch.'

'Get him on the phone!'

'Yes, sir.'

He went through to his office and sat down in his chair, and when the phone rang, he picked up the receiver.

'Officer of the Watch, sir,' a voice said.

The man composed himself and let his frustration slide past.

'I believe I am Admiral French. Is that correct?'

'Yes, sir.'

'So, when I give an order or a command, it is to be carried out to the letter. Is that correct? So, very discreetly remove the guard on Daisy May's gangplank. Do you understand what I am saying?'

'Yes, sir.'

'Good, do it!' He hung up the receiver.

I got off the train, turned and looked at Trevor, 'What is your last name, Trevor?'

'Evans, sir.'

'Follow me, lad.'

We walked back to the *Daisy May*. She had been turned around and was now facing down the river. She looked the same as when I had left her, but some things were different. Her rigging was unusual, and her sails looked new, but they were still dirty grey. Looking at the Plimsoll line on her hull, she appeared to be fully loaded. The Cat was waiting at the top of the gangplank.

I turned around to young Trevor, 'That is Cat. His name is Cat, don't try and touch him; he has sharp claws.'

We walked up to the gangplank onto the main deck. Jacko, Ted, Michael, and Les were standing with their backs to us. I shouted out as loud as I could, 'Don't just stand there! Get back to work!' They all spun around.

Jacko said in a loud voice, 'Well, the party is over now, the Skipper is back!'. They all chuckled.

'This is Trevor. He will be joining the crew. Get him stowed away, Jacko.'

Jacko just nodded to Trevor and walked off towards the forecastle. I followed Les to the galley, and he handed me coffee in my mug. I took a sip. I had missed this black tar!

I saw three young men sitting on the hatch cover. They would have all been in their thirties and appeared to be very fit and healthy. There were two other men I did not recognise. Jacko was coming out of the forecastle with Trevor behind him. 'Trevor, make yourself known to these blokes until I call you.'

I walked over to the galley, Les and my usual crew followed me. I had noticed new stores on the deck; tinned food, bully beef, spam, potatoes, vegetables and fruit. There were spare sail canvas and extra ropes in coils still with the lashing around them. There were new oilskin coats and jackets, woollen trousers and jumpers and light boots of good leather. I sat down on the bench with my hand under my chin. We had new sails, but they weren't white, they were a dirty grey, but high-quality canvas. It was war, and there was an acute lack of cloth. What was going on? I looked up at Ted.

'*Daisy May* has been in dry dock,' Ted said. 'They have re-corked her hull, replaced copper sheeting and anti-fouled her hull. They have got the motor working. New fuel tank, repacked the stern gland and did some work on the cabins. We also got a new radio.'

Les chuckled, 'I've got a new Aga stove, pots, pans and utensils and new carving knives and a lot more stores than I could use on three voyages around the world!'

They were more confused than I was, and I was somewhat confused! Once again, I was not in control of my vessel. Jacko could not contain himself.

'Has someone got a queer sense of humour Skipper or are we are getting set up for something nobody's told us about?'

'I don't know Jacko, but I may find out tomorrow. Get all the stores stowed away. Get that sailcloth below decks with the ropes and rigging. We will get a good night's sleep and find out tomorrow. Colin stow the gangplank for tonight. Jacko, you take the first watch.'

I wanted time to myself, I needed time to think, but I couldn't find any answers. Jacko's words, *Are we being set up?* echoed in my mind. Why is there a new cabin? I looked into the other cabin; it had been painted out in a beautiful fresh white, with a new mattress, blankets folded up neatly in a pile with new, clean pillows. There was a hand basin and mirror, drawers under the bunk and side drawers on one side of the hand basin. There was also a bench above that with bookshelves and curtains and a new latch on the window. I saw a new wall clock that had different times on the face for places all over the world.

I was confused and frustrated. What is happening? Why have they spent all this money? There is a war on! There is a shortage of everything. Why had we got everything? I walked back to my cabin and opened the door. My cabin had been freshly painted as well. It had a new mattress, new blankets, and pillows, a new radio on the wall. I hadn't seen one like this before. I needed sleep. I needed to shut the world out for just a few hours then I would take over from Jacko's watch when there won't be anybody on deck. Perhaps I could think more clearly in the early hours of the morning.

As I lay in my bunk, trying to sleep, my mind was racing back and forth. I thought of the young mother on the train, her innocence untouched and unspoiled by the turmoil of life. I would fight for her. She is Australia!

Why have they spent so much money on *Daisy May*? Who were the three new young men on board? Why the new cabin? So many questions without any answers.

I awoke suddenly. It was my watch. I climbed out of my bunk and looked around at the white panels. They were beautiful timber before. Damn them! It was my cabin; they had no right to paint it white.

I walked out of my cabin into the wheelhouse and out onto the deck. I looked up to the top of the wheelhouse where I knew Jacko would be, with a blanket over his shoulders watching. I went into the galley made two cups of coffee, walked back out onto the deck.

Jacko was waiting for me. 'Funny things have been happening that I don't understand. When we were in dry dock, nobody would talk to us, except the man in charge. He kept asking Ted all sorts of funny questions about *Daisy May,* and when the new sails turned up, they were on a Navy truck. They had refloated *Daisy May,* and when she was brought back to this side of the river, there was a Navy guard on the gangplank.'

I put my hand on Jacko's shoulder. 'We've got lots to sort out tomorrow; go and get some sleep, Jacko. I think it is going to be a big day.'

'Yes, Boss.' Jacko looked at me with a sad look in his eyes. 'Did you find Mum's grave?'

'Yes, I did. I told her how much we loved and missed her.' Jacko nodded and went to get some sleep.

I was standing with my hands behind my back, looking at the dry dock on the other side of the river. A hand touched me on the shoulder. I spun around. It was Colin. His shoulders were slightly bent forward, and he had a weary look on his face. 'Would you like me to get the crew up? Some of them have got a lot to learn in minimal time.'

'Yes, let's get them to work.'

I watched Trevor and Michael. Michael seemed to have taken young Trevor under his wing as a big brother would. I walked up to the three men who appeared to be out of place on the *Daisy May.* 'What are your names?'

'I am Dominick,' answered the first one. I put my hand out and shook his.

'I am Reno,' replied the second man. I shook his hand. The third young man replied that his name was Philip.

'Good to have the three of you on board. Now, why are you three on this vessel?' They all moved slightly on their feet, their heads bent down. It left me with an uneasy feeling. Dominick and Reno looked at Philip, as though he was their spokesman.

'We want to learn all about sailing vessels while we can, for our future as this is what we all want to do in the future.'

'I'll accept that, but as long as you are aware that as I am the captain of this vessel, don't cross me. Do you understand gentlemen?' They all stood erect.

'Yes, sir,' they all replied.

However, I felt uneasy. I was not happy about something, but I didn't know what. I turned to Ted, 'Get these three topside; better they learn now while she's in the dock.'

I spoke to the rest of the crew briefly. They were seasoned crew, old hands on a sailing vessel. By this time it was eight o'clock. I picked up my leather satchel, nodded to Jacko and Colin. Ted walked down the gangplank with me. There was Cat at the bottom, I stared at him, *What do you know that we don't?* Cat moved to one side as though he had read my thoughts.

I walked up Flinders Street, passed the Halfords store, passed under the railway bridge and then up to Spencer Street. I walked into the shipping office building, and went to their room on the top floor; there I met the same two gentlemen I had met on the previous occasion.

'Good morning, Captain.'

'Good morning, gentlemen.'

'Well, Captain, we have another voyage for you with a cargo of wool and muttonbird oil. Your destination is Liverpool, England. They need the wool for soldiers' uniforms, ninety-five days Captain, we would say. That would be a pleasant voyage.'

'Yes, sir.'

'We have found your crew.'

'I would like to add another onto the crew, sir, a Trevor Evans, fifteen years of age, from Bairnsdale.'

'That will be quite alright, Captain. Here is your old logbook but we are also giving you a new logbook. In your new logbook Captain, could you keep things as brief as possible. I know that it will be hard because you are a meticulous man for detail. You will also find a new radio in your cabin and on this small chain is the key to it. We would like you to put this around your neck. Never give it to anyone else and only use it if your vessel is sinking!'

I nodded to acknowledge I'd understood what he had said.

'Here are some papers for Mr Ted Coe, please give them to him.' He handed me a large envelope. I had seen this type of envelope before, but couldn't remember where.

'Here are your papers and the instructions we'd like you to carry out. There is a high tide at three o'clock this afternoon, Captain. We would like you to sail then. Good morning Captain. That will be all.'

The other gentleman stepped forward. 'May I have a word with you in the foyer please, Captain?' I hesitated for one moment. I was dismissed, and now someone wants a word in the foyer?

'Yes, certainly.' We both went and sat in the foyer. This arrogant man had now become soft and gentle.

'Captain, my son was a supervisor working on your vessel. He said that you had pulled him up sharply and put him back in his place. His mother has spoiled him. She wanted a girl!' He put his hand on his lap, and his head went forward.

'I need my son to be a man for the responsibilities he is going to take on when I pass over. He has to understand people, to have compassion and understanding, but still be strong. I would appreciate it sir if you would take him to sea with you and make a man of him. He does not know that he has signed these papers'.

He drew out a white envelope from his inside pocket and handed it to me.

'Will he be on board when we set sail?'

'Yes, sir, I shall arrange it.'

He got up from the chair and walked over to the woman at the desk.

'You have the names of the crew on the *Daisy May*?' I had added Trevor Evans, fifteen years of age. He hesitated, and I knew what he was thinking, *How do I tell his mother?* He shook himself and added his son's name to the list.

'The Captain has had his papers signed,' he told the woman.

He turned and faced me, put out his hand, and I shook it, I nodded to him. He turned and went back into his office. The young lady gave me the piece of paper in an envelope. I put it in my bag with the rest of the documents and returned to the *Daisy May*.

I did not board her straight away but walked down to the wharf to watch a ship being unloaded. I found the dock foreman, Johnny Young. I had put some money in the palm of my hand. When Johnny turned around and faced me, I put out my hand, and he shook it. The money disappeared. 'Did you load the *Daisy May*?'

'No, we didn't. There is a shortage of men on the wharf. My brothers have joined the Army and Navy.' He hesitated for a moment. 'I was paid to stay away from her.'

He reached out his hand. 'I don't need this. You've always looked after my brothers and me.'

He put the money back in my hand and walked off. I thought to myself; this jigsaw puzzle is getting bigger and bigger. I returned to the

Daisy May, went on board and into the wheelhouse. Jacko and Ted were there waiting.

'High tide is at three o'clock. I want to be out on the Bay as soon as possible so we can sort a few things out before we are at sea.'

They both nodded happily and disappeared. I noticed Mr Fraser coming on board.

'Welcome aboard, Mr Fraser.' The young man who I was supposed to make a man of was also coming on board, they both walked into the wheelhouse. The young man couldn't contain his enthusiasm.

'Captain sir,' he started, 'my father said I could sail with you to Port Phillip heads.'

'That's correct young man. If you would like to go and get a cup of coffee from the galley and sit on top of the hatchway over there, you can enjoy the scenery.'

He scampered off to get himself a cup of coffee.

'Mr Fraser, I suppose you want to see my papers?'

'No, sir, I have already been briefed.' He took me entirely by surprise. Another loose end! *I have already been briefed?*

'Well, Mr Fraser, we will set sail then.'

'There is a small tug to take you down the river; it should be here shortly.'

The naval boat that had been tied up in front of us had now gone. The tug arrived, and soon we were back at Williamstown and Jolimont.

Coming down the river, I had asked Ted to get the three men aloft to see how they could handle the height. I had also asked Michael to see how far young Trevor could climb.

Calm water, no sails, I watched the three young men climb up. You would have thought they had been doing it all their lives. Young Trevor climbed as far as a full mast and stopped. In the meantime, I was going through my papers, scanning them briefly so that I could think about any problems that may occur. I walked out of the wheelhouse leaving

DAISY MAY

Jacko at the wheel, he was happy there, at the helm. Ted and Michael were instantly at my side.

'Michael, what sails would you like to see on her first?' He looked at me briefly, scanned the masts and then looked at the sea. A strong wind was blowing.

'Flying jib first, spinnaker for a sail, main topmast staysail, mainsail forward, top galley and sail main top gallant.'

Ted didn't wait for any commands; he just shouted out the commands to others.

The three new men must have studied their ships and rigging because they went straight to work, watching the others and copying them. I noticed Trevor was still up at the top of the mast. He waved at me as though he was enjoying it. Ted glanced at me and looked up.

'Leave him there Ted. He seems to be enjoying himself.'

We were heading up the bay to Arthur's Seat, Mt Martha. I had quickly counted the crew. I had ten, not including myself. I had two more than I needed, but even so, I could only count nine on board. I walked back into the wheelhouse, picked up the Crew List and went down the names. Lesley Johnson spelled with y. They had spelled that wrong!

'Ted, where is Lesley Johnson?'

Jacko shouted out, 'Your place to tell him, Ted. I'm just the helmsman!'

Ted put his head down.

'We were waiting for the right time to tell you, Skipper. "He" is a "she"!'

'Say that again? "He" is a "she"? Could you explain that to me, Ted? And Jacko, you shut up!'

'I think you had better meet her yourself, Captain.'

'Skipper!' Michael's voice broke in. 'The spinnaker needs a little tightening, but the others are alright. They might stretch a bit, but new sheets always do.'

Ted was glad to get the mainsail, main upper topsail, fore upper top-sail, and main-upper topsail up, this was his chance to escape. He darted away from my side and was busy shouting out his orders. Again, it hit me. Colin's name was not on the Crew List I had, but he was on board. Where was he? Ted was busy. Michael was busy. Jacko had his hands full. I raced over to Les.

'Where is Colin?' He seemed to freeze for a moment; then I saw those shoulders start to shudder. He wiped his face with his apron, wiping away the tears.

'Down alongside the big motor.'

I ran to the stern, to the small hatch where the motor was and clambered down the stairs. Les followed me. I could see Colin sitting on a pile of rags with Cat sitting on his lap. Colin had a piece of bloody cloth in his hand. I went down on my knees. I shouted, 'Colin, oh Colin. Can I do anything to help you?' He looked up.

'Nothing, Skipper. I need to be left alone with my best friend, my mate and to be able to die in my way.'

I knew what he meant. I turned around, pressed my head into Les's shoulder.

Back on deck I went into the wheelhouse. Mr Fraser was standing with his hands behind his back. I looked at Jacko and shouted at him.

'Why didn't you tell me?'

His mouth started to quiver, tears pouring from his eyes. 'What could you have done with all the problems that you had? He asked us not to tell you until we were at sea.'

Mr Fraser looked confused. He didn't know what we were talking about, and it was best that he didn't.

I noticed Jacko looking over my shoulder and spun around expecting to see Ted. To my surprise, there was a face, that took my breath away – dark curly hair down to her shoulders, a small perfect little nose and red cheeks. I looked straight into her eyes. They were bright and alert. She wore a beautiful colourful jumper and a warm black pair of trousers and good leather boots.

'Hello, Captain. My name is Lesley Johnson. I do hope I haven't inconvenienced you at the wrong time.'

I had trouble finding words. I don't usually talk to ladies. I snapped myself back; there was too much going on.

Ted walked up behind me, 'Excuse me for a moment.'

'Yes!' I said.

'Michael would like to put the fore royal and the main royal on her.'

'Yes,' I replied. 'But no more. Let's see how the new rigging is holding up. I don't want any trouble back through the "Eye of the Needle". We won't have any water to play in.'

'Aye Skipper.'

'Miss Johnson, come through to my cabin. Could you tell me what a woman is doing on board my vessel?'

'I believe you have a letter in your files, sir.'

I went back into the wheelhouse, found the envelope, ripped it open, and read the letter.'

Captain Farquhar, Lesley Johnson is a member of your crew. She is to work her passage in any position you think fit. She is a news reporter writing a series of articles for magazines. We also employ her in other parts of our organisation. She is entirely under your command.

The paper had been signed with the standard signatures.

I went back to my cabin and looked at her with a severe face, and thought for a moment.

'Do you have any medical knowledge?'

'Yes, I do Captain.'

'Well, if you could please go and get the medicine chest and check out what is in there, then go to Les, our cook. He will take you down to the engine room to see what you can do for the man down there. I would be very grateful to you if you could keep this to yourself.'

She didn't answer me but turned and took the medical chest, walked out of my cabin, over to the galley and spoke to Les. I felt a wave of frustration start to move over me.

CHAPTER 7

Daisy May was free. She was under full sail, with new rigging, a clean hull and a spirit to guide her. I turned around to find Jacko looking at me.

'Pull it together, Boss; we've got too much to do.' I shook my head. How does he always know what's going on in my head?

My eyes caught the young man, Jarrett, whose father wanted him on board. Did I have the right to take him to sea against his will? Just then I noticed the jib boom start to quiver; it stuck out over the bow and held the flying jib and the triangular sails over the hull.

'Michael! Michael!' I called.

He spun around, looking straight at me. The jib bent. He looked straightforward and shouted at one of his men, then grabbed a marlin spike and ran forward to tighten the rigging.

My mind returned to the young man. He was working hard, assisting wherever he could, doing precisely as instructed.

'He looks like he will be a good man,' I said to Jacko

Jacko caught the direction of my eyes but didn't say anything. I noticed Lesley coming out of the engine room hatch. She came straight to the wheelhouse and put a bundle of rags to one side and put the medicine chest back. She took out a syringe and a bottle of morphine and disappeared again down the hatch.

I looked over the bow to Hovell Pile, trying to gauge the time we had. I tried to measure the wind, the movement of the water, the direction of the howling wind as it whipped up the water of the South Channel. I walked over to Jarrett.

'How are you enjoying yourself, Jarrett?

'The best day of my life, Captain. The best day of my life.'

'Could you come into the wheelhouse please Jarrett?'

I walked over to Ted. 'Get them ready to jive; everybody knows what they have to do.'

'Aye, Captain'.

'This is a tight turn, Ted.' I patted him on his shoulder and went back into the wheelhouse, picked up Jarrett's papers and the letter from his father and handed them to him. Lesley appeared again in the cabin.

'I've done all I can, Captain.'

She showed me the bottle before going back into the cabin where she put everything back into the chest, picked up the bundle of rags and went into the galley.

Before I could think, my emotions got the better of me. Then young Jarrett burst into tears. This little arrogant upstart young man fell to pieces. I put my hand on his shoulder.

'You can leave with the pilot boat if you wish.'

He turned to face me. 'But my father said I can stay on board *Daisy May*. He always said he'd look after me. He took me away from my mother. She always wanted a girl, not a boy. She always called me Geraldine, not Jarrett. She was always fussing over me, brushing my hair, telling me what I could do, what I couldn't. What I've got to eat or not eat. She was always coming into the bathroom interfering; a man has to have some privacy. I would very much appreciate it Captain if I could stay on board as one of your crew.'

I walked out of the wheelhouse and shouted to Ted, 'You have another crew member!'

'Get to work young man; you have a lot to learn!'

'Yes sir, thank you.' He ran back to his post.

I noticed Lesley had taken up a position on the web line. Sisal rope and manila rope could cut your hands to pieces if they were not hardened with calluses. I reached behind the wheel and grabbed two pairs of gloves and gave them to Jarrett and Lesley.

'Put them on and don't argue.'

I scanned the sails and masts where the men were. I shouted to one of the men, 'Get it together now, do your job or you will answer to me!' and flashed my eyes at him.

Then I noticed Colin leaning on the rail supporting himself on the stern; the morphine must have helped him. The Cat was at his feet. I stared at Colin for a moment and remembered the first words he said to me when we first came on board, 'Don't give me any trouble!'

I slowly turned towards the wheelhouse. Jacko was staring at me. He moved his head slowly from side to side.

'Yes, Jacko, you're right again.'

I walked to the starboard side watching the wind; it was going to drop off slightly and should be a calm night on the Bay, but a cold one. I went back to the wheelhouse. Ted had the three men up to the top of the masts with two others, ready to reef the sails if needed. *Now the fun begins*, I thought. The turn into the channel under sail was very tight. The channel was narrow at this point with sand and mud banks on either side. We had to keep Hovell Pile on our starboard, jive at the next pile. Keep it on our starboard at a forty-five degree angle.

'Are you ready, Mr Fraser?'

'Yes, Captain,' he replied.

I noticed Lesley already on the whip liner, her concentration on Ted and Michael. Looks like she will turn out alright. She looked up at the mast to the men on the top. I don't know what she was thinking, but they were going to have one hell of a ride. I was watching the surface of the water to see how the wind was affecting it, how fast the current was running. We were now level with Hovell Pile.

I stepped behind Mr Fraser. 'Hard to starboard Mr Fraser.'

'Hard to starboard helmsman.'

Jacko shouted. 'Hard to starboard, sir.' I thought to myself that he could be a cocky little sod.

I left the wheelhouse. Ted and Michael were already shouting out orders. All the yardarms and spas were coming to starboard just right. I looked up at the mast; the three men were still there, and so were the other two. I took a deep breath and said to myself, *Thank God for that, thank God for that! Daisy May* had slid around perfectly; she was now heading down the Channel. Jacko and Mr Fraser had her on course. Her hull was free. There was nothing to hold her back.

Then I felt it. The shudder. Then another slight shudder. I spun around to the wheelhouse and saw Jacko was fighting the wheel. Something was wrong with the steering and the rudder. I ran into the wheelhouse, thinking to myself, *Not here, not in the Channel.*

I lifted the small hatch on the floor of the wheelhouse so that I could see the steering mechanism. They had replaced the chain that ran over the sprocket, and it was loose so that when Jacko had put pressure on the wheel and was holding back against the wind and current, it was slipping.

I shouted out to Michael, but he was already there by my side with a marlin spike in his hand. He pushed me aside and disappeared down the hatch. Michael was turning a turnbuckle on the chain. Then I heard Jacko shout out, 'That's fixed it, boss.'

I sat back for a moment. I wondered what would I do without Michael. He came back out of the hatch, grease all over his face and hands.

'They didn't want that to rust, Skipper!'

I stood up quickly. 'Michael, if you wanted my boots, I would give them to you gladly.' Then I lightly punched him on the shoulder.

Again, I could see people on the beaches. They stopped walking and watched the *Daisy May*. I felt a deep sense of pride go through me, *Yes, Daisy; they think you are something special, and you are indeed!*

Sorrento and Portsea were coming up on the port side. She was sliding through the water, so gracefully, so majestically. The quarantine station was on our port side where many vessels were burned and sunk to stop diseases plaguing the city. We now could see Pope's Eye clearly on our starboard side; we were now passing the last channel marker on our port side. I walked out onto the deck.

'Ted, it looks like the wind will be from her stern; she will love that.' I walked back into the wheelhouse. Mr Fraser had already altered her course slightly to port. Jacko grinned to me and flipped his eyes up the channel. There was the little fishing boat again, and her crew was busy pulling up their anchor. They had spotted us coming up the channel, and they were not going to get caught again.

Mr Fraser turned towards me. 'That will take care of the problem in the future Skipper!'

My emotions started to swell again. I put my hand on Jacko's shoulder. 'I didn't think this would ever happen again!' *Daisy May* was returning to the sea, to her freedom. I glanced at Mr Fraser.

He nodded his head and shouted, 'South West twenty-two degrees.'

Jacko's voice bounced back, 'South West twenty two degrees.' Then his voice boomed out in one of his Aboriginal chants.

I heard Ted yelling commands, and all the spas turned so that she was catching the wind from her stern. Point Lonsdale was on our starboard side. Lesley walked to the stern where she could see the lighthouse.

Admiral French, stood on the observatory in the lighthouse, next to the man recording all the shipping. He raised his binoculars to his eyes, watching Daisy May. He thought to himself, 'Will we get away with it? God only knows.' Then he saw her, standing on the stern next to an elderly gentleman. He saw her raise a hand and wipe her forehead with only three fingers showing.

He grinned to himself and said out loud, 'That means all is shipshape.'

The man alongside him said, 'I beg your pardon, sir?'

'I was thinking out loud young man. Do not record Daisy May leaving Port Melbourne.'

I told Jacko to have a break and took the wheel from him. He walked out of the wheelhouse, stopped and turned to watch Lesley's back; he saw her hand come up to her forehead. There was something wrong. Was she wiping her brow or was she saluting Melbourne goodbye? Lesley turned and saw Jacko looking at her. She turned around, looking over the stern again. Lesley thought to herself, *He is a scary little fellow isn't he?*

Mr Fraser turned to me. 'Thank you, Captain Farquhar. I will never forget you or your vessel. I'm going to Sydney in the next troopship to do extra training. We are meeting it coming in. I will be piloting her into Melbourne.'

I shook his hand. 'Good Luck, Mr Fraser. I think you might find yourself in command of a ship.'

'That's what they tell me, sir, thank you.'

'Thank you, Mr Fraser.' His pilot boat had come alongside. He disappeared over the side. I saw him on the stern of the vessel looking back at *Daisy May*, free and under full sail.

CHAPTER 8

My mind snapped back into gear again. I glanced at the barometer. We were now at sea, and it would give me an actual reading. 30/1020, fair. The barometer is the guide to the weather patterns coming up, and as a captain of a sailing vessel, you are always watching your barometer. I have two barometers, this one, and Jacko. He is always in first; he is always in front of the barometer; he has that knowing! Now the course. What course? I went back through the paperwork again, picked up the envelope marked *Ted Coe*, and briefly put it to one side. I found the document I was looking for and read through it. A quarter of the way down the text was the recommended course. *Opposite to Macquarie*. I read it aloud so that Jacko could hear me: 'Recommended course opposite to Macquarie.' What the hell does that mean?

Ted walked into the wheelhouse just as Jacko burst out laughing. He grabbed Ted's hand and put it on the wheel. Ted looked surprised.

Jacko went into my cabin and came back with a book, opened it and flipped through the pages.

'Here it is Boss! Macquarie was the first Governor of Sydney, New South Wales. Governor Macquarie was the first man to lay out

Sydney as a city. They have the documents of the course he took from England to New South Wales. We can't exactly take that course, as this is September, but if we go across to Perth, the trade winds there will be finicky, but there will be winds. If we follow the trade currents and winds into the Indian Ocean, come back around to Madagascar and come close to Port Elizabeth North London, that will give us the winds in our favour. From there to Cape Town, we will be playing games with the wind; then we will be in the Atlantic Ocean and heading up to our destination.'

It also stated in the report that we do not make landfall, but they have left that to my discretion. I suddenly realised where I'd seen the envelope before. I had one just like it! I stared at Ted for a few moments.

'Ted, what happened when you were in port?'

'What do you mean Skipper?'

'Were you taken anywhere to answer questions?'

'Yes, I was.'

'Who took you there?'

'Padre Oliver. He took me to an office in the city, something to do with ships. I sat down in front of some gentlemen, and they asked me a lot of questions about the sea, about ships, ports, harbours, channel markers, and questions I didn't have the answer to, so I just said that I didn't know. Then Padre Oliver brought me back here.'

I knew then what the envelope was. I was so proud of him and handed him the envelope labelled with his name. He opened it very carefully, took the papers out, and started to read them.

'The Padre gave me another big package for you,' said Jacko.

He nodded to me to take over the wheel and darted off. Ted looked up from the papers, tears flowing. I'd never seen him cry before. He stared at it.

'It says, it says Captain Ted Coe, and it gives a lot of other information. I don't believe it.'

He walked up to me with the papers in his hand, put both his hands on my shoulders and just kept shaking me, saying over and over again, 'Captain Ted Coe, Captain Ted Coe, Captain Ted Coe!' He stopped and wiped the tears from his face.

Jacko turned up with the big package, put it on the bench and couldn't help himself; he started to rip off the paper. Ted stood alongside him, not believing what he was seeing. It was a captain's uniform and a captain's hat! He put his arms around Jacko's shoulders.

'I wouldn't have this if it wasn't for you. You kept asking me all those damn questions all of the time, over and over and over.'

With the papers in his hand, he went to Colin, who was sitting in a chair at the stern, Cat at his feet. Lesley was standing alongside him. Ted gave him the papers. Colin took his glasses out of his top pocket, put them on the end of his nose and read the articles. He handed the papers back to Ted and pulled himself up onto his feet with Lesley's help. He shook Ted's hand, and in a gruff voice said, 'Captain Ted Coe, sir. You have certainly earned that title, Captain Ted Coe.'

He sat back down in his chair and with a deep sigh, said, 'I've done my job. I'm satisfied. Thank you, Ted.'

Ted came back into the wheelhouse. I laughed and pointed to the wheel. '*My* wheel. *My* wheel. *My* vessel. Captain Ted Coe!' We both just laughed.

'Ted, I've been watching the clouds; the wind is going to pick up on our port side. The Eye of the Needle again. Could you get the crew together for me, but make sure that Lesley stays on the stern.'

The crew gathered around. 'Now that we have a woman on board, there will be no swearing. You will treat her with the utmost respect, and there's to be no *pissing* over the side. We now have a toilet on board, use it or use a bucket very discreetly. You all know what happens when you break my rules! We are not going around the Horn but around the Cape of Good Hope. Those of you who are familiar with the finicky winds and storms they can produce will know what is in store. Thank you for your attention.'

I turned and went back to the wheelhouse. The wind was coming across from our stern, port side. Her spas and braces are set. *Daisy May* seemed to be happy.

'Jacko you take the first watch; let me know when you see the lighthouse.'

'Right Boss.'

Ted and Michael had everything organised on deck, so I went back to my cabin and lay down. I don't know whether it was the movement of *Daisy May*, but I fell into a deep sleep. I awoke to the sound of the bell. It was the change of watch for the deck crew. I walked into the wheelhouse.

'All's well, Jacko?'

'All's well Skipper. The wind has stayed at the same strength in the same quarter.'

'Coffee, Jacko?'

'Yes, Boss.'

I walked over to the galley and came back with two cups of coffee and sat them down on the bench. Jacko took a sip from his. I sipped mine. Jacko turned and looked at me.

'Bill, too many things happening. Nothing makes any sense. You make any sense of it?'

'No, not yet, but I am the skipper of this vessel, and I will find out. I've got to go over everything in my mind. Lots of money had been spent on her. Johnny tells me they didn't load her, and he doesn't lie. His loyalty to his brothers is too strong. A woman on board? Money spent on her cabin. My cabin has been painted white, all these extra stores. Why are our sails a dirty grey? Why haven't they done anything to her appearance?'

'I was thinking of Snowy, Bill. He said I looked like a roo. A roo is the same colour as those sails. He blends into the bush. Can you see him? Would you see our sails at sea Boss?'

'No, you wouldn't Jacko. With white sails, you couldn't miss us. But there's a war on; wouldn't that be the best way to be?'

'I suppose,' replied Jacko.

We didn't say anything more, just drank our coffee. We didn't have any answers.

Suddenly there were flashes, three seconds' duration with fifty percent of darkness the entire period. The lantern had three flashes every revolution. Every two minutes and thirty-nine seconds. Cape Otway Lighthouse. I entered it in my logbook, the log time, longitude, latitude, course, wind strength and wind direction.

The crew on deck were resting. I stopped. Colin? I glanced over my shoulder, looking towards the stern. He was sitting there with Cat. I got him a cup of coffee and handed it to him. He took it with both his hands. 'Are you warm enough, Colin?'

'Yes, young William.'

He hadn't called me that for a long time.

'How is the pain?' I found myself biting my lip. Stupid question.

'Lesley seems to have taken care of that for me. It is nice to have a woman on board, especially one like Lesley, young William. *Daisy May* has come back to life; she is herself again; she is beautiful. But young William, you must watch the wind in your sails; it is not all it seems. I have taught you to read the stars, the wind, and the clouds, the seagulls and other birds of the sea, the dolphins, porpoises, and whales; everything depends upon the sea. It tells you its own story to help you survive.'

He paused for a while, as though his thoughts were being put back together.

'But I can't give you what Jacko's got, and in a sense, it is as though he is nature itself. He belongs to you, and will never leave you, so you have that precious gift to call on.'

He bent his head forward, and he was asleep.

'I'm going to take these papers and try to read through them to see if I've missed anything,' I told Jacko.

I returned to my cabin, sat down at my small desk and started to read everything I could in the papers. And what wasn't in the documents, it was what was between the lines.

Before I knew it, it was daylight, and I still had no answers. Back in the wheelhouse, I checked my logbook time at the Otway Lighthouse and jotted them down. I picked up my sexton and took my bearings, jotting them down and recording them in my logbook and did a few calculations, then grinned to myself. I tapped Jacko on the back, but thought to myself; he is reticent. I called out to Ted. He turned up alongside me. I handed him the sexton and glanced down at my logbook.

'Could you check those figures?'

He looked at me, his eyes narrowed.

'Always pays to check the calculations, Ted.'

He walked back out onto the deck, came back in, picked up a pencil, and started to write the figures down; he looked up at me.

'I was worried for a moment Skipper; I thought you were one degree out. But I was wrong; you were right.' He pushed me with his shoulder, laughed and went back on deck.

Why was Jacko so quiet? Then I noticed the papers on the bench, a small leather satchel, a tin, and Colin's pipe. I gasped for breath and shouted out, 'Oh no, Colin!'

I ran to the stern. The chair was there with Colin's coat hanging over its back, his hat resting on top of his jacket. The Cat was curled up on the chair. There was a pain that I could not fathom, so deep down inside me. I had never known my father and Colin had been the only father that I had known. He had gone the way he wanted, to the sea. It was his home. That is where he belonged. Ted and Michael turned up alongside me, and Ted put his arms around my shoulders and just held me. I slowly turned around, and there was Les, his hands were on his lap, his head bent forward, and he was sobbing loudly. He didn't care that he was showing all his emotions. How long had we known each other? I don't know. I went back into the wheelhouse and looked at Jacko.

'You knew, didn't you, Jacko?'

He turned and looked at me. His eyes were red with tears.

'Yes, Bill.' He looked at the wheel, and I took the spokes. He walked back to the stern, looking at the bulwarks, and started to chant a prayer in his words. Then he returned to me. He just stood there, staring at me. A small grin came over his face.

'He hasn't gone, he hasn't gone! His spirit is here!'

He turned back to the wheel, took his place, and I checked the clock. I went over to the chart and recorded the time in the logbook.

'Jacko, West, South West 260 degrees,' I shouted, 'come about to starboard.'

The crew snapped back to work. I walked up to the three men standing together. 'Good morning Reno, Philip and Dominic. Did you enjoy your ride yesterday up there?' Philip stepped forward; he took me by surprise by the way he stepped forward.

'Yes, Skipper.'

'I would have liked to have left you up there, but as we were going through the heads, we needed you on deck. It is a dangerous stretch of water. I wanted you all to experience what it would be like to be at sea when the boat is rolling around in a gale. You did well lads.'

I turned and looked at the stern again. I had lost Colin. We had all lost Colin, but not his spirit.

CHAPTER 9

We were playing games with the winds. We were still under the influence of the Roaring Forties; we had to get above them. The latitude was 35°S. *Daisy May* was now free; she could move as she wanted to, and we could keep more sail on her. We kept tacking back and forth. We were on the right course and everything was going well.

Jacko and I were playing chess in the wheelhouse when we heard Michael asking Lesley to come into the wheelhouse. He had a piece of cardboard and a pencil, he asked Lesley to place both hands on the cardboard, and he drew around her fingers. Her fingers were neither long nor short, just in between. Michael disappeared. Lesley looked down at the chessboard and grinned.

'Could I play the winner?'

Jacko and I just looked at each other and smiled. We both said 'Yes' together. Then Jacko suddenly stood up straight.

'Take the wheel, Boss.'

He ran out of the wheelhouse to the foremast and climbed it rapidly, with the greatest of ease and grace. Michael and Ted looked up at the mast. There was Trevor, hanging on to a rope, swinging dangerously. Jacko reached him but didn't race forward.

'How are you doing mate?' he said in a soft, warm voice. 'I'll show you what to do.'

He put his hand on the reefing rope. Trevor was holding on tight, with fear in his eyes; the movement of the ship made him sway back and forth.

'Put your leg around the rope like I'm doing,' Jacko said. Trevor copied him. 'Now, make sure the rope is over your foot, like mine.' Trevor again copied him. 'Now, put your other foot on top of the rope on your foot.' Trevor did so. 'Now relieve the pressure on your right arm, slowly. Watch me.' Jacko wound his arm around the rope taking it back in his hand. Trevor copied him. 'You are doing well mate. Do you feel safer now?'

'Yes, I do Jacko.'

Jacko gave him a warm smile, and those big white eyes seemed to put Trevor at ease. 'Can you feel her underneath you, the gentle movement? If you learn to understand her, you will enjoy every moment of her. We will play around with some ropes later, and I'll show you how to be alive in the rigging.' Trevor just nodded at him, by this time Michael was with them. He glanced at Jacko and winked his eye.

'I've just come up to check this fore top galley and sail. She seems to be doing well, and the canvas hasn't stretched too much.' Then he and Jacko helped Trevor back down to the deck. Lesley had been watching with the others, but they had gone back to their duties.

Jacko walked past Lesley, 'Nice day *Gidgee* isn't it? I'll get a coffee, Boss.'

I nodded at him and shook my head. Lesley came back in and stood alongside me.

'How did he know Trevor was in trouble? You can't see from here.'

I sighed, 'He has a sixth sense that we don't have. When we were on a Cattle station on the Diamantina River...'

Lesley froze! Memories came flooding back, Bill, Bill? The boy on the veranda! How could she forget those eyes? How serious he was. She had never forgotten her first crush, the old feelings came rushing back to her, but she had been trained to hide her feelings, she felt he was seeing something too, should she tell him? No, she couldn't, she must keep her secret to herself.

Bill did see something in her eyes but didn't understand what, he saw her cheeks flush; she fidgeted and kept flicking her hair from her face.

Bill kept on talking, 'they would give three or four Aborigines a horse and some food, which they called "grub", fifty or sixty cows, and they would disappear with them into the bush. They knew where the green grasses were, and would move with the cows as nature itself would move. Just before the rainy season, they would be back with the cows, fat and healthy, no white man could do that. Lock them up in jail, or a room with four walls and they die. They must be free. If they are not their whole system is out of control.

'Mum used to say the Aborigine has to migrate like the birds, kangaroos or the fish in the ocean. He has something so precious that we do not have; he can survive anywhere. His senses are totally in tune with his surroundings. Jacko's father was one of the elders, a brilliant man, and very, very clairvoyant. Nobody, man or woman, would break the rules. They knew he would enforce them for their survival.

'We are destroying their way of life, and I fear we may destroy them also. Jacko didn't know who his mother was; we think she died giving birth to him, but the old man gave him to my mum, and she brought us up as brothers. I don't look after him. He looks after me. But you play chess with him, and you'll find it fascinating. Play the game with your inner senses, as you would be with nature itself.'

Jacko walked in with two cups of coffee, with that silly grin all over his face.

The next day I played a game of chess with Lesley. She studied every move so carefully, and when she was satisfied, she would move her chess pieces with determination. It was so different from playing with Jacko. Jacko was always at ease; he had you on a string, playing with you as if you were a toy. However, when Lesley played, you had to play with all your wits, keeping you sharp. Each time I studied her, I enjoyed what I was seeing in her personality and her movements. The way her head would go backwards, slightly to one side, her eyes would widen and then narrow. Then she would sit up straight and make her move. Something inside me I had never experienced before was happening. What, I do not know.

We heard a shout, 'Whales, starboard side!'

Lesley said, 'Excuse me, Captain,' and ran to the starboard side. Although she was still a very composed woman, you could see the little girl in her. There was that feeling in me again that I could not understand!

I opened my logbook and recorded the time and location of the whales, a pod of six heading in the opposite direction, very early in the season.

Jacko walked up alongside me. 'Don't like this Boss. They know something we don't!' I wanted to write his comments down in the log-book, but I didn't.

Darkness fell. Then we saw it, groups of four flashes of light every twenty seconds. Cape Byron Lighthouse was on Kangaroo Island, the only square lighthouse I know; it was the entrance to Adelaide. We were on course. The beam range was twelve nautical miles. It was a clear night, and we could easily make the flashes out. Time to alter course again. Stay on Latitude 35°. That will keep us right away from Little Island, which is a small island off Western Australia, opposite Esperance.

The next morning the wind had increased. *Daisy May* was pushing into a massive swell. We had stowed the sails to keep the pressure off her masts; many sailing clippers have pushed a mast right through their hulls trying to keep up too much speed in a heavy sea. Each time her bow plunged into another swell, it put too much pressure on her rigging. Our three young men were learning so much about the pleasures of sailing on a vessel like this.

Lesley and I were playing chess again. The games were getting more serious. She was winning too many. In my forty years at sea, I was not used to a woman beating me. Get it together, Bill, sharpen up, you are the Captain!

Nevertheless, I was enjoying it. I had never experienced this before. Lesley didn't wear perfume; her smell was different. It wasn't like a man's smell; it was something so much more inviting.

Just then Michael came into the cabin with a pair of gloves, beautifully made with padded palms and fingers and holes to let the air in on the back He handed them to Lesley.

'Try these on Lesley.'

They fitted perfectly; she started to stand up. I thought she was going to hug him for a moment, but she stopped herself.

'Thank you, Michael, thank you. I've never had anyone make me a pair of gloves like these. Thank you.'

Michael nodded and walked back out of the cabin. That feeling again, that I couldn't understand.

Michael and Jacko had taken young Trevor under their wing. He was now swinging around on the rigging, assisting the others to reef the sails in or let them go free. Michael was acting like a big brother, teaching him to sew and understand sail making.

As I was changing watch with Jacko, he said, 'Boss, the crew are having a bit of trouble with Jarrett. You'd better talk to Ted and Michael.'

I asked Ted and Michael to come into my cabin.

'What's happened to young Jarrett?'

Ted moved his mouth to one side.

'I was just thinking how to sort him out myself.'

'So, what is the problem, Ted?'

'Well, he is becoming arrogant, a little bit contentious and letting everybody know about his education and remarking how his father owns the vessel. The crew don't like it, and I don't want the crew sorting it out if you know what I mean Skipper.'

'I do. Get everybody up on deck Michael and keep an eye on young Trevor. I don't want his mind bruised.'

Everybody was on deck. Every one of the old crew knew what was about to happen. Ted, knowing the procedure, stood alongside me. I noticed the three men standing together as brothers. Philip seemed to be in control, but they did what they were instructed to do; they never gave any trouble at all. Jarrett stepped forward in front of me.

'Now let's get this straight,' I said to him, 'I am the Captain of this vessel. When it is not in its home port, I own it! It is mine, it belongs to no-one else until I have it back to its owners, and you are no better than anyone. You are just as equal as anyone on board this vessel, and they are equal to you. When we hit bad weather, you must work as a team., Now stop arguing because your life depends on it. The lives of everybody else on this vessel depends on you doing as you are told, instantly, at once, without question. If Captain Coe or Michael give you a command and you hesitate, I will give the crew orders to keelhaul you. For your information, keelhauling is where we tie a rope on one leg, and another rope on the other, throw you over the bow, drag you underneath the vessel and pull you up to the stern. If you are still alive, you would be a fortunate person. Have I made myself clear, Jarrett?'

His head went forward; his eyes flitted around the crew.

'Have I made myself clear?'

'Yes, sir.'

'Thank you, gentlemen, return to your duties.'

Everybody disappeared. Young Jarrett walked to the stern and stood there gazing over the back. Ten to fifteen minutes later, he was still there. I thought I had better go and talk with him. As I walked out of the wheelhouse towards the stern Lesley's voice was behind me.

'Do you mind if I talk to him, Skipper?'

I was still angry inside and spun around, ready to snap, but something in the expression on her face and the way she stood there, stopped me. I hesitated. I don't do that!

'Yes, if you would, please.'

She walked to where Jarrett was standing. I stood there looking at them. I shook my head, went into my cabin and closed the door. As I sat down I felt that emotional, tender feeling again.

Daisy May. Lesley Johnson. Colin. I have no answers.

CHAPTER 10

I was trying to put my thoughts and emotions in check so that I could command my vessel. I awoke to the sound of the bell. It was my watch. I got out of my bunk, dressed and went into the wheelhouse to that familiar voice.

'Good morning, Skipper.'

'Good morning, Ted, a good night?'

'Yes, Skipper. You surprised me yesterday. Captain Ted Coe; I've never heard myself called that before on deck.'

I grinned at him. 'Did I make a point in the right direction?'

'I think so Skipper.' Then he disappeared to his bunk.

I checked the compass on course. My eyes went to the documents on the other end of the bench. I'd been avoiding them. I stared at the pipe on top of the papers and the two leather folders and the tin. I suddenly thought, *Where is Cat? I haven't seen him for the last couple of days.*

I reached across and picked up the pipe. I felt that pain, deep down inside of me. I squeezed the pipe tighter. I shouted out in frustration, 'Stinking damn thing!' and gently placed it on the window ledge in front of the wheel. Then I picked up the tin and looked inside. There were some photos of a well-dressed lady and a gentleman in a military suit with his hat underneath his arm. Two young children stood in front of him, a boy about nine years old, and a girl a little younger. There were other photos of people, and a picture of a large house, like an English manor house. I put the top back on the tin, picked up the white envelope and took out a piece of paper. It was hard to read, written by somebody with a very shaky hand.

William my time has come, I must leave you and Daisy May. She has been my lover, my companion throughout the years. The sea has been my very soul, so I must stay at sea, with the sea. As Jacko would say, I am part of the sea itself. All of the items that are in the safety deposit box are yours. The documents I hold in trust, please give them to my sister. They are now rightfully hers. I will always be with the Daisy May. I will always be with Jacko, and I will always be with you. You are my sons, I cherish you both. Take good care of my best friend; Colin signed it.

I read the letter again and again. I put it down on the desk, picked up the leather case and opened the flap. There was a small pouch with a pocket watch inside, a very, very expensive piece of work. I opened it up and looked at the hands. I looked at the clock on the wall, rewound the pocket watch and said to myself, *right time*, then I looked at the back of the watch. The engraving said, *To my son Colin on your 21st Birthday – Your father.* There was a small note inside. *Please give this to Jacko for he is my son and it is rightfully his,* signed Colin Matthew Henderson. I put the watch back in the pouch with the document. There was also a birth certificate and a marriage certificate, as well as a photo of a beautiful young lady. I knew nothing of Colin's past or where he had come from.

I opened the other leather folder and took out the first document. It was Colin's last will, and he had left everything to me to sort out as I felt fit. It had been drawn up in England when we were last there, three years ago. The other documents were his lawyer's instructions, all papers and reports would be returned to his sister. Colin had informed his lawyers that I would do so.

There was another envelope, a letter and a key. *This is the key to my deposit box, which is now yours.* The address on the back was in London. I stared at them, trying to put it all together in my mind. *Who was Colin? What had happened to him and the beautiful young lady? What made him choose the sea?* There was another piece of paper not in an envelope, dust on it, written on one side, *Please read these words at the stern of the Daisy May.* I opened the piece of paper and re-read the phrase again. I said to myself, *Yes, yes.*

I saw Les going into the galley. I shouted out to him to come over to me. He picked up a cup of coffee and walked into the wheelhouse.

'Where is Cat, Les?'

'He's down next to the big engine curled up on Colin's jacket. He's grieving.'

'Is he eating Les?'

'No, Skipper, he isn't.' Les went back to his galley.

Daylight was well upon us now; the three young men were exercising on deck. Lesley had joined them. They were bending and stretching, jogging up and down, something I hadn't seen before on *Daisy May*. I looked at Lesley; I hadn't been this close to a female for so long; no wonder my emotions were all over the place. *Put it in perspective Bill*, I told myself. Jacko walked in and stood behind the wheel, relieving me of my watch.

I went to the stern, and down the hatch, I saw Cat. He was lying on Colin's jacket. Cat looked up at me. I shook my finger at him and shouted, 'If we have to put our grief to one side and do our job, so will you!'

I snatched Colin's jacket from underneath him and took it with me to the wheelhouse. As I folded it neatly, I could smell Colin, could smell his pipe. I turned and faced Jacko, shook my head and put the jacket on the bench where Cat usually slept. Then to my surprise, Cat jumped up on the counter and sat down on Colin's jacket. I shook my head at Cat.

'So we have an understanding, do we?' I turned to face Jacko.

'What are you grinning about?'

Jacko replied, 'I never thought I'd see you talking to a Cat!'

I called Ted and Michael to my cabin.

'I cut Jarrett down a peg or two, but he will always be a little arrogant; it is his upbringing. But he is a smart lad and has had a good education so let's work on that. Ted, you work with him for an hour a day on the rules of the sea. Michael, teach him about rigging and the sails, not mending them, but how they work. I will work with him on navigation. Jacko will question him. Let's see if we can make something of him.'

I left my cabin.

'Jacko, we are going to work with young Jarrett. We will be giving him all the information that he needs to know about the sea; I'd like you to question him and see that he has it right.'

'Do it over and over again. Boss, Ted was hard enough, but Jarrett!' He said a few words in Aborigine. I just laughed; I knew what he meant.

I looked down at the leather folder; the pain of loss was there again. I picked up the letter and handed it to Jacko. He read it slowly and looked at me, folded the letter and put it on the bench in front of the wheel. He stood there staring at the pipe.

I handed the leather pouch to him. He took the pocket watch out and for a moment just stood looking at it, he then read the letter. He turned to me, tears flowing from his eyes. He was shaking. His grief had burst right open, and he was out of control. He put the watch back in the leather pouch then ran to the forward mast, climbed to the very top and just sat there. An hour passed, then I saw Michael climb to the top of the mast, and with profound relief, I saw them climbing back down. They came over to me.

'Colin asked me to do one thing for him, and now I am going to do it. Ted get all the crew on deck. Lesley take the wheel, please. Gather around lads. As you all know, we have lost a shipmate; his time had come, and he ended it the way he wanted to. He asked me to read out these words, and I do so know in his honour …

The Lord is my Shepherd; I shall not want

He maketh me to lie down in green pastures: He leadeth me beside the still waters.

He restoreth my soul: He leadeth me in the path of righteousness for his name's sake.

Yea, though I walk through the valley of the shadow of death, I will fear no evil: for thou art with me; thy rod and thy staff they comfort me.

Thou preparest a table before me in the presence of mine enemies: thou anointest my head with oil; my cup runneth over.

Surely goodness and mercy shall follow me all the days of my life: and I will dwell in

the house of the Lord forever.

May he rest in peace. Thank you, gentlemen.'

I went back to my cabin and put my thoughts and emotions in check so that I could be the Captain and be in command.

CHAPTER 11

The days seemed to slide past. Sometimes the wind was finicky, other days it was strong. The crew appeared to get along well; everyone knew what their duties were. And I enjoyed my chess games with Lesley. She would say, 'Jacko's good, you never know what move he is going to make next, he certainly sharpens me up and makes my mind work in different directions.'

I noticed how well she was getting on with Les, helping him in the galley; they would talk and laugh a lot; we all saw the woman's touch in preparing the food. You would see her playing cards with the crew, enjoying every moment of it. She was relaxed and at peace with herself. The worry she had when she came on board had gone.

Michael had indeed taken Trevor under his wing and was being Big Brother. Everybody was pushing Jarrett hard, and he seemed to be enjoying every bit of it. It had opened another part of his mind. He would ask the crew questions, debate and discuss things with them, and I could see he was becoming a part of them. I often saw them laughing together. Ted taught him to use the sextant and the compass; how to study the charts, read longitude and latitude, time and date. And I gave him one of Colin's notebooks.

'Jarrett use this as a logbook; record everything in it.'

'Thank you! Captain, why are you giving me all this attention?'

'Your father asked me to make a man of you. He told me that you were going to take on significant responsibilities, so we must prepare you for the future. That is what we are trying to do. I think your father would be very proud of you if he were here. It is going to be a clear night tonight, so be back here after dark. You will have a long night; the stars have a lot to teach you.'

He nodded, picked up the notebook, and went back to his duties.

I studied my charts again and took another reading before the sun had set. I asked Ted to check it; we both looked at the map. We dropped back down to Latitude 36°S because we had to avoid an island called Eclipse One and the Muddy Reef. *Daisy May* had all her canvas on, and she was doing well. I took the first watch; working with Jarrett. Jacko took the next one, and we altered course again. I wanted to be at Longitude 115°E, Latitude 35.5°S. That should be just before daylight.

The next day was a beautiful day, *Daisy May's* sails were looking full and majestic, she seemed to glide through the water. Jacko walked into the wheelhouse with two cups of coffee and half a sticky bun sticking out of his mouth. I took one of the cups of coffee then quickly reached out and snatched the half sticky bun out of his mouth, a muffled sound came out of this mouth, it was an Aboriginal word, and I fully understood what it meant! I laughed. 'Jacko, take the first watch. Call me when you see the lighthouse. Ted and Michael have everything under control on deck.'

I went into my cabin, sat down at my desk and opened my logbook. I remembered them telling me to write as little as possible. I wrote that *Daisy May* departed Melbourne, the date and time, and Port Phillip Heads. I picked up the pieces of paper with the crew names on them.

Ted Coe – Bosun, Ted is as strong as an oak tree, tall, thin and wiry, his untidy hair straggled down to his shoulders and he always wore his seaman's hat. He was a man totally devoted to his position on board. A man of few words but when he was talking to Jacko he would joke with him, teasing him and laughing at the answers that came back. He didn't do this with any of the other crew members. When Ted went ashore he would always pick a woman who didn't want small talk; he just wanted to get on with the pleasure and then return to *Daisy May* where he was safe and in control of his environment.

Michael Theodore, Sailmaker, Rigging master. Michael was one of those interesting men, women were his biggest problem, he was built like a Greek God, thick black hair swept back, and he shaved before going ashore but always had a good moustache. His eyes were his biggest enemy; once a woman looked into them, it was as if he had already made love to her. Women could not resist him. He would buy them small personal gifts to make them feel special, a red rose, the best bottle of wine he could find. Then, just before *Daisy May* left her berth he would stand on the jetty and tell them how beautiful they were and how much he was going to miss them, while they stood there in tears. I would look at them on the jetty and wonder how he did it. They are always the most beautiful women in the port.

Jacko – Helmsman. Jacko was about five foot six, a little on the thin side with a bit of a potbelly, probably from too many sticky buns. His hair was white and wiry; his beard was also white. When Jacko first came on board as a young man, his hair and beard were black, the wind, sun and sea had turned them white. Leave Jacko at the helm, and he was totally at home, he knew everything before it had happened. Never dismiss what Jacko said, he was totally in tune with nature. When Ted and Michael came back on board, they would run their fingers through his hair, pull his beard, tease and tickle him, and he thoroughly enjoyed it. The three of them were as one.

Terry, I didn't know his last name. Terry was six foot tall, reasonably built, and always did his job well. He was a very private, individual man who kept to himself.

The next name puzzled me, Lesley Johnson. Lesley was spelled wrong, it was spelled in a masculine way, she obviously wanted it that way, so that's how I wrote it. She was about five foot six tall, with curly hair about shoulder length, and it was very well fashioned. Lesley had an English complexion; the sun and wind had not withered her looks. I remembered her standing on the stern of *Daisy May* with her hands clasped behind her back. She appeared to be totally in control of herself. Lesley said she was a reporter writing articles for magazines. When she said that a small smile came over her face and her eyes flittered down to the deck. What was I seeing? I didn't know. I didn't have any knowledge of women, their facial expressions, movements, I knew nothing! I did love the colour of her jumper, a beautiful blue that reminded me of the sea. She wore what appeared to be expensive slacks that fitted her very well. Everything about her was in proportion, my eyes drifted down to her chest, I shook my head, I don't know whether she noticed or not, but I liked what I saw. Mum never wore earrings, neither did Lesley. Her ears were tiny and very neat, they reminded me of mum. I grinned, *put as little as possible in the logbook!*

I wrote down the names of the remainder of the crew, closed the log-book and lay down on my bunk. I went into a deep sleep.

I woke to the sound of the bell. I leaned on the bench, and there was Cat sitting on Colin's coat. Cat lifted his head and stared at me. Jacko's voice broke in.

'There she is Boss, right where she should be, flashing every seven-and-a-half seconds, Cape Leeuwin Lighthouse.'

We were now heading into the Indian Ocean, past Perth; following the Gulfstream Tradewinds. The weather would start to get warm now, and the winds would become more unpredictable. A large pod of dolphins played around us. Lesley, Trevor and Jarrett seemed to enjoy every moment of their company, laughing and shouting. Suddenly the dolphins disappeared.

'Something's wrong Boss!' Jacko said.

Then he turned sharply, looking over the stern.

'That's what's wrong Boss.'

There was another ship coming up behind us. I looked through my telescope, then handed it to Jacko.

'Big navy ship Boss; big guns, and she's coming up fast.'

The wind was coming from our port side; all our sails are fully rigged. The destroyer came up on our starboard side, too close for my comfort. The crew had gone to the starboard side, fascinated to see the big warship. Ted came to the door.

'I wonder what she wants, Skipper?'

'I don't know Ted, but I'm pleased that she's British, look at her flags.'

The warship had reduced speed to match ours. A naval officer was standing on the wing. He lifted a loudhailer to his mouth.

'Captain, we are checking all shipping. We are satisfied who you are and wish you a safe voyage.'

As quickly as it arrived, it had left.

'I suppose it's the war,' Ted remarked and then walked back out on the deck.

The captain of the warship walked back into the wheelhouse and looked at his second officer, who was holding his binoculars.

'Yes, it's the woman. She wiped her forehead with three fingers showing, thank you number one.'

The Admiral walked into the radio room.

'Message for Command: "Admiral French very much enjoyed our night out, but I will stick to three fingers of scotch in my glass next time, getting too old for more." Send this straight away!'

There was a knock at Admiral French's office door.

'Come.'

The Communications Officer walked in with an envelope, handed it to the Admiral who took it, tore it open and read it.

'That will be all. Thank you.'

The door closed behind the officer; the admiral sighed to himself, So far so good! He opened his diary and wrote down three, put a circle around it and wrote, All is well.

Lesley stood watching a man on the wing of the battleship; she reached up to brush the hair from her forehead with three fingers. Then she felt a shiver run down her spine. She turned and looked towards the wheelhouse. Jacko was staring at her. Lesley turned around to face the destroyer. She could feel a cold sweat coming over her and shivered. Was this fear?

CHAPTER 12

Jacko and I stood watching the beautiful sunset. We had all the canvas on her, every sail set. *Daisy May* eased herself back and forth with a gentle roll from side to side. The crew seemed to be at total peace with her; carrying out their duties. The young men, Trevor and Jarrett, appeared to be practising a game of self-defence, laughing and shouting at each other and enjoying each other's company. Lesley and Les were in the galley laughing and talking, patting each other on the back with warm friendship. Lesley had her hands covered in flour and both her cheeks were covered as well.

Watching her and seeing the sunlight in her hair, the warmth, and compassion within her, I felt a loneliness within me. Something, I'd never felt or understood. Jacko broke my thoughts.

'Why would a British destroyer check on us in Australian waters? You would think it would be an Australian warship.'

'Yes, Jacko, I was thinking the same thing.'

Another loose end.

That night I worked with Jarrett, we talked about the stars. I pointed out different constellations in the sky and explained their locations and meanings; how you could use them for navigation. It was one of those beautiful nights when you felt so small under the canopy of those twinkling lights.

The next morning was the same. The night had been a good one. Everybody seemed to be rested and relaxed. I saw Cat stand up, turn and stare at me. Then I heard his voice. *'Sharpen up boy, sharpen up.'* It was Colin's voice in my head.

Jacko turned and looked at the barometer; then looked at me with a worried face.

'The barometer has dropped to very low air pressure; we are going to hit trouble, big trouble.'

Jacko was looking at the sails; they suddenly went slack. There wasn't any wind. Then, just as suddenly, they filled with wind again as if nothing had happened. Jacko and I both knew what this meant. I went out on the deck where Ted and Michael were looking into the distance. There was a thin black line on the horizon right around us. We all looked at each other, knowing what was in store. I walked into to the galley.

'Les, I think we're in for a bit of a blow., Could you prepare everything?' I said in a calm voice.

Ted's voice broke in, 'There they are Boss.'

You could only barely make out the white fluffy clouds on the horizon. They were right around us.

'This looks like it will be a real blow. Get the canvas off her rigging; prepare for stormy weather. You and you, lash everything down that could move.'

I looked at the clouds again and could see the black tips on them. The wind hadn't increased yet but I knew once it did, it would come as a significant force, churning up the water. White waves of water would come crashing down on us, throwing us violently up into the air. *Daisy May* would crash down the other side, ready to meet the next wave. What did we have to do to prepare the ship? Then I thought of the motor. They had worked on her, but I'd stopped relying on that a long time ago.

'Michael, did they start the motor?'

'No, Skipper. We were in dry dock. They changed the oil filters, fuel filters and put a new diesel tank in her. They could not start her as there wasn't any water for the cooling system.'

'Try and start her now, Michael.'

He disappeared below. *Daisy May* was rigged to meet the storm.

'Young Trevor come here. I want you to get some blankets, a bucket, biscuits, and water. Wedge yourself under the bench in the wheelhouse and get one of those fancy jackets on; I believe they are supposed to keep you afloat if you fall overboard. Don't stare at me lad, do it now! Lesley, would you please do the same.'

'Have I got something to worry about Skipper?' she asked.

'No, just be prepared. Put on some warm clothing and tie yourself in your bunk.'

I walked up to the three young men.

'I want two of you to operate the pump, one of you to rest and be ready to relieve one of the others when the time comes. Lash yourself to something. Put some warm clothes on and your oilskins.'

I heard the motor turning over, but it didn't start. Michael appeared back on deck and shook his head at me.

The fore-topmast staysail had been set on her bow; the foresail on her mainmast had been reefed. The spinnaker on her stern was set. Just enough sail to give her steerage and not put too much pressure on her rigging. I gave Ted a hand to put the shutters on the wheelhouse windows. Michael was doing the same to the galley windows. Les was passing out hot soup before he shut his stove down so that everyone had some food in their stomachs for what was about to happen.

Then we felt the gust of wind which comes before the storm. Massive black clouds were rolling in over the horizon; a black that felt evil and chilled you to your very bones, because you knew what was in store. Then we saw it. A wall of white water was coming before the storm. The crew was still lashing ropes across the deck so that they had something to anchor to.

'Brace yourselves, lads, here it is,' I yelled.

Daisy May's bow hit the wall of white water. She shuddered and shook. Her bow was thrust upwards, up and up as if she wasn't going to stop, then she crashed down the other side, going down and down. She hit the bottom of the trough; she shook and vibrated, then the next wave crashed into her. Her bow rose back up and spray from the wind engulfed her then she went back down the other side of the wave.

Colin's coat slid off the bench onto the floor. I heard Colin's voice again in my head, '*She was built for this boy. She'll handle it; no worries!*'

The sound of the wind was deafening; the rolling, the pitching, and shaking, the shutters vibrating in the wind. I could see the two crewmen, wearing oilskins were working on the pumps; ropes were tied securely around their waists. They were the only men on deck There was a cross-brace with two handles on either side so that you put a hand on each handle, one pushed up, the other pushed down, and rhythm developed. I could see Ted lashed to the mainmast facing the stern. This nightmare seemed to go on and on. The fearful, ominous dark grey-green waves kept on coming. I wondered when it was going to stop, would we survive. *Pull it together, Bill, this is just another storm, there will be plenty more.* *Daisy May* reached the crest of another wave again. Looking out of the wheelhouse window I froze at what I was witnessing.

'No, no, no, we don't want that!' Jacko said shaking his head.

There was a cross wave on our starboard side. It was coming in sideways as we slid down the wave we were on. The cross wave hit our starboard side and *Daisy May* listed to her port side; her bow was now facing sideways in a trough. The next wave crashed into her, she shuddered and shook, then rolled over onto her side, being pushed sideways.

Jacko was lying on his side with ropes holding him in tightly. He screamed out in his native language as he gripped the wheel. I was thrown sideways and landed on Colin's jacket, which was on the wheelhouse deck. Then the next wave hit us, I slid under the bench alongside Trevor, his eyes were as big as saucers, he was screaming, but no sounds came from his mouth. The weight of *Daisy May*'s cargo forced her violently upright. The spinnaker on her stern filled with wind.

Jacko was holding tight onto the wheel, and the rudder, being in the right position turned *Daisy May* to face the next wave, but instead of going over the top if it, she plunged into it, shaking and vibrating. She tossed the wave over the top of her bow, the decks were awash, I scrambled to my feet just as her bow was rising to meet the next wave. I looked over at Jacko, he was alright. I shouted out 'Ted, Ted,' but I knew he couldn't hear me. I looked at the main mast; there was Ted looking at the wheelhouse with his thumb in the air. The two men on the pumps were still there, with the ropes slashed around them, but they weren't looking too healthy.

The wind started to ease, and the waves seemed to be less violent. The troughs in the waves were wider, *Daisy May* had more time to meet the next wave. Ted replaced the two men on the pumps with four men. He knew we had water in our hull; it was swirling around in the bilge. All I wanted now was to get my bearings and see how far the storm had pushed us off course.

'Ted, could you take a reading and check my figures?'

He did so and looked at me with a deep frown.

'I was worried for a moment Skipper. I thought you were a degree out.' He laughed out loud and turned to walk out of the wheelhouse, 'But I was wrong.'

He walked back out of the wheelhouse, giving instructions and orders to the crew to check everything.

'Trevor, you can come out from underneath the bench now. You have weathered your first real storm. Go and get yourself some food from the galley. Take the bucket with you and dispose of the contents. Don't be embarrassed. I half filled a bucket like that once, many years ago.'

I tapped Jacko on the shoulder. He winked at me, 'I filled one too.'

I knocked on Lesley's cabin door.

'Come in.'

She was sitting with her legs over the bunk.

'Are you alright?' I asked her.

'No, I'm not! My hair is all over the place, and I look terrible., It feels like somebody has put a stick of dynamite in my stomach. Les has brought me some soup and biscuits.'

I looked for her bucket, but Les had already taken it.

Daisy May weighed 254 tonnes payload, she was 114 feet long and twenty five feet in beam. Weighing that much and being tossed around in a rough sea, her mast would have been whipped back and forth. When I got back on deck, Ted and Michael were tightening the wedges in the mast.

'How are they, Ted?'

'Not bad considering the storm. I hope we don't meet any more like that Skipper. She wouldn't have survived it if she hadn't been refitted!'

'How are the shrouds?' The wind was putting pressure on one side of the mast, so looking at them on the lee side, you could see if there was any slack in them.

Michael replied, 'Could need a bit of tightening Skipper. The forward and aft stays seem to be OK.'

'Yes, I agree, the stays seem to be alright.'

I asked Michael what he thought about the foremast aft rig that supports the tri sails.

Michael shrugged. 'I believe that we had better keep an eye on them, Skipper.'

'What about the spinnaker? It looks a bit loose.'

'Yes, Skipper, it took a beating during the storm. I think it should be replaced.'

'Very well, Michael, go ahead.'

I walked up to the three young men.

'Reno, are you alright?'

'Yes, sir.'

The word 'sir' took me by surprise.

'Dominic?'

'Yes, I'm alright; my stomach is a bit tight.'

'Philip, are you alright? You don't look too good.'

I heard the others chuckle.

'I'm still a little bit sick. I'm not too good at all, but if I can get away from these two laughing jackasses, I'll be alright.'

I turned and looked at the other two and winked.

'Well, Philip, the best place is on top of the forward mast.'

I turned and walked away. The other two were still chuckling. I spoke to the rest of the crew one by one. Malcolm had a cut on his arm, quite deep. The towel was bloody.

'Come with me, Malcolm. Lesley, could you please attend to this man for me?'

Lesley disappeared into my cabin and came out with what she needed.

'Trevor, could you please get me a bucket of salt water? Lesley asked. Michael get me some warm water, please.'

She unwrapped the towel and studied the wound. Lesley looked at the men.

'I think we had better find somewhere to sit down.'

She washed the wound with salt water.

'Captain, this is going to need some stitches. He will need to rest for at least two weeks.'

I put my arms on Malcolm's shoulders.

'Well, Malcolm, we will have to work you harder when you are back on deck! Just take it easy and do as Lesley tells you. Les will get you anything you want.'

I turned and winked at Lesley and went back to fill out my logbook. I found myself thinking of how she looked before the storm with the flour on her face and the sunlight shining in her hair.

CHAPTER 13

I picked up Colin's coat and put it back on the bench next to the window. Cat appeared out of nowhere and jumped up onto it. Then I noticed Jacko. He looked very weary and tired. His head kept dropping forward, then his eyes would flash back to the compass. He'd been there for nearly twelve hours through the storm; the rope was still lashed around his waist. I beckoned to Jarrett.

'Take the wheel, lad.'

I stood behind Jacko, put my arms under his arms, and took him back to my cabin and laid him down on the bunk. He curled up in a tight ball and was instantly sound asleep, totally exhausted. I sat on the edge of the bed and put my hand on his head. I thought of my mum, how she had loved him from a baby, how she had nursed him. She would sit and talk to him when the world was cold and didn't have any understanding or compassion. He is my brother. I knew not to cover him with a blanket; his body temperature worked differently to mine. I went back out on the deck.

'Ted, get some rest. You've been up too many hours.'

'So, have you, Captain.'

'You've been out in the weather, Ted; I have not. Get some rest!'

'Aye, aye Captain!' He gave me that far Eastern wave.

'Michael, could you keep an eye on Jarrett? I'm going to put my head down for a couple of hours. Please wake me.'

I walked into my cabin, sat in my chair, put my head in my arms on the desk, and slept. But I found myself in a nightmare. A nightmare about everything that had happened since we had sailed into Port Melbourne. Nothing made any sense – all the events that had occurred, all the things that were unexpectedly put right on *Daisy May*. The money, the secrecy, the people that don't belong, my emotions for a lady on board, a woman on board, a woman on board, all this going around in my head, the storm, the words of the woman on the train, '*Why aren't you in the war?*' The young mother with the children, '*Take my son and make a man of him.*'

I suddenly awoke. There was a hand on my shoulder. I looked up, and there was Lesley with a cup of coffee in her hand.

'You asked to be woken, Skipper.'

'Yes, yes.' I stared at her for a moment, trying to get my thoughts together, then I took the coffee from her.

'Thank you, Lesley.'

As she turned to walk out of my cabin, she gently reached out and touched Jacko and turned her head slightly back towards me.

'He is certainly different from any other man I've known, but he is the other half of you, isn't he?'

'Yes, he is my brother; he is part of my mother.'

She turned and left the cabin.

I checked out our bearings again; we were still on course. I handed Jarrett the sexton.

'Check our position and our course and record the figures in your logbook.'

I slept for another two hours. This time it was a sound, deep sleep. I awoke once and found Jacko behind the wheel, his big, white eyes and that cheeky grin brought me back to where my mind should be.

'Well, what do you think, Jacko? *Daisy May* found that storm a piece of cake.'

He chuckled to himself and gave one of those funny chants again.

'Michael, get everybody on deck,' I said.

When the crew gathered on deck, I addressed them.

'Well, lads, we came through the storm well.'

My eyes caught Terry. He was not standing correctly; he was leaning slightly to one side and didn't look well.

'We are now entering dangerous waters. We are going to pass the Mauritius Islands, just a few nautical miles from Madagascar. We will head down to East London, around the Cape into the Atlantic Ocean. Around the Cape the winds are finicky; the currents are strong, and there are many reefs. You can't count the number of shipwrecks along this stretch of coast. I want all of you to rest as much as you can, but be ready to move, to change sails as quickly as you can. We are now passing the Tropic of Capricorn. Storms can come out of nowhere. Suddenly warm waters are hitting cold currents. Thank you, lads. Michael, could you please rest up? You're going to need all your resources. Terry, what's wrong?'

'Nothing, Skipper.'

'I will ask you again, Terry, what's wrong?'

Terry replied, 'my back is a bit sore, and I have a bit of pain down the back of my leg.'

'What happened?' I asked.

'During the storm, I was thrown up against the bunk and hit the middle of my back.'

'Ted, could you lay this man down on his back. Wedge him in so that he can't roll. I will get Jacko to look at him.'

Ted nodded to me and helped Terry below.

'I'm sorry, Skipper,' Terry shouted.

'No, Terry, it is I who is sorry you are hurt.'

Dusk was moving in fast; the rays of the setting sun were glinting on the water with a golden shimmer. We watched the sun slowly drift down over the horizon.

'There's land to our starboard side Skipper,' Jacko said.

I could see the sunlight on it; the birds were heading there to roost. Darkness came quickly in this part of the world. In half an hour it would be dark.

'Lighthouse port side off the bow,' a voice shouted out from aloft, 'two flashes every ten seconds. Repeated it, two white flashes every ten seconds.'

'Good man!' I shouted up at him.

Now we were looking for a second lighthouse. The Pointe aux Caves Lighthouse and we could make it out on our stern. We had just slid past it. My nerves were slightly on edge, waiting, scanning the horizon. Should I alter course to starboard ten degrees or wait? I walked towards the bow, searching the darkness. I found myself tapping my foot on the deck. Then I heard his voice again in my head, '*She's there boy, you know she's there. Have faith in yourself.*'

'Lighthouse on our port side. Two white flashes every six seconds,' the voice shouted from aloft again, 'two white flashes every six seconds.'

My worries subsided. I shook my head and walked back to the galley where Les was grumbling and moaning, banging saucepans.

'What's wrong, Les?'

'Those damn shipwrights can't get anything right. My Aga stove is loose, it can move.' He pushed it violently and it just slightly moved. I shook my head.

'I'll get it fixed in the morning for you, Les.'

'I could wreck the *Daisy May* on a reef, that doesn't matter, but a whisker of movement in Les's Aga stove and it is the end of the world! I should be getting my priorities, right.'

I saw Jacko grin at me.

'Are you talking to me Skipper, or Cat?'

I shrugged my shoulders in frustration.

'Terry has hurt his back. In your own time, when you are not busy stuffing your face with sticky buns, could you go and have a look at him?'

The wind dropped to a gentle breeze during the night. I was pleased the crew could rest. The temperature was moderate, and the current was still with us, but the winds and currents could start to work against us at any time, trying to draw us back down into the Roaring Forties. I had to get closer inshore to East London to be able to pick up the winds coming down the mainland from Mozambique. I worked on my charts and studied my currents and tides. We could come down to Latitude 30°.

Ted walked into the wheelhouse.

'Calm night, William.'

'Yes, Ted.'

I liked this time in the night being able to talk to Ted. We could talk to each other not as Captain and crew, but as friends.

Ted took a deep sigh.

'We are back at sea with cargo. What happens when we get to England and the war?'

'Yes,' I replied, 'it leaves us back in no man's land, doesn't it? Let's wait and see.'

Ted took another sigh.

'I now have my "Masters Ticket" What will they do with me? They haven't given me a ticket for no reason.'

Another loose end, I thought.

I nodded at the papers on the bench.

'Ted if you will just look over that for me. Good night.'

'Goodnight William.'

I awoke to find the breeze had picked up. We were still under full sail. Jacko walked up to Lesley.

'Gidgee,' he said.

Lesley frowned at him.

'Do you have any of that funny stuff, morphine?'

'Yes, we do,' she replied.

'Terry's back is bad. I've had a look at him. He needs something to relax him. Got no grog on board.'

I walked up to them.

'Good morning, Lesley, did you sleep well?'

'Yes, thank you,' she replied. 'Do you mind if we give Terry a little bit of morphine to relax him?'

'Did Jacko ask you?'

'Yes he did. He said Terry needs it to relax him.'

'Go ahead,' I replied. 'Lesley, when we were on Cattle stations, the drovers and the jackaroos would come to Mum with their problems. She would bind their broken limbs, put their backs into place, fix any dislocations. She taught Jacko all she knew and Jacko has that gift to heal.'

Lesley disappeared below with the morphine, and a few minutes later she reappeared with Jacko at her side. They were laughing with each other.

'That's fixed him Boss. Give him a couple of days, he will be back on deck again.'

'Thanks, Gidgee.' He went to get some grub.

Lesley looked at me with a frown on her face.

'Why does he keep calling me that name? Is he trying to be funny?'

'No, no, it's Aboriginal. They have one word that means many things. They don't have an English dictionary, so when he called you that name it could mean, "cool water, gentle breeze, sweet honey, good tucker, new baby, a warm fire or sweet yams". He is trying to say he likes you.'

'And I like him.'

She turned to hide the tears and walked to the stern and said to herself in a soft voice, *'What's happening to me? I was totally in control of myself, fully in charge of my emotions. I knew how to be heard, to get where I wanted to be, and I had achieved it. No woman has gone as far as I have. Something has happened to me on board this vessel, and I like it! But what exactly do I like?'*

Before her thoughts and emotions could go any further, the three young men turned up alongside her.

'The weather seems to be holding with us so far, and I am enjoying the voyage,' she said as she glanced at them.

'Yes, we are also enjoying the journey and learning many new skills,' answered Philip.

'I think the next four days will be exciting, but after that, we may learn a lot more.'

Philip nodded at her.

'Good evening, Lesley.'

Lesley gave them a stern look.

'Good evening, gentlemen.'

She left the three men and went back to the galley to give Les a hand with the evening meal.

For the next two days, we tacked back and forth, taking readings, making sure we knew where we were. I had noticed a few more vessels to our port and starboard but did not make any radio contact; I just touched the key around my neck to remind myself of my instructions, '*Do not make radio contact with any vessel unless you are sinking!*'

The crew had gone back to the easy way of life, enjoying each other's company, just enjoying the moment. I heard Lesley laughing and giggling. A woman's laugh was something warm and inviting, it seemed to do something for the crew. I'd see a gentle smile on their faces; something not usually seen on a sailing vessel with all men. Terry turned up at the door to the wheelhouse.

'Permission to come back and work on deck Skipper.'

I saw Jacko's eyes flash at me.

'I don't want you lifting and bending for a couple more days. You can read and write, can't you?'

'Yes, Skipper.'

'Well, you have been with me for about sixteen years now.'

'Actually, Skipper, it is eighteen years.'

'What makes you sure it is eighteen years?' I replied.

'You remember being in Bangkok Skipper? You had to get out fast because Colin had got into a bit of trouble, too much gambling and some woman wanted him to marry her. Her daddy was the wrong man to be tangled up with.'

'I remember it well; he was a big man in the port. I didn't go back there for many years. When we got back to sea, Colin had brought you on board. The only thing I could do is make you one of the crew.'

His head tipped slightly forward. I could see him biting his lip, there was a smear of blood. He tapped the wheelhouse with the palm of his hand.

'It was not Colin who got into trouble. It was me! He saved my life by putting me on the *Daisy May*. My death wouldn't have been a pleasant one. That was eighteen years ago.'

'I've always noticed that you write letters for the crew just before we are going into a port. How well educated are you?' I was curious.

'I've had a good education Skipper I had good parents, and I let them down. *Daisy May* became my home. Nobody asked me any questions, they just accepted me for who I was.'

'You've hidden it well,' I said as I picked up a notebook and a pencil. 'Make a list of everything we have on board, below decks. Look into every corner; check on everything. That should keep you busy for a couple of days and give your back a chance to settle down. If you need anything lifted young Trevor will do it for you.'

I called out to Trevor, and he sprinted over.

'I want you to work with Terry. Do any bending or lifting for him.'

I nodded at them and went to turn away when a thought came into my mind.

'Trevor, do you have trouble reading and writing?'

He looked uneasy.

'Yes, I do.'

'Then, Terry, you have work to do.'

'It will be a pleasure, Skipper,' he said smiling.

'If the wind should pick up, lay down again. Do you hear me?'

'Yes, Skipper,' he answered.

'Thank you, lads.'

'Looking for answers?' Jacko said looking at me gravely.

'Yes, Jacko, I am. What the hell is Lesley doing on this sailing vessel? She is too quick, too sharp. That chessboard, she's got us both worked out. When was the last time you won a game?'

He grinned.

'I wasn't winning. I knew I had to change the game, but it's not a game anymore. It's like life or death. I'm back in the desert and I've got to survive. Looking for drawings in the rocks to show me where the freshwater is, where the Dreamtime people, in the time before the time, had prepared us for the future. So I have to play in her mind.'

The severe look went from his face, and those big white eyes flashed at me, and a big grin came over his face.

'But you like her, don't you Skipper?'

'Yes, I do. There's something in Lesley, something I don't understand. I have worked with men all my life. I know men, but women are something else.'

Just then, both of us felt the wind change. There was a little more pressure on the rudder, and another current had picked us up and was pushing us. Ted and Michael were standing on the deck, looking at the sails and the surface of the water.

'Leave the sails as they are Ted, you can rest. Michael, stay on watch. Jacko, could you get some sleep? I'll take the wheel. Jarrett take some bearings and readings with the sexton.'

We were now near Latitude 30° Longitude 40°. I changed course slightly, knowing I was heading for East London to the Cape of Good Hope and playing a far-reaching game with the wind. No man, captain or seafarer could say that he understood the winds. It would be foolhardy arrogance. She taught me something every day.

However, I did know *Daisy May*!

Jarrett returned to the wheelhouse. He did not look at me, just went to the bench and started to write down all his figures and calculations. He was engrossed in getting it right. He opened his logbook, slightly turned to look at me, not staring, just acknowledging I was there. He wrote everything down in his logbook. He was completely in control of what he was doing.

'May I have a look at your logbook please Jarrett?'

He hesitated slightly. I took the logbook and opened it. He had recorded everything. Winds, tides, latitude, longitude, right down to the last degree, the time when he took the readings, sail changes, and what sails had been reefed to half sail. I was very impressed, but I also noticed he'd made comments about members of the crew, not criticising or condemning them, but the value of their position on *Daisy May*. I thought to myself that he would make a good skipper one day. I've got more work to do with this young lad. Then I remembered his father's words, '*He will be taking on greater responsibilities.*'

'How are you coping on board, Jarrett?'

He turned to me with a light in his eyes and a pleasant smile on his face.

'I'm fascinated with everything, Captain. I can't learn enough. Everybody on board wants to help me learn, and when my job gets too hard, there's always somebody there. When we are changing sails and I'm up there with cold fingers, wet through from the sea spray, or rain pounding my face and the mast swaying back and forth from side to side, there is always somebody there to help and support me.

'When I get back down to the galley, there is always some hot soup, fresh bread rolls and biscuits. Everybody laughs and jokes about the storm and the things that happened to us when we were aloft. I don't want it to stop. I know we're going to get to England and that fascinates me. I've always wanted to go to England, to see the castles, churches and little villages, the small harbours and fancy houses. I would very much like to meet the King. He has a lovely daughter. I've seen the photos.'

'Which daughter Jarrett?'

'Princess Elizabeth.'

'You have a good eye for women,' I replied.

Young men! Do I destroy his dreams? And mention the war and confusion, the turmoil that it will bring? No, not yet.

'Well, young man, we will see, we will see. Get some rest. I think the wind will be changing soon as we get closer to the shore. We will need to have all our strength.'

'Will we see much of the Cape Captain?'

'No, they want us to be in England in ninety-three days. They need the wool for men's uniforms and blankets and the mutton bird oil for machinery.' I patted him on the shoulder. 'You're doing well, young man. Go and get some rest.'

I found myself studying his figures, his calculations and then checking them with mine and how the results were the same. He seemed to have a quick way, a sharper way than mine. Mine is the way of an old sea dog; his style is that of a well-educated young man. He is undoubtedly the future and I liked the way he was thinking.

The wind changed again, and we had all the sails on *Daisy May*. She seemed to love it. She gently eased up to the swell to suit herself. She'd rise onto a swell with gentleness; on the top of the swell she would ease slightly to starboard and with the way the wind was pushing into her sails she would ease back down the swell and come back to port with a gentle rhythm. Lesley appeared alongside me.

'I can't sleep, Captain. Too much going on in my mind.'

I picked up Jarrett's logbook and handed it to Lesley.

'You say you're writing magazine articles for the owners of this vessel, read through this, it might help you.'

She looked at me with a serious look; she seemed puzzled and snapped herself together.

'Yes, that would be interesting.'

She took the logbook and started to read. She read it with a deep concentration on her face. When she had finished reading, she looked up at me and back at the logbook.

'Does this logbook have to stay with you?'

'No, it's Jarrett's, but while it's on this vessel at sea, it belongs to this wheelhouse and *Daisy May*.'

'He has a beneficial future,' she said as she lifted her head and looked straight into my eyes. She then looked back at the logbook; her mind was deep in thought. She snapped herself back together.

'Well, what about that chess game?' she smiled.

Before I could answer, the board had already been set out, and she had moved her first piece. My mind raced back to when I talked about writing articles for the magazine and the look on her face. And the question about the logbook. *Jarrett has a good future.* Something wasn't quite right—another frustrating loose end. We had finished the game and I had nearly won, but at the last moment, I lost!

The bell rang. It was a change of watch. Jacko appeared out of nowhere, as per usual.

'How are you going, Gidgee?'

Lesley remembered what the word meant and kissed him on the forehead. Jacko stood there with a silly grin all over his face. He glanced at the chessboard with a serious look on his face.

'We play a game?'

'Yes, Jacko, I'd love to,' Lesley replied.

I walked to my cabin, closed the sliding door, kicked my boots off and remembered Jacko's words, '*Have got to go back to the desert and survive.*' Well, Lesley, now you have to sharpen up! I closed my eyes and was asleep.

The bells of the watch startled me. I put my boots on, slid back the door. There were Lesley and Jacko still playing chess!

'Well, who's winning?' I asked.

Lesley's face turned to me, her eyes flashing. 'We are trying to play chess Captain. Could you please leave us?'

Jacko's eyes flashed to the compass and back to the chessboard. I didn't say a word, just went into the galley. Les handed me a cup of coffee and a sticky bun. My eyes scanned the sails; we still had all the canvas on her. Michael walked up alongside me.

'The winds have been holding Skipper. What's wrong with those two in the wheelhouse?'

'Nothing Michael, the game has got more serious; she's been baiting Jacko.'

'If he gets into her head, she won't win. He got into mine, and I've given up!' Michael laughed as he walked away.

I went back into the wheelhouse, picked up my sexton, and took my calculations; checked the time then went back in and checked my figures. I called out to Jarrett. He was there instantly. I handed him the sexton.

'Check my numbers.'

'Yes, Captain.'

I gently pushed Jacko away from the wheel. He gave me a little nudge in the ribs with his elbow; cheeky little sod is going to win. He's playing games with Lesley. He is in her mind. She reached out to move a chess piece; then stopped herself. She looked at Jacko, her face was full of anger and rage, then it softened, and the tears started.

'You handsome, spooky little man. We've played this game for hours, but before we even started you had been playing games with me, not the chessboard, but with me. Whichever way I move, you've won. We've been playing for over four hours, the same game, and now you've won.'

'I haven't won yet. You haven't moved your last chess piece,' Jacko grinned.

Lesley picked up her chess piece, took his hand, put the chess piece in the palm of his hand, closed his fingers around it and then kissed him on the forehead.

'I think you and your people won a long time ago. It is we who have lost. We tried to change you because we didn't know that precious gift that you have and we still don't. Now I'm going to sleep and I know this time I will sleep.'

With a chuckle, she disappeared into her cabin.

'Pleased with yourself, Jacko?'

'Yes, Boss. But no, she won, but in a different way.'

I looked at him puzzled. Then Jarrett's voice cut in with a laugh.

'She's a woman Jacko. You will never win!'

Jacko and I just looked at each other. We hadn't had any experience with women. It was something new. I shook my head.

'Have you got your figures there, Jarrett?'

'Yes, Captain and they are the same as yours.'

I walked into my cabin, took my telescope off the shelf and stopped for a moment. I reached down to the bottom drawer. I hadn't opened this drawer for a long time. I took out the telescope that Captain Walter Wright had given me many years ago. There was another telescope in the drawer, but I left it there. I placed the telescope in Jarrett's hand and told him to follow me. We went to the bow, starboard side, and I focused my telescope on the horizon, and Jarrett did the same.

'What are we looking for young Jarrett?'

'Well, Captain, according to my calculations and yours, we should see land in half an hour or so.'

'That is correct. We won't see the Seal Point Lighthouse if there are dark clouds. Normally the white of the lighthouse and the glitter of its light would show up. But not today. See that haze on the horizon?'

Jarrett looked more closely with his telescope.

'The grey clouds on the horizon?'

'Yes, they are the clouds on the land, or just above the land. We will stay on this course for another three hours; then we will alter course starboard five degrees. It is now 7:30 am. At 10:30 am we change course. I want you to be here every half an hour with this telescope. Scan the land and keep doing it until you're satisfied that you have not missed anything. Study the sea in front of us. You are looking for something that does not belong. Report any white caps on the surface, rocks, or if the sea seems to have a different colour. We are looking for sandbanks, and they are tough to see on the surface. The water may be different, see how the sun is reflecting off it, this gives a different type of colour. If you wish to stay here and keep a good, sharp eye, that is up to you. I will have coffee, cake and biscuits brought to you.'

I tapped him on the shoulder and walked away.

'Ted, I'm going to do some paperwork in my cabin for half an hour.' I looked down at the compass. 'At 10:30 am if the wind stays with us, we will change course five degrees to starboard. Michael has a man aloft with a sharp eye.'

'Aye, aye, Captain.'

I went back into my cabin but did not close the sliding door. I sat down and did my calculations, figures and reports. I checked my 24-hour clock and recorded the times in my logbook. To the crew, time was morning, daylight, evening, dark; when their food was ready or when the bell rang for the change of watch. Where they were in the world didn't seem to matter, as long as they were at sea. However, what I wanted now was to see Cape Recife Lighthouse at Port Elizabeth. I had read of many shipwrecks here. No explanations were found. Ships washed up on beaches or rocky outcrops. Some said piracy; others said the fickle finger of fate. Maybe sailing vessels with holes in the rigging that had become tired but nobody had spent money on them to keep them afloat.

'Is all well Ted?'

'Just watching the horizon; looks like a bit of a blow coming in,' Ted answered.

'Yes, it does. Let's get the topsails off *Daisy May*, the four royal and the main royal, main topgallant sail and the fore topgallant sail. We'll keep her rigged low in case there are any problems. It will be much easier on the crew.'

I knew Jacko was on top of the wheelhouse, stretched out getting as much sun as he could. I knew there was cold weather about to come. The barometer had started to fall. Jacko was also a living barometer. If Jacko looked at the setting sun or the rising of a new moon, he could tell by the colours surrounding them what was happening in the upper atmosphere. He could watch the formation of the clouds and the direction of the migrating birds and know what the weather would do.

Suddenly the wind became brisk, biting cold and sharp. Jacko swung off the wheelhouse roof and landed lightly on his feet.

'This wind wants to push us to starboard.'

I stood aside and let him have the wheel.

'Keep on this course and see what happens when we pass Danger Point.'

I saw Jacko shiver.

'Don't like this place, Skipper. Widgee is in the wind, and he's never happy.'

'Then talk to him, Jacko. Tell him what an incredible wind he is. Perhaps you can get some favours for us.'

We held her on course for the next four hours. I had two hours rest. Darkness was starting to fall, and the wind had dropped off to a very gentle breeze.

'Ted, just keep the sails as they are and send five of the crew to rest.'

'Aye Skipper,' he replied.

I paced back and forth across the deck, waiting for the unpredictable, playing chess with this widgee Jacko talked about. I was pleased to see the lights of a steamer coming towards us. It put me at ease. We were on the right course.

I jumped with a start. I heard a man's voice on the radio.

'To the vessel on my port side, good to see your sails.'

I wanted to answer him but I couldn't. Frustration seemed to take over me again. Why not?

'Game of chess Skipper?' Lesley said as she appeared alongside me.

'Yes.'

I played the game, but my mind wasn't on it. I was too busy watching the wind, trying to listen to the man aloft. Michael was alongside the wheelhouse; he would be about to change the man aloft.

He shouted out the man's name. 'Change the watch.'

'Lighthouse on the starboard side forward,' he shouted half an hour later.

This lighthouse was called Danger Point, off Port Elizabeth. Colin's favourite girlfriend lived there. She always looked after him when we were in port. He never gave me any information, just grinned, and chuckled at me.

The days slid past. There was the Roman Rock Lighthouse, best lighthouse ever built, every sea captain appreciated it. Around every lighthouse, there are politics. Instead of just building it, politicians had to get their name involved in it somewhere.

I was relieved that we were leaving Cape Town behind us and heading into the Atlantic Ocean. At Longitude 15° I changed course again. I wanted to be at Longitude 5° before altering the course. I was tired and weary. I had finished playing a frightening game with the winds, tides, and currents of the Cape.

We were heading back up to the Tropic of Capricorn, back out into the open sea.

'Ted, I need to sleep; take over command.'

He nodded at me and glanced at the chart.

'You're in trouble now, Jacko! I'm in command,' he said as he tapped Jacko on the shoulder.

'Yes, Ted, I'm in trouble now. You're in command; now, my worries start.' Jacko gave a small chuckle and chatted a few words in his native language. They both laughed.

I slept soundly for six hours then I felt a slight movement from the bottom of my bunk. I swung my head around, off the pillow to see who was there. There wasn't anyone. Then I smelled it, Colin's pipe. The smell was not offensive anymore. I felt something comforting deep down inside me. I shook my head, and the hairs on the back of my hand started to stand up. There was a knock at the door. It slid open, and there was Les warmly smiling. He had coffee and a meal; it smelled so good. He placed the food and coffee on my desk.

'I'm having trouble with your coffee cup. Lesley keeps using it!' He turned around and walked out.

I ate the meal and drank the coffee. I was now awake. My stomach was full; I was ready once more. I didn't have to play the scary game with the winds, tides, and currents that could suck me onto a reef or rocky outcrop.

CHAPTER 14

Night had fallen once again.

'Why don't you get some rest, Jacko?'

'I can't relax Boss; it's here again, Boss. I stay here!'

I learned a long time ago what Jacko meant. The fog was rolling in across the darkness of the water. The stars were gone, and Jacko could not see the horizon. All his senses were lost and gone. He was out of control. However, all the time he stayed at the wheel and watched the compass he felt safe in his mind. Lock an Aboriginal in a dark room with no windows; he will lie down and die. If you put a bird in a box with no light, it will die. The fog was like a box with no windows with nowhere to escape.

I put my hands on his shoulders.

'Hold on Jacko. The sun will return; hang on.'

I went back out on the deck.

'Michael, Jacko knows the fog is coming.'

'Yes, Captain, the wind is dropping, and you can feel the dampness in the air.'

An hour later, the wind had dropped entirely. The fog becalmed us. It was dark, and the dampness of water was dripping off everything. It had an eerie, unnatural feeling that felt utterly evil. Lesley appeared alongside me.

'Lesley, could you please stand in the wheelhouse with Jacko and talk to him about anything you like; just talk to him, your voice will calm him.'

Then I noticed she was drinking coffee from my cup. She walked through the door and started talking to Jacko.

Daylight never seemed to come. There was just a grey mist that swirled around us, giving us a feeling that we were lost in time. Our foghorn boomed out that sorrowful, lonely sound, and we waited for it to bounce back to us, letting us know that another ship, land or the devil himself was out there. The fog stayed with us all the next day and the next night. I walked up to the three young men, and Jarrett turned up out of nowhere.

'Are you coping with the fog, all right?'

'Not too well Skipper, it's nothing like we've ever experienced before. How long do you think it will last?' Philip said as he stepped slightly forward.

'I believe that by morning it will have passed. If you look at the ripple on the sea and look at the sails, you will notice we are starting to move again just gently. This slight breeze will lift the fog. If you all walk aft to the wheelhouse and ask Jacko, he'll tell you.'

I thought that would keep Jacko busy. The next day we had a gentle breeze and clear blue skies. The air was still damp and heavy though. Jacko was sound asleep on top of the wheelhouse, happy and content. I asked Les how his new Aga stove was going.

'It's the best present anyone ever gave me. I can cook things properly on it. It's magic,' he replied.

'Has Lesley got my cup again?' I said as I noticed my cup was missing from the rack.

'Yes, Skipper.'

'Why?' I asked.

'You don't know anything about women, do you Skipper?'

He took me entirely by surprise.

'No, I don't.'

'It's the only way she can get close to you, to be a part of you, to be with you.'

I wanted to say *'Why would she want to do that?'*, but I stopped myself. I was puzzled and confused, caught up in my emotions.

'Skipper, we've been at sea for forty-eight days now. In another forty-five days, she will leave this vessel and probably never return. The events in the future will change all of our lives. How can she let you know her feelings for you? You are the Skipper; you must stay above people's inner feelings; you have to keep *Daisy May* afloat.'

He reached up and took another cup down, filled it with coffee and handed it to me.

'This is the cup Lesley used when she first came on board; she brought it with her.'

He walked back into his galley. I found myself just staring at the cup. I put both my hands around the cup and gripped it tightly.

The days slid past; we tacked back and forth, still keeping on our course. I watched Ted and Michael working with Jarrett. Jacko's questions challenged Jarrett; he wanted Jarrett to get his mind working.

Sometime later, I found Jacko looking over the stern.

'What's wrong, Jacko?'

'Don't know Boss, but big fish, he's been following us for a while. You could see white water coming from his blowhole.'

All that day I would see Jacko looking over the stern. Ted and Michael had noticed him also.

'What's the spooky little fellow know now? Michael asked.

'I don't know, but it's starting to concern me.'

The wind increased during the day. It was a cold wind and I'd noticed Jacko on top of the wheelhouse with a blanket over his shoulders, looking at the stern. He came and had his meal, then went and took his position in the wheelhouse. Lesley had joined him. They were talking and laughing together. Lesley's laugh was warm, sincere, and relaxing as if she didn't have a care in the world. I didn't want to disturb them, but I needed to rest. I gently slid past Lesley to get to my sliding door. We didn't touch, but she lifted her head slightly. I felt frozen in time. What could I see in her eyes and the look on her face? Then she broke away.

'I'd better get some sleep Skipper. I'm sure there will be more sail changes tonight.' She got up and slowly disappeared into her cabin.

'Wake me in three hours, Jacko.'

I noticed Cat looking at me and thought he knew something. Jacko and that damn Cat! How do I put them in the logbook? What could I write? They would think I was crazy! I found myself sitting on the edge of my bunk, thinking about the look on Lesley's face. I had never seen that look before—but maybe I had. When the old Aborigine put Jacko into Mum's arms, she had the same look on her face.

The next thing I knew Jacko was shaking me. 'You're a funny looking fellow when you're asleep!' he said.

'Why don't you go and get coffees? You're a damn cockatoo, always squawking!'

He walked away, laughing and went back into the wheelhouse. Daylight had just started to come over the horizon.

'Jarrett take the reading coordinates,' I said as I handed him the sexton. 'Show me your star calculations from last night.'

Most of the crew were up. The three young men were doing exercises on the deck with Lesley and Trevor. I had to admit they were far fitter than I was!

Then, in total surprise, Cat stood up on all four legs, and arched his back. He started to hiss. You could see his teeth as his mouth opened wide and he stared directly at Jacko. Jacko's head swung to the starboard side; his eyes were wide open, and all his senses were as alert as Cat's. Then I heard sounds I'd never heard before. It was not a sandbank or the sound of tide waters. It was a sound with warning all over it! It was the sound of water bubbling, of huge air bubbles boiling to the surface. Then a big black object started to rise to the surface. Brown with rusty streaks running down its side, it had what appeared to be a chimney at its rear. Then a long metal body appeared from underneath. I realised this monster was a submarine. A man surfaced on top of the conning tower. He had a loud-hailer to his mouth. A voice boomed out in German; I didn't understand what he was saying. Then his voice boomed out again in English.

'Heave to your vessel, stop your vessel Captain.'

A man appeared on the front of the submarine. He was carrying something. I then noticed a cannon on the front. The man was carrying a shell.

'Jacko, turn her into the wind! Turn into the wind, starboard!'

We were now one hundred feet in front of the submarine, its bow was pointing directly at our starboard side. We had come to a complete stop. The crew was standing on the starboard side of the vessel. Lesley and the three young men were standing on the stern, to the starboard side. Lesley had both her hands on the top of her head, it all seemed perfectly natural, but the next moment we were shocked, confused and bewildered entirely by what we were seeing.

The stern of the submarine, just behind the conning tower, lifted high out of the water. You could look at its propellers. Then it crashed down into the sea with a bubbling, hissing and roaring and you could hear the tearing sound of metal. The bow of the submarine had a big number fourteen painted on it. The submarine disappeared into the water. The man on the bow had dived back into the hatch as the sub rolled onto one side towards us. There was more of the sounds of tearing metal, the hissing and bubbling of air, then the submarine lay down in the water and disappeared beneath the surface. Turbulent water was swirling all around us, and for a brief moment, I stood frozen.

'Get back into the wind!' I shouted.

Jacko stood staring over the side as we started to glide away. Like the rest of the crew, I was confused. I thought this was the end; that they were going to sink *Daisy May*. Then I heard a voice behind me which put things back into perspective. *'That fixed them young Bill.'* I spun around in total surprise. I expected to see Colin standing behind me, but he wasn't. The Cat was sitting behind me. I stood staring at him as he looked towards the stern. Lesley was standing at the stern, looking out to sea, wiping her forehead with her hand. The rest of the crew were standing there. I knew they wanted me to give them answers, but what could I tell them? I don't know what just happened, but it was a German submarine, and that is all I can say. I don't know what happened to her, but thank God it did.

'Jarrett, give me your figures and the coordinates.'

I checked the figures. Jarrett was shaking. I then saw my hands on the bench; they were also trembling.

'Yes, Jarrett, it has frightened the hell out of all of us.'

I jotted down in my logbook *German submarine fourteen sunk*, then closed my logbook.

The British naval captain stood peering through his periscope. He could see the German submarine rising alongside Daisy May. They had picked up the

sound of the props during the night. He could see the woman on the stern. He shouted out to his First Officer.

'Clear all personnel from the torpedo room! Close all watertight doors!'

The First Officer hesitated and started to ask a question, but the Captain cut him short.

'Carry out my damn orders.'

He shouted out the orders again, and he then saw the woman put her hands on the top of her head. He knew then exactly what he had to do.

He gave the helmsman the coordinates. 'Dive twenty feet, full ahead, brace for the collision,' he shouted the order to the helmsman.

The First Officer in a quiet voice questioned his command, but the Captain ignored him. He could hear her props vibrating, giving her full power. Her turbines were screaming. They were racing forward in the water and struck the German submarine just behind the conning tower.

As it hit, he shouted, 'Surface twenty feet, hard astern.'

There was a sound of tearing metal, banging and cracking. The water was boiling and hissing. The vibration seemed to go right through the submarine; her turbines were still screaming. They had only done this in sea trials. The Captain was looking at his watch.

'Dive to seventy feet.' He was counting. 'Half, speed.'

'Half, speed, Captain.'

That was the first time in this incident he had to repeat his command. Time was of the essence.

'All, Stop!'

'All Stop Sir'

'Damage report.'

They both walked into his quarters.

He spun around on his First Officer and shook a finger in his face.

'You ever dare question my command again!' he said at the top of his voice. Still shaking his finger in the face of the First Officer, he realised he was out of control. He snapped himself out of it and in a calmer voice said, 'If I had fired *a torpedo into that German submarine, the concussion would have blown all the caulking out between Daisy May's planks, and she would have sunk. My orders are to keep her afloat at all costs, even if I have to sacrifice…'*

He did not finish, just left it unsaid.

'That German submarine was an old submarine, built just after the last war. It doesn't have any bulkheads, and it was built with fragile metal plate. We, however, are a class 'S' submarine. We have bulkheads and a thick plate designed to break the ice. We weigh twice as much as that German submarine. I take my orders from the Daisy May, so don't ever question my command again!'

He went back onto the bridge, gave the coordinates, 'Periscope depth!'

'Periscope, depth, sir!'

He found himself pushing his thumbnail into one of his fingers. He had tightness in his chest as he was standing before the periscope. He could see the stern of the Daisy May and the woman standing there. He saw her wipe her forehead with her hand, exposing three fingers, and he found himself relaxing.

'Down, periscope!'

He muttered to himself, 'So we now follow the phantom again; she just disappears into the sea.'

Darkness had fallen. The Captain gave the command to surface and turned around to his First Officer.

'Take the crew forward on deck and give me a damage report.'

He stood on top of the conning tower, just making out the bow of the submarine. He heard some banging and some splashes in the water. The crew must have removed some twisted handrail. Somebody appeared alongside him. He didn't take much notice. He was more concerned with getting on their way. The man alongside him took a cigarette out of a packet and put it to his mouth, took out a lighter and started to flick the lighter to light his cigarette. The flame flashed. The Captain was suddenly aware of what the man was doing and snapped it out of his hand.

'You should know better than that; you will see that flame for miles.'

'Damage control, sir; no superstructure damage sir, some small dents and scratches, but nothing serious, sir,' one of the crew member's said.

'All crew below decks.'

'Yes, sir.'

'Dive to periscope depth.'

I was standing on the stern of the *Daisy May* staring into the darkness. I felt that within myself I was out of control. My mind kept going back to the German submarine. What had happened? It was a German submarine, what did they want? Was it our stores? If they hadn't wanted anything, we would have been on the bottom now. Jacko's voice was in my mind, *'Big fish following us, Boss.'* Was that the big fish? I was angry and frustrated. I had no answers. Then I saw it. My mind snapped back to a flash of light, far in the distance; not on the horizon but halfway between the horizon and us. Perhaps two miles from us. Was it another vessel? Was that vessel a ship? If it were a ship, you would see its green or red lights and the white light on the mast of the stern. Damn, damn, damn, another loose end, something else with no answers. I clenched my fist and thumped it on the baulkworks with frustration. I went back into the wheelhouse and stood alongside Jacko.

'That big fish Jacko, was it a submarine?'

'There is another big fish, Boss, a big, big one.'

I stood there, thinking the worst. There's another submarine? A cold shiver went down my spine. I looked back at my chart.

'Jacko, I want to swing wide of Cape Verde, a couple of days west of Dakar. Latitude 15°, Longitude 25°, sail out to Longitude 30°.'

Jacko laughed. 'Remember the sandbank Boss when we slid down alongside one? That was scary!'

'You warned me the day before Jacko, but I didn't take any notice of you.'

Jacko gave a little dance. The sea and tide push the sand up into rows, maybe two hundred feet long, maybe more.

We were not aware on that distant day we were heading directly for the same sand bank. We lay over to one side, and the next minute, we were upright again and then as the light hit the sandbank from a different direction we saw them. The Gods were with us on that day. I wanted to give the sandbanks a wide berth, so I gave Jacko the course. He swung the wheel onto that course and the sails filled with air. *Daisy May* was happy. I would never forget those coordinates. Every time I look at that chart, the memories come flashing back as nightmares. What could have happened?

Another night and another day and the crew had returned to their usual friendly attitude. Jarrett and Trevor were working with Michael with the sails over their laps repairing the corner eyes. Lesley was laughing with Les; the three young men were on the bow scrubbing the deck. Ted had others carrying out other duties. But Jacko looked worried and concerned.

'What's wrong, Jacko?'

'Things are not good Boss.'

'What is wrong?'

'The birds, fish and dolphins are not happy Boss. The seas are not happy Boss. All wrong.'

He shook his head and did one of those little chants. I knew this was protection for all of us. The night slid by into a calm morning. The wind had dropped to a very slight breeze. Some of the crew were doing exercises as usual. I noticed Jacko sniffing the air. I looked at him with a question in my mind. He stared at me for a moment.

'The air is not good Boss, smells funny!'

Your greatest fear on board a vessel is fire. I scanned *Daisy May* looking for something that wasn't right, smoke, anything. I looked directly at the galley. Les seemed to be quite happy in what he was doing. Then

Jacko pointed to the bow. I saw black smoke on the horizon, rising in a long column to the sky. I stood staring at it. By this time, everybody had noticed what we were doing and were looking at it as well. I grabbed my telescope and aimed it onto the smoke.

'She is on fire Boss; that ship's on fire,' Jacko said.

The unwritten law of the sea is that you always go to the aid of another vessel; you always assist those in peril at sea.

'Alter course, Jacko.'

I watched through the telescope, and young Jarrett observed through his telescope as well.

'That ship has sunk Captain,' he said quietly.

I just stood there, trying to think of what to do next. What sunk the ship? What caused the fire? Has it hit an object in the sea or a sandbank? Are there any survivors?

'Standby to rescue survivors. Get the rope ladders down each side.'

Then we saw them. Three white lifeboats bobbing around on the surface of the black oil-slick. We also saw whispers of smoke from some of the oil on the surface and debris everywhere. I nodded to Ted; he gave the order for sails to be reefed and stowed.

We got alongside the lifeboats. Jacko turned *Daisy May* to the wind, and we came to a gentle stop. The men in the lifeboats slowly rowed to our side, we threw ropes to them and they slowly started to climb on board. They were covered in oil. Some had burns. Others were covered in blood from cuts. One man came on board covered in oil and with his face blackened.

'We have a man here with a broken leg, Captain.'

I nodded to Michael and straight away he had a bosun's chair lowered over the side, and two of the rescued men remained in the lifeboats.

'Ease him into the boson's chair.'

Finally, all ten men were on board. I watched the last man as he entered the gate then I looked at the man on deck with a broken leg.

Lesley and two of the other young men had stripped off his trousers and Lesley, and one of the men held him down as Philip pulled and twisted his ankle. The man screamed out in pain. They put splints on either side of his leg and wrapped a bandage tightly around it. Les had hot coffee ready to give to him, but Lesley gently stopped him.

'Just a little bit of water Les, we don't want him throwing up. He has had a shot of morphine.'

I looked back at the man who had come on board last. He was breathing very heavily. He put out his hand to mine.

'Captain Fox.'

'Captain Farquhar, my name is Bill.'

'My name is Jack,' he replied.

He took the coffee from Les, and he then started to shake. I put my hands on his shoulders to steady him. I could see him trying to hold back his tears and emotions.

'Let's get that oil off you and get you some clean clothes. Michael get some canvas on those lifeboats, so they don't fill up with water. Ted take those lifeboats in tow. Jacko, turn her back to the wind.'

The crew went to work cleaning the men up. I went back to Jack Fox.

'Your ship was *The Castle*?'

'Yes.'

'We met in the South Channel in Port Phillip Bay.'

'That is correct,' Jack replied.

'You were once a crewman on this vessel?'

'I was, many years ago,' Jack answered.

'Very pleased to have you on board, Jack.'

He dropped his head slightly forward; his body seemed to shake. Then he slowly went down on his knees, and he sobbed.

'I lost my best mate, my ship. A torpedo struck us. I tried to keep her afloat. The German submarine surfaced and finished her off with their deck gun.'

I slowly helped him to stand. Lesley appeared with a bucket and some rags and started to clean him up. He looked at Lesley, surprised.

'Your wife, Bill?'

'No, Lesley is a working passenger.'

I left them both to it and checked the rest of the crew. I went back to the wheelhouse and opened my logbook. Young Jarrett walked into the wheelhouse, picked up the sexton, and started to take readings and bearings. I thought to myself, *You're doing well young man, you're doing well.*

Captain Jack Fox came into the wheelhouse after Lesley had cleaned him up. He looked at me sharply.

'Damn woman wants to shave my beard off! Women always want to interfere. A man's got to be a man! She's not touching my beard!'

I thought of how many times she had won the chess game. I shook my head and went back to what I was doing.

'You've got ten crew, a significant number?'

He looked at me with pain in his eyes.

'My orders were to follow a convoy of ships after we rounded the Horn. Everything was going to plan. Two Navy destroyers, and fourteen of us cargo vessels in convoy. Then it happened. Loud explosions were coming from the other ships, burning oil, screams from the dying men. We were told to keep moving, not to stop. By the time daylight had come on the second day, we were alone. I stopped during the night and picked up three survivors in a life raft.'

He took three deep breaths and paused for a moment. He seemed to be letting it all pass out of his mind, but his eyes told another story. That pain would stay with him for the rest of his life. He shook his head.

'Yes, yes, the logbook. What are the names of your crew?'

Jack gave me the names, and I wrote them down in the logbook.

'What are the names of the other survivors?' I wrote these down.

'And one man who is a passenger trying to get back to England,' added Jack.

'You didn't lose any of your crew?'

'No. Thank God for that.'

Jarrett gave me the coordinates. I didn't check his figures, just wrote them down, and tapped him on the shoulder.

'Thank you, Jarrett.'

To our total surprise Cat, who was sitting on the bench, stood up sharply on all four legs. His nose was twitching as if he was sniffing the air. He looked straight at Jacko, it was as though they were talking to each other. Jacko laughed, gave one of his funny little chants, and said to Cat, 'Could be right.'

The Cat jumped off the bench and went trotting out onto the deck, over to a man sitting by the baulk works with a coat wrapped around him. Cat sat down alongside him, his tail and ears twitching back and forth. He was sniffing the air. Then a Cat's head appeared out of the overcoat. The young man tried to stop it, but it wriggled out. Cat stood up, the young man reached out.

'Whisky, it looks like you have found a friend!' he said in a warm, friendly voice.

Cat led Whisky, a female Cat, to the galley to the water bowl and Whisky drank, drank, and drank some more; she didn't seem to want to stop. They then both walked back into the wheelhouse and curled up on the bench on Colin's coat.

'So, all my crew are safe and sound, and so is my Cat!' Captain Jack Fox said. Then the tears started, and he just stood there sobbing.

I went over to Michael.

'Michael, that man over there, his name is Mr Brown. He is a passenger. The others are all crew. Give them some small tasks to do to keep their minds away from the turmoil and the nightmare they've just been through.'

CHAPTER 15

Over the next few days, everything seemed to settle down; everybody found their place on *Daisy May*. Mr Brown kept to himself, reading anything he could find. I saw Lesley trying to talk to him, but he just walked away and left her standing there. He was incredibly arrogant and annoying; the crew seemed to be uncomfortable around him.

Jacko, Jack Fox and I were all standing in the wheelhouse; Jack asked where Colin was.

'Colin's body has passed away, but his spirit is still here, Boss,' Jacko replied.

'You always phrase things differently, Jacko,' Jack answered.

He laughed and tapped Jacko on the shoulder. Cat lifted his head and looked at Jacko. Just then, Ted came into the wheelhouse. He looked at Captain Jack Fox and looked at me.

'Too many captains on board!' he laughed and shook his head.

Jack looked at him with a startled expression.

I chuckled to myself and said to him, 'Meet Captain Ted Coe.'

Jack reached out and shook Ted's hand.

'I think they'll put you to work Jack, you know too much about the sea.' Jacko laughed. 'Do you still say there is the same amount of calories in a bottle of beer as there is in a T-bone steak?'

'My oath I do, and when we get to England, I'll buy you a T-bone steak at the bar, and it'll be a cold one!'

Lesley appeared in the wheelhouse with a small smile on her face.

'Jack, I've still got a pair of scissors!'

Jack pulled his head back. 'Don't you touch my beard!'

We all laughed. Lesley then looked solemn.

'What do you know about your passenger Jack?'

'All I know is that he is an Englishman wanting to get back to England to his family. Apart from that I don't know anything about him; we can't get him to talk. He came on board at the last minute. He presented his papers; I couldn't argue as I had spare cabins.'

'Why do you ask that, Lesley?' I was puzzled.

She hesitated. 'Mr Brown confuses me. He tells me he is English, but he doesn't act English. If you would excuse me, I think Les wants me. A woman's work is never done!' and with that, she disappeared.

'What was your cargo, Jack?' I asked.

'Mutton bird oil and wool.'

The same cargo as mine. I shouted out to Terry, and he came to the door.

'Have you finished that list for me?'

'Yes, Captain.' He handed me the notebook. 'The last two pages are not my writing Captain; they are Trevor's.'

'I'm pleased to hear that. Did you find anything out of the ordinary?'

'No, Captain, we didn't.' He hesitated. I gave him a severe look.

'Well, Captain, some of the bales of wool are not as tidy as they could have been; they were stored very tightly packed.'

'Thank you, Terry, keep working with young Trevor.'

'I will Skipper.'

I found myself biting the inside of my gum. Nothing makes sense. I could feel the tension within me. I couldn't shake it off. I looked at Cat, *At least you're happy you ratbag*. His tail twitched back and forth. I shook my head and walked out on the deck.

'Les, do we have plenty of supplies?'

'Yes, Skipper.'

I studied him for a moment; he looked happy and content. His world was cooking, and he had plenty of that to do. He also had a companion with whom he could chat and laugh.

'Has Lesley been trimming your moustache?'

'Yes, Skipper, she has.'

'You would never notice Les.'

I winked at him. He shook his head and disappeared into his galley. Les had a small scar on his lip, which is why he wore a moustache, but only I knew that.

Darkness was once again falling; it had become cold. Everybody was wearing jumpers and oilskins. We were nearing Longitude 45°, and there was a slight drizzle coming in. It was going to be a cold night. The breeze was holding strong; we had tacked twice during the day. We should be back on course heading into the evening. Ted walked up alongside me.

'Those three lifeboats Skipper seem to be yawing backwards and for-wards. I will let out a little more towline, maybe another hundred feet.'

I thought about it for a moment. 'Have one at hundred feet, the second sixty feet behind that, the last one another sixty feet behind.'

Michael had put the covers over them so they wouldn't take in water from the spray. As salvage, they would be worth a bob or two to us.

'Go ahead, Ted.'

He disappeared to the stern. Jack walked back out onto the deck.

'Bill, I never thought how good it would be to be back under canvas. I'm back at sea where you have to have your wits about you and to be sharp. You have to tack backwards and forwards with the wind and play the game; not like that cramped old steamer of mine; keep her on course, and that's all. Yes, you have your problems, but it's not like being under canvas. Here you are alive; every part of you is working to survive. Your life has a greater purpose.'

'Jack, I once met an old man on a train. He said he had been the skipper of a four-master. I noticed the way he looked at me. He had lived a full life and was content. I wish I could have brought him back on board to where he truly wanted to be.'

Jack sighed. 'Yes, yes, I understand. Now I had better go and check on my three crewmen who were injured before I turn in.' He put his hand on my shoulder, turned, and walked away.

I went back to the galley and poured myself a cup of coffee. Lesley was still washing dishes.

'Woman's work never done, Lesley?' She turned and smiled at me.

'Something like that, Skipper.'

I saw the sadness in her eyes. She looked up at me.

'Skipper I've never experienced anything like what I've experienced on *Daisy May*. I don't think you'd find it anywhere else in the world. It is hard work everybody has a job to do, no matter how much it hurts, how cold it is, how tired you are, it's the way you all do it together. You don't complain or grumble; you are a part of each other; you see the funny things, laugh with each other, and laugh at yourself. I don't want it to stop. I know that in a few days it will. I have learned so much about myself. *Daisy May* will always be a part of me as will each member of the crew.'

I wanted to say something to her, but I knew deep down to leave it alone, for she was talking from somewhere deep down inside her, where I cannot go. I looked at her. I wanted desperately to be a part of her. I desperately needed to connect with her, but I knew that I could not touch her or hold her. I knew I must walk away.

She looked at me with sadness.

'Can I get you another cup of coffee?'

'Yes, please, Lesley. Yes, please.'

We made three sail changes during the night. Nobody got much sleep; everybody was weary and a little cold. The sky was overcast, the light drizzling rain there one minute, gone the next. We had a pleasant breeze. There was no chance of *Daisy May* being seen. We had all the canvas on her, so she gently leaned over to one side. *Daisy May* seemed happy; she was built for this. Daylight was starting to creep in. I had the wheelhouse door closed to keep the rain out. Then Jacko's voice boomed out.

'We've got trouble, Boss, we've got trouble.'

'Where, Jacko?'

'Portside, Boss.'

I slid the door back. Four men were climbing all over the baulk works, all dressed in military uniforms, with machine guns over their shoulders. I saw the bow of the other vessel easing back from *Daisy May*'s side. They had come alongside us through the mist and rain and caught everyone off-guard. One of them shouted at me in German. I shook my head to let him know that I didn't understand; then he cried out in English.

'You are the Captain?'

'I am.'

'Get your crew on deck.'

I carried out his orders; everyone was on deck. I didn't like the machine guns or the Luger he was carrying in his hand. Mr Brown appeared on deck, looked at the German soldiers and started to laugh out loud. He then burst into German, waving his arms in the air, talking in German and laughing again. The three soldiers and the officer laughed with him. Then they noticed Lesley.

'This is your wife Captain?'

I didn't know quite what to say.

'No, a passenger.'

'A little bit of fluff to keep you warm.' The officer laughed.

The soldiers laughed again. That is where they made their mistake.

The three young men, after a nod from Lesley, dashed forward. Before the German soldiers had time to think, they were dead. A knife blade had done the work. Philip and Reno had taken care of the officer. His Luger fell to the deck in seconds. We threw their bodies overboard.

The craft that brought them on board was now six-hundred to seven-hundred feet behind us. They couldn't come any closer to our stern because of the lifeboats. Mr Brown, now realising what had happened to his colleagues, knew his only escape was the vessel behind us. He ran to the stern and, but as he jumped, he hit the towrope. It spun him into an unnatural dive. *Daisy May*'s speed was about six knots, and the lifeboats struck him as he hit the water. Lesley ran to the stern and put both her hands on her head in alarm for what she saw.

The crew on the boat following had not seen what had happened to their men, and the rain had distorted anything they did see. Some of the crew ran to the stern of the vessel looking for the man. Captain Jack Fox was standing alongside me. Ted and Michael were waiting for orders. Jacko had his head out of the wheelhouse, trying to see what was happening. Then to our total disbelief, the stern of the vessel following us rose up in the water and just seemed to shatter. Then it disappeared. We had left it behind. All of us just stared at the scene, totally confused.

The British Naval Captain stood at the periscope. He could barely make out Daisy May as the night was drawing in close. She was back on course, but then she would tack again, and then tack back again. She was a nightmare. They had followed her back and forth, port to starboard, back to port again.

She was like a phantom or a ghost, prone to disappear. He was starting to get to know her, beginning to respect her. He could not tell when she was there, as there wasn't any noise from her props. And no sounds came from her hull, the ten inch planks deadened any sound, but he knew they were in the open sea. How many times would she tack during the night? Darkness had fallen.

'Down, Periscope. Surface.'

There was a loud noise, escaping air. The Captain stood on top of the conning tower taking in the fresh air, feeling the cold spray and the wind and drizzle on his face. His First Officer came over and stood alongside him.

'When I signed up for a submarine, I didn't expect this – playing nursemaid to an old sailing ship, something from the Dark Ages,' he said in a quiet, gentle voice.

The Captain replied with a small chuckle, 'Yes, I know what you mean. I think it will be over shortly, just a few more days. Then we might get to fire a torpedo or two. However, for now, we have to get the Daisy May phantom safely to England. Why? I don't know. You take the first watch.'

He went below, leaving the First Officer to the refreshing air.

A short time later the First Officer came into the Captain's cabin.

'Excuse me, sir.' The Captain awoke from a deep sleep.

'Yes, yes, what do you want?'

'We have propeller noise on sonar, sir.'

The Captain got up, and they went to the Navigation Room. Both men stood watching the sonar.

'It's a high-speed vessel I would say, a mile to a mile and a half from us. Periscope depth. Up, periscope.'

The Captain put both the handles down quickly, put his face to the eyepiece and spun it around quickly. Daylight had just started to come. It would be an overcast day with drizzling rain. He saw Daisy May with full sails. Then he saw something else, for just a moment. He froze. His mind was in turmoil. What is going to happen? What can I do? If I arm a torpedo, I cannot fire it, not this close to Daisy May.

The torpedo boat had not positioned herself to fire at Daisy May's side but was coming to the stern. He'd come down to Daisy's *speed, which was five-and-a-half knots. The three lifeboats were behind Daisy May, one behind the other, which seemed to be stopping the torpedo boat getting too close. She moved on to the port side. He switched to high magnification. Then he saw the men on the torpedo boat's bow; he saw them climbing on board. Then a plan of attack came into his mind.*

'Increase speed to eight knots. Clear the torpedo room. Close all watertight doors.'

Nobody argued or questioned. They just did their job. He had positioned the submarine slightly to the starboard side of the torpedo boat. All those on the torpedo boat were looking toward Daisy May. The next moment he saw a man jump overboard and wave to the torpedo boat. Then he saw her. Her hands were on the top of her head. He shouted his orders.

'Port twelve degrees, full ahead.'

They felt the submarine surge forward.

'Surface. All stop!'

Then they felt the shudder, the banging and cracking.

'Hard astern. Dive!' The Captain counted to twenty four. Then he gave the command.

'All, stop! Damage control.'

'No damage, sir.'

'Periscope depth.'

The sound of rushing air.

'Up, periscope.'

He could see the stern of the Daisy May. She was still moving on course; she had not stopped. He turned to high magnification again, and he could see the woman on the stern with three fingers exposed. He gave a deep sigh.

'Thank God for that.'

He turned to the First Officer. Put his hand on his shoulder.

'I wish we had a bar on board. I need one!' And he went back to his cabin to fill out his log book. Or was it to be alone?

Daisy May seemed to be enjoying the stiff breeze, but with that slight drizzle, the crew were now on edge. There were too many questions that there were no answers for. Not even I could answer them. Ted and Michael walked up alongside me.

'Skipper all the ropes and rigging are soaked through with water. Do you think we should slacken them?'

When ropes get wet, they shrink and tighten, so they have to be slackened off. We discussed the ropes some more and Ted said that he would get the crew busy.

'Leave the three young men with me. Philip, Reno, and Dominic, the three of you come to my cabin.'

I noticed Lesley staring at us from the galley. I sat down in my chair.

'Sit down, gentlemen. Now explain to me why you're on this vessel and who you are.'

Reno and Dominic's shoulders seemed to tighten; their heads appeared to come to attention. Then Philip spoke.

'We are British Naval Marines travelling to Britain. Any more than that, sir, we cannot discuss as we are under the National Security Act, carrying out our orders.'

I studied them for a moment. Something had suddenly changed.

'Sir, you are the skipper of this vessel. We are under your command.'

'So you are in command of these two gentlemen Philip?'

'Yes, sir.'

'Well, that explains everything, but explains nothing!'

'Sir, we probably won't get the opportunity to say this, so I'd like to say it now. What you and your vessel have taught us in these last weeks at sea, we will always cherish. All the way, you have shown us another side of life. You have put things in a different perspective. You have shown us different attitudes and points of view. You have shown us how to work with other men, to trust them and have faith in them even when you're swaying around a hundred feet in the air with only whitecapped water underneath, and forty knot winds. If I ever become a training officer, I'll have my trainees doing that. I know that'll make men of them.'

The other two laughed briefly. Philip stood to attention; the other two did the same.

'Permission to return to our duties, sir.'

I just nodded my head.

'What do I put in my log book?'

Then I heard the words. *'As least as possible in your logbook, Captain.'*

'Get out of my cabin, you three.'

They left quickly. I sat there with too many unanswered questions— too many.

The three young men were no longer a part of the crew; they were separate. I sat trying to get my thoughts together about the four men who had died. Was it all a daydream? A nightmare? I knew it had happened. There was a knock on the door.

'Excuse me, Captain. My name is Freddie Lees. I was the Chief Engineer on board *The Castle*. My trade is a mechanic. Michael tells me that you've had trouble with the Gardner motor. May I have a look at it, sir?'

I stared at him for a moment, trying to get my thoughts together.

'Yes, I would very much appreciate that.'

I walked back out on the deck.

'Michael, please work with this man on the motor.'

138

They both disappeared below.

The German man, who had jumped over the stern, had slung a hammock on one side of the engine where he could be alone. There was a leather satchel on the hammock, beautifully made. Michael took the hammock down, rolled it up with the leather satchel inside it, and put them to one side.

Freddie examined the motor. He then checked the oil and the freshwater tank and opened the seacock so that the salt water could cool the freshwater tank. Michael turned the fuel on and put a small handle in the flywheel of the auxiliary motor. He checked its oil and water and lifted the compression lever on top of the engine. Then he wound the handle on the flywheel, dropped the compression bar, and the little motor came to life. The compressor filled the air tank, and when the gauge got to the correct pressure, the small motor automatically dropped back in revs.

Freddie lifted the compression lever on the big engine, opened the air valve and the big motor started. He dropped the compression lever, the engine fired but only on one or two cylinders. He picked up the large screwdriver, placed the handle to his ear, bent down and put the end of the screwdriver on each cylinder to listen. The air tank ran too low on pressure to be able to turn the big motor over. Freddie turned off the valve, and the little engine started to build up the air in the tank again.

'I don't quite understand it. They've replaced everything on this motor – new injectors, new water pump, new hoses, new fuel tank and they may have replaced the rings in the cylinder. These Gardner motors run forever, there is nothing to go wrong, but I believe somebody has altered the timing.'

Michael just stared at Freddie's face.

'Can you repair the timing?'

'Yes, I can, but I want to know whether the Captain has the maintenance manual. Get the timing wrong; you can do too much damage.'

They both walked into the wheelhouse.

'Captain, do you have the manual for the Gardner motor?'

I turned around to look at Jacko.

'Yes, Boss, in the drawer under your bunk.'

I came back with the manual. 'I didn't know that I had it.'

I handed it to Freddie and he disappeared back down the hatch with Michael. An hour later, we heard the big Gardiner motor startup. Black smoke streamed out of the exhaust on our port side; it settled down to a gentle blue. Freddie and Michael came back to the wheelhouse, Freddie had a puzzled look on his face.

'Why would they spend so much money on the motor and then alter the timing so it would not start?'

Listening to it now, it was purring away like a kitten.

Lesley appeared with four cups of coffee. She had been watching and prayed to herself, *Please don't put it into gear and turn on the propeller. Please don't do it.* She had to find a way of getting into the wheelhouse. She said to herself, *Coffee!* and in a minute she was in the wheelhouse with the coffee, she stood listening to the conversation.

Jacko said, 'Grey sails are like a kangaroo. You can't see *Daisy May* at sea as her grey sails blend with the sea like a kangaroo blends in with its environment in the bush. They haven't painted *Daisy May*'s hull, so she still looks tired and worn out. And they gave us a course which we wouldn't have normally taken. Big fish following us.'

Jack's voice broke in, '*Daisy May* makes no noise!'

Lesley could not contain herself. 'If her propellers were turning, she would broadcast where she was!'

I stared at Lesley. Somehow, there was an answer to the jigsaw. Jacko's words came racing back to me. *'Are we being set up Skipper? Are we being set up?'*

'Freddie, could you turn the motor off for us, please?'

He left the wheelhouse, and we heard the big Gardner motor shut down. I turned to Jack and Jacko. Lesley had walked back to the galley. It's as if they don't want us to exist. They? Who are they? Another unanswered question. Why are we so important? Why are those three naval officers on board? If the submarine or the torpedo boat wanted to sink us, they could have. Why not? Is there someone on board who is very important or something? Who? What? So many unanswered questions. Too many.

CHAPTER 16

The captain of the submarine was watching the Daisy May through his periscope. Night was starting to fall, and big black clouds were rolling in. Flashes of lightning were illuminating everything, and Daisy May again became the ghost he had been following for so many days and nights. One moment she was gone, and the next, she was illuminated by the flashes of lightning. The sails bounced back the light in such a way she appeared to have an eerie aura around her. She would then disappear back into the darkness. He asked himself if he was dreaming; was this a nightmare? Will he wake up?

He shook himself and shouted out, 'Down, Periscope.'

His first officer walked up to him. 'Excuse me, sir. Sparks would like to have a word with you.'

He walked up to the man wearing headphones and sitting in front of an instrument panel. He put both his hands on Sparky's shoulders.

'What's up, Sparky?'

'Sir, before we reached the torpedoed cargo boat I was getting these little blips on the scanner. Do you see them up here sir? Well, we were told to ignore them; that they were most probably interference from the ship or the submarine. They are called 'anomalies', so I didn't take much notice, but just before *that torpedo boat arrived, they were there again. Then they were gone, but now, they're back!'*

The captain stood, thinking for a while. How did that torpedo boat, in inclement weather, go directly to her? She was near invisible in that weather.

'Sparky send this message: The three stars are alive tonight, but I need to turn out the light.'

He tapped Sparky on the shoulders. 'Good work.'

He then went back to his cabin to fill out his log book.

Lesley stood with Bill and Jacko watching the lightning as it illuminated the *Daisy May*. *Daisy May* seemed to come alive as if in another time and another dimension. Jacko burst out laughing, gave one of his little dances and chanted a funny song.

The dream-time people Kiichi are dancing in the sky telling us all is well; they are dancing and banging on the clouds.

Jacko was jubilant. The two Cats sat up and stared at him. He stopped dancing, and you would swear he was talking to them. He turned to look at me.

'Very serious trouble in the morning Bill. Nothing will be the same.'

He turned and looked at Lesley, and there were tears in his eyes. He turned back to the wheel and the compass. Lesley and I looked at each other.

As Lesley started to walk out of the wheelhouse, she said, 'You are a very spooky little fella.'

She disappeared into the galley. I just stood there looking at him. I knew I had to be on guard. He was seldom wrong.

'I'm going to shut my eyes for a while Jacko. Wake me on the next watch.'

The winds stayed with us all night; just a moderate breeze, no swell and so *Daisy May* just glided through the water. She kept an average speed, and in the early hours of the morning, the wind died off to just a gentle breeze. *Daisy May* still had a full sail and was doing well.

Just on daylight, I saw Lesley and the three men on deck. Lesley walked straight to the wheelhouse. She put her hand on the door.

'Captain, the man with the broken leg, seems to be having trouble. I don't know what to do.'

I shouted out, 'Jarrett, take the wheel.'

I looked up to the top of the wheelhouse, 'Jacko! Follow me.'

He bounced down, as usual, landing on his feet. We went below. The injured man was lying on his bunk propped up with pillows. Sweat was coming from his forehead, and he had been vomiting. Concern and worry came over me. I needed three more days to get him to a hospital. Jacko knelt alongside him. He touched the man's toes with his fingers. I knew he was feeling the blood pressure in his legs and watching the colour of his toes.

'Have you had that funny stuff, mate?'

'Yes, Jacko.'

'And you've never been on a sailing vessel before?'

'No, Jacko, I haven't. *Daisy May* is my first sailing vessel. The only other vessel I've been on is *The Castle*.'

'You are seasick, and what's more that funny stuff doesn't help! Can we get him on deck, Skipper?'

He shouted at me, 'It's here, Boss; it's here!'

And with that, he was running back on deck. I followed him, and Lesley and Jack Fox followed me. Back on deck, we found Jacko looking over the bow.

'What's wrong, Jacko?'

He didn't answer me but turned and ran back to the top of the wheelhouse looking over the bow still. He pointed to the horizon, but we couldn't see anything. Then slowly, we could see an aircraft coming directly towards us. It was a British Naval Aircraft.

Jack Fox shouted out, 'It's a Catalina Flying boat!'

It came down to our mast height and flew around us three times. I noticed Lesley, she had a hand raised above her head with three fingers exposed, stretched out wide. She was turning around as the aircraft flew around us. The plane took off to our stern. About three miles away, it turned and flew directly back to our stern. From the nose of the aircraft, there was a flashing light. Philip had a pen and a notebook and was writing something down. Lesley was talking to him, all the while watching the aircraft. As the plane started coming in closer, she raised her hand, three fingers in the air. The plane headed back to where it had come from and disappeared.

Lesley gave a command to the three marines. 'Find it!'

She pointed to the back hatch to where the motor was. I walked up to her, wanting some answers. She turned to me; her face was like a stone; she wasn't the same person.

'Not now, Captain!'

I was stunned, taken entirely by shock.

The three men reappeared on deck. Philip placed a leather bag on the deck and opened the flap. He took out a waterproof bag and inside there was a beautiful wooden box about the same size as a cigar box. The box contained two notebooks, two writing pens and a pill box. Philip picked up one of the writing pens and gently unscrewed the end. A small Allen key appeared. He turned the other end of the pen, and it bent sideways, he picked up the little wooden box and handed them both to Lesley. Her manner was arrogant as though she didn't have to answer to anyone. She turned the box around, and there was a small hole into which she put the Allen key and using the pen, she turned it like she was winding up a clock.

The three men were looking through the books and nodded to Lesley. She answered, 'Yes'. They put the books back into the watertight bag.

Lesley walked into the galley, picked up a biscuit tin, emptied all the biscuits, then put the little box, notebooks, writing pens and pill box into the biscuit tin and resealed the tin. Lesley walked to the stern, held the tin high in the air and then gently lowered it into the water. She then raised her two hands high above her head and then placed them on top of her head.

I stood staring, what had just happened? Who is she? Who are they? I saw Jack Fox staring at me as well as Ted and Michael. None of us had any answers. Jacko walked up to Lesley as she was staring over the stern, watching the tin box bouncing on the water. He put his hand on hers. She turned and faced him with a cold, hard face.

'Yes, Gidgee, it's over. For now, You can't go back, not yet. But *Daisy May* has planted something in you which you will always cherish, like a cool desert breeze or the smile on a baby's face.'

I walked up alongside her and put my hands on the baulk works.

'I am the skipper of the *Daisy May*. I do not know what games you are playing, but I am the Captain of this vessel. Do you hear me? I have to get her into port. We are now in dangerous waters. Do you hear me?'

Lesley looked at me with a very stern face, but I saw her hands were twitching. She didn't want to say this, but she had no choice.

'You are the Captain of this vessel, William Farquhar, and I will respect your command, but I outrank you!'

She turned and walked back to her cabin, closing the door behind her. She could see Les's face in her mind. How do I tell him, how do I tell him? I must return as an officer in His Majesty's British Navy. I am the highest ranking woman in the Navy. Then the tears started to flow down her cheeks; I must let my tears flow and then return to my command.

'Ted, could you get everybody on deck, including the man with the broken leg.'

Les appeared at the galley door.

'Coffee, Skipper?'

'Yes, please, Les. My cup has gone again.' I looked at him questioningly.

'She's got it, Skipper. I don't understand Skipper; what's happening?'

'I don't know Les. I don't know.'

I took my coffee and walked over to my men, my crew.

'Lads, I don't have any answers for you. I don't know what is going on. So much has happened on this voyage; we are tangled up in something big. We can only do our part, deliver our passengers and cargo safely to their destination. If I find out any answers, I will let you know. Thank you, gentlemen. Ted put the man with the broken leg in my cabin and give him a big bucket!'

Ted grinned at me. I went into the wheelhouse and spread out my chart on the bench.

'Jarrett, take the readings.'

'Aye, aye, Skipper.'

'Jacko at daylight tomorrow I want to be at Longitude 9°, Latitude 50. It will bring us to the entrance of St. George's Channel, but I need the tides to be with me.'

The captain of the submarine was watching through his periscope. He could see the aircraft circling Daisy May. He watched Lesley on the stern and could see her holding something above her head. He turned the periscope onto higher magnification. Then he saw her lower what appeared to be a tin into the water. She gave him the appropriate signals. 'All is right; all is in place.' His orders were not to surface in daylight.

Sparks yelled out to him, 'We've got that signal loud and clear, sir.'

'Sparky, that homing signal is coming from a tin on the surface. We've got to follow it and retrieve it.'

It had been a long day, but finally, darkness fell. He ordered the submarine to surface. They could just make out the tin bobbing up and down on the surface of the water, and they successfully retrieved it.

'Down to periscope depth.'

The captain took the lid off of the tin and removed the contents. He took out the small wooden box and slowly prised it open. Inside was a clock-like mechanism. Turning an Allen key wound the mechanism up, and it turned a little electrical device which gave out a pulse. The captain took a toothpick from his top pocket and placed it in the mechanism. Everything stopped. Then he took another one out of his pocket and gently removed the spring.

With a grin all over his face, he said, 'You would never think I was a watchmaker before the war, would you?'

He opened the first book. It was full of information about Port Phillip Bay. How many guns and what their firing range was. About Western Port and where the guns were at in Queenscliff. The other book gave information on Sydney Harbour and the naval base. All sorts of information was there extending right down the New South Wales coast. He put everything back in the tin and felt very pleased with himself. Following Daisy May had a purpose, a very practical purpose.

I woke to the sound of bells. Not being used to sleeping in a hammock, I was stiff and sore. I grinned to myself and thought, *Be careful man. It's a long time since you got out of a hammock. You'll find yourself face down on the deck; take it easy.*

Nevertheless, I was soon standing upright. On deck, the air was cold, and we had a gentle breeze with us. *Daisy May* had a full sail on her.

Ted's voice came from behind me.

'Good morning.'

'Good morning, Ted.'

Ted put his hand on my shoulder.

'She seems to be pushing against the tide so it must be the last of the run-out tide. That will give us a good tide back into the channel.'

'Yes, Ted, I've never liked the tides here. They are so strong and unpredictable.'

'We do have an ace up our sleeves now Skipper. We have a motor and a propeller,' Ted chuckled.

'Yes, it does put your mind at ease a bit, doesn't it? I think the wind will drop off at daylight.'

'Skipper, I'm a bit concerned about the men with the burns on their bodies. They are turning a funny yellow, and some of them look quite sick and are getting a fever.'

'Yes, Ted, I've noticed that, but it may be two more days before we can get them to a hospital. The only thing we can do is to keep them all warm. That burn on Fox's arm, it's bad, but he tries to make out it isn't a problem. You know we used to call him "Foxy" because he could survive anywhere.'

He put his arm back over my shoulder and looked at me very seriously.

'A lot can happen in two days Bill. What are they going to do with us?'

He left the question in the air and walked off to the galley. I noticed Jacko on top of the wheelhouse with two blankets over his shoulders. He was just staring at me.

'Too damn cold Jacko!'

I went back into the wheelhouse. I was surprised to see Lesley there, and so was Michael. They had been talking.

Michael, in this gentle voice, said, 'Lesley, you came on board this vessel to do a job more serious than we would ever understand. You stepped on board *Daisy May,* and you touched us all. You became part of us; you became one of us. You obviously have to return to your world.'

Ted walked into the cabin alongside me. Lesley looked straight ahead. We knew she was in command. Lesley folded her hands behind her back.

'Gentlemen, I am very proud to have been part of your crew. I will always cherish the memories. I train others to take command, and what I have learned from you and your professional men of the seas I will install in the minds of my officers in the future. Events will now happen over which I have no control. Thank you, gentlemen.'

She walked out of the wheelhouse and went back to her cabin.

We didn't say anything. We had nothing to say; we just returned to our duties. Jacko was there alongside me.

'Well Boss, I think we're just pawns in one big chess game. We are just one small piece on the chessboard.'

CHAPTER 17

'Jarrett, could you take the readings, please?'

'Aye, aye, sir.'

I looked at the leather satchel on the bench which had belonged to the German. I opened the flap and looked inside. There were places for pens and notebooks, but it was empty. It was beautifully made, something you would be very proud to own. I closed the flap and put it back on the bench. Cat was resting his head on Whisky.

'You have found what you wanted, haven't you?'

Cat rolled his head slightly to me; he seemed to be acknowledging me. He understood. Jarrett returned with the readings and jotted them down in his notebook. Longitude 9°, Latitude 50°.

'No other figures, Jarrett?'

'No, Skipper.'

'Spot on!' I looked at Jacko and gave him a grin.

'You call me spooky Boss, but you're spooky as well!' Jacko said.

We were now at the entrance to St. George's Channel. I filled out my logbook and was just about to close it when Cat stood up straight. Jacko stared at him.

'It's all happening Boss. They are here.'

'Who is here?'

He pointed to the port side, and I saw a sizeable naval destroyer. Then I looked to our starboard side, and there was a Navy frigate. They pulled in quite close to us. A naval officer with a loudhailer called out.

'Good morning, Captain William Farquhar.'

I went to the starboard side and gestured to him.

'Captain do not use your radio. Follow us.'

Then he came sharply to attention and saluted.

'Good morning, ma'am.'

Lesley was standing alongside me dressed in her naval uniform, her rating status on her lapels; all the different colours of a high-ranking officer. The other three, also dressed in their naval uniforms, were standing behind her. She gestured to the Navy Captain that she acknowledged his orders and turned and looked at me. I don't have a choice, do I?

I turned to the frigate and shouted, 'I am a vessel under wind power!'

The voice came booming back.

'Understand perfectly, Captain.'

With that, the frigate altered course towards the English Channel. I went back to the wheelhouse.

The large destroyer was at our stern, too close for comfort. I saw Lesley and the three officers walk to the stern. Philip had two semaphore sticks in his hand. He started to wave them back and forth at the destroyer. Lesley had a notebook in her hand. A man walked onto the wing of the ship and started flashing a light at them. Lesley was busy writing on her notepad. She spoke to Philip, and he moved his flags once more. They had finished. Ted and Michael were standing in the wheelhouse watching them.

Michael chuckled. 'I haven't seen semaphore used since I was in the boy scouts.'

'Did you understand it, Michael?'

'No, too quick for me, but I can tell you this, Lesley was in command,' he replied.

Lesley walked into the wheelhouse and glanced at Ted and Michael.

'Leave us!' she said in a commanding voice.

'No, no,' she took a deep sigh. 'I'm sorry. I want to talk to Bill. I would appreciate it if you could leave us for a while.'

She glanced at both of them; they could see the pain on her face. They both walked out and went into the galley.

Lesley turned to me. 'In exactly four hours, I would like you to start your motor and proceed under power. Strip all your sails off her.'

She stopped, turned, and looked out of the window; you could see the pain deep within her. She put her hand on Jacko's shoulder.

'Take all the sails off *Daisy May* and stow them below, separate them from the cargo. And brace all your yardarms. We will be tying up on your port side. Thank you, Captain.'

She turned and walked back to her cabin before he could see the tears in her eyes.

Les walked out of the galley with two cups of coffee and a plate of sticky buns with red jam centres. He placed them on the wheelhouse table and then returned to the galley for another cup of coffee and more sticky buns. He walked over to Lesley's cabin and knocked on her door. It opened, and he walked in, closing the door behind him.

'Please sit down, Les.'

He sat down, and she sat down on her bunk then placed both her hands on his.

'How do I explain all of this to you? You have become my closest friend. You gave me back something I had lost. You showed me how to laugh again; how to cook beautiful food; how to be the me I was before I was in the Navy. You taught me how to serve and look after others; how to feed them and know what they liked and what they didn't. I don't want to lose you as a friend.'

Les patted her on her hand. 'You fell in love with Daisy May, you fell in love with her crew, and the hardest thing for you of all, is that you fell in love with her captain. And he has fallen in love with you. But you can't have each other, not yet. You both have jobs to do.'

He stood up, took a cloth out of his apron and wiped the tears from her eyes. Then he lifted her to her feet and put his arms around her.

'If you will be my daughter, I will be your friend forever.'

She nestled her head into his shoulders, gaining the strength that she needed for the future.

'I will leave his cup with you!'

I kept glancing at the door to Lesley's cabin, wondering what they were talking about. Finally, Les came out and returned to his galley. Ted and Michael returned to the wheelhouse and Ted nudged Jacko as he entered.

'You sound like four possums munching a loaf of bread!'

Jacko just put his thumb in the air. His mouth was too full of warm sticky bun filled with jam.

'Michael, in three hours would you and Freddie go down and start up the Gardner motor. Ted, I've been told to take all the sails off *Daisy May* and stow them below. I don't want to stow damp sails so could you start stripping her topsails off now. They want all the yardarms and spas braced on our port side. They say we will be unloading from portside, so slacken all the necessary ropes off anything on the decks and stow them below.

Ted, could you have the crew up on deck, please.'

I walked to the galley. 'A coffee please Les. I noticed my mug was gone. Again.'

'She has it, Boss.'

He reached up and took her mug from the rack, filled it with coffee and handed it to me. I wrapped my hands around the mug and walked back to the men who were standing; waiting.

'Well, I can't tell you much; only that we have been told to start the Gardner motor and to take all the sails off *Daisy May* and to stow them below, away from the cargo. I want to get them off dry. Stow everything below deck. I do not know if our destination is Plymouth or Southampton. I do not know what's going to happen when we are in port, but I want to say you have been the best crew, the very best. Under tough circumstances, you have not questioned but just carried out my commands. *Daisy May* and I are very proud to have been with you on this voyage. Thank you, gentlemen.'

I heard the big Gardner start. Michael and Freddie came back on deck.

'Michael, Ted, take the gear shift and put her into gear!'

We felt *Daisy May* shudder and her movements changed as the sails were taken off her. She was no longer a barque sailing clipper.

The Gardner pushed her gently through the water. We passed Prawle Point and altered course and were now heading towards Torquay. Lesley appeared in the wheelhouse.

'We will be taking her into Dartmouth; there will be a small tug waiting to assist you. The mouth of the river is quite narrow.'

We saw the large destroyer signalling to the frigate, and the ship then altered course.

Darkness was starting to come, but we could still see the big chimney on the hill, with the openings in the bottom.

Lesley said, 'We don't know who built it, we think it was the Romans. It may have been a lighthouse marking the entrance to the channel, but we don't know.'

As we got closer to the channel, we saw the green and red lights of a small tug. Ted and Michael went to the bow to prepare a towline. The little tug was in front of us, and smoke from its funnel lit up the night sky. We saw a small castle protecting the entrance and Lesley told us that there had once been a massive chain across the entry so that ships could not leave or enter unless the chain was lowered to the bottom. Henry VIII had installed it.

There were high cliffs on either side; I could see houses painted white. Due to the blackout restrictions, there were no lights on, just darkness. Lesley pointed to our port side.

'That is where the *Mayflower* originally sailed from.'

We passed a ferry boat going back and forth. Lesley pointed to a wharf.

'That is where we are berthing.'

Army trucks were on the dock, and a squadron of men were waiting there, both Navy and army. The three naval marines were waiting at the hatch to the baulk works.

Lesley's voice was sharp and in command, 'Captain, your crew will stay on board; stay out of the way. I have asked them not to call me by my first name but to call me either Miss Johnson or Ma'am.'

Daisy May's bow and stern lines were tied up to the wharf. We were now in England.

What is going to happen today? I asked myself.

My world had been turned upside down. I felt anger and frustration rise within me. I had been Captain of this vessel for over thirty years, protecting her, loving her. She had become my wife. Walter Wright had given me this responsibility, and I had given him my word. I could see Lesley standing at the gangplank with the three naval marines. I slapped my hand on the bench in the wheelhouse and said to myself, *No, no, I am the Captain of the Daisy May!*

I shouted to Ted, 'Follow me.'

I walked past the three naval officers and stood alongside Lesley. A man in a captain's uniform started to walk up the gangplank, and other men began to follow. I stepped forward so they could not board *Daisy May.*

'You are?'

The man stopped abruptly, glanced towards Lesley, then seeing who she was, and her rank saluted her. She saluted back.

He replied, 'I am the captain! I am the captain of this port. Your name?'

He looked at me with such arrogance.

I repeated my words. 'You are?'

He glanced at Lesley. She just raised her eyebrows. He looked back at me, staring me directly in the face.

'I am Captain Williams!'

He started to walk towards me, to come on deck. I stood my ground and did not move. He stopped abruptly, just one pace from me.

'Is there something you wish to say to me?'

'What is the correct procedure before boarding another captain's vessel?'

His eyes widened, and I saw the men behind him grinning. His head went backwards and with arrogance in his voice, he said, 'Permission to come on board sir?'

'You have my permission.' I stepped aside, putting my hand out, 'Captain William Farquhar.'

He just nodded but did not shake my hand.

'Before we go any further, Captain Williams, I have injured men on board. One with a broken leg. Other crew with bad burns. We will need to attend to them first.'

Captain Williams glanced at Lesley; she nodded to him. He turned to the men standing at the top of the gangplank.

'If your men would work with Captains Ted Coe and Jack Fox,' I said. Ted and Jack stepped forward, 'I would appreciate that. Please follow me into the wheelhouse, Captain Williams.'

Lesley followed us into the wheelhouse. I took out my papers and my logbook and placed them on the bench, turning to Captain Williams.

'Your papers, sir?' He looked at me, confused. 'I do not hand over my cargo to anybody who does not have the correct paperwork. Get it!' He looked at Lesley.

'Well, Captain, he is correct, is he not?' she said.

He turned and looked straight at me.

'Excuse me; I will be back shortly.'

He walked off *Daisy May* down the gangplank, Lesley burst out laughing.

'I was at the Naval Academy with that arrogant self-centred sod. He was born with a silver spoon in his mouth. I'm enjoying this.'

I walked out of the wheelhouse and stood at the gangplank and said my goodbyes to each man leaving *Daisy May*. There were three ambulances on the dock.

'Goodbye, Jack, I've enjoyed our short time together. I hope we'll meet again under better circumstances, but good luck, Jack.' He stood there, looking into my eyes.

Then he said in a quiet voice, 'I lost her, I lost *The Castle*.'

I put my hand on his shoulder.

'Jack, Jack, it was beyond your control. It wasn't a reef or a sandbank. It was the war. I'm quite sure you will have another ship.'

His lips tightened, and his eyes had a sorrowful look. He shook his head, turned, and started to walk off the gangplank.

Lesley's voice broke in, 'Goodbye, Captain.'

He nodded to her, then nodded to Ted and Michael and disappeared down the gangplank.

Jacko was standing on the rigging.

'Have another T-bone steak for me!' Jack waved back to him.

Captain Williams returned on deck and walked into the wheelhouse. By then, Jacko was standing behind me, holding my overcoat.

'Put this on Bill; it's too cold.'

I put it on and walked into the wheelhouse. Captain Williams gave me his papers. I read through them and found them confusing. I turned to Lesley.

'My cargo belongs to the British Government, and it's under the Secrecy Act? What exactly does that mean?'

Lesley replied, 'Exactly what it says. It belongs to the British Government. The cargo is under the British Secrecy Act. I cannot divulge any more than that.'

'And the vessel *Daisy May* is owned by the British Navy?'

'That is correct, Captain.'

I found myself just staring at her. My emotions and thoughts were totally out of control. I didn't have a logical answer in my mind. The lady was Lesley but was not Lesley. She is Miss Johnson, a naval officer. The cargo belongs to the British Government. *Daisy May* belongs to the British Navy. Her voice snapped me back.

'I know Captain, this is all very confusing, but we carry out our orders and do not ask questions. Do we Captain Williams?'

'No, ma'am.'

'I've got my cargo manifest,' I said. 'This is my cargo. If you could sign here, here and here, I will sign it and hand the cargo over to you, Captain Williams.'

We signed all the paperwork. I put the papers together and started to give it to Captain Williams but Lesley's hand shot out, and she took the documents.

Les walked into the wheelhouse with three cups of coffee. Lesley took one cup – my cup. I picked up both the other cups of coffee, stepped out of the wheelhouse door and handed one cup to Jacko, who was on top of the wheelhouse.

I put my hand on Les's shoulder. 'Thank you, Les.'

Lesley's hand shot up to her mouth, covering it.

'Follow me, Captain Williams.'

We both walked out of the wheelhouse. 'Ted, could you remove the covers off the hatches? The captain's crew will be unloading her, so send our lads down to rest. I will talk to them in the morning.'

I noticed two men wearing white coats, carrying little boxes. A wire was coming from them, attached to a small stick. They were making a click, click, click noise.

Captain Williams looked at me. 'They are not my men.'

I turned around and looked at Lesley, who was in the wheelhouse. She nodded at him.

'They are hers, not mine.'

I said to myself *The cargo is not mine; it belongs to them!*

I walked to the galley. 'Les, could you give the crew a good breakfast at six in the morning?' He nodded at me. I slapped my hand on the door in frustration and walked back to my wheelhouse. Lesley looked at me with a grave look on her face, like a stone. Then she broke out into a warm smile and started to laugh.

'I have been waiting so long to see that. You are the only man I know who could bring him down, and when you took the cup of coffee and handed it to Jacko, you said everything. Good night Captain!' and with that, she walked out with my mug.

Jacko swung down off the top of the wheelhouse. He'd been listening to everything. I looked at him.

'Nothing makes any sense Jacko, but I do know it's a big plan, something gigantic.'

I noticed there was only Cat on the bench. Whisky had gone. I turned to Jacko.

'Yes, the young man took Whisky with him, but Cat hasn't gone!' Jacko stood there with his head slightly bent forward. 'Bill, I will always be with you whenever you need me; just talk to me!' Tears were pouring from his eyes. 'Talk to me, Bill. I'll be looking over the horizon for you, Bill, always.'

He turned and walked out of the wheelhouse. What does he see, what does he know? Then I heard Colin's voice loud and clear, '*Don't worry; I'll take care of him, don't worry young Bill.*' I spun around. Cat was staring at me. I'd had enough. Enough for one day, I went to my cabin and lay down on my bunk.

I awoke at about 5:30 am. My mind had been full of dreams, disturbing dreams. I dreamed of Jacko, and he had been talking to me. I dreamed of Lesley. We were sitting under a beautiful weeping willow tree by a small stream. But I had also been with Colin, we were just there talking, and I listened to him. I could smell his pipe. I could hear his gentle voice telling me it would all end in the right way; that I would find what I was looking for. I didn't wake as I usually did. I didn't seem to have any worries. My mind appeared to be at rest. Jacko came in with two buckets of hot water, towels, and a pair of scissors.

'I think we had better clean you up, Boss.'

He had pressed my suit and put out clean underclothes. I didn't argue with him. He fussed about with my hair until I finally stopped him.

'That's enough, Jacko! Mum certainly taught you well, didn't she?'

I walked back out into the wheelhouse. Cat was still there on the bench, but the leather satchel had gone.

'Where is the leather satchel?'

'That captain took it.'

'When?'

'Early hours of this morning when they'd finished unloading. I put the other papers in the drawer so nobody could read them.'

'I'll be back shortly,' I said.

I went to the gangplank and spoke to the guard at the bottom of it.

'Excuse me, could you tell me where the Captain's office is?'

'Yes, it's over there, but you will need to make an appointment to see him.'

'Thank you,' I replied and walked towards the office. I went through the door. A man was sitting at the desk; I noticed the name on the far door: Captain Williams.

The man sitting at the desk asked, 'May I help you?'

I ignored him and walked up to the door, opened it and walked in. Captain Williams was sitting at his desk. He had been working all night. I noticed the leather bag on the chair by his desk. He stood up sharply.

'What's this?'

I ignored him, walked up to the leather bag and picked it up. It was heavy. I opened it, and inside there were papers, pencils, folders and other documents. I turned it upside down on his desk and shook it. Most of the stuff fell out. I removed everything else and threw them down on his desk. He just stood there staring at me. I turned around and walked out of his office and went back to *Daisy May*, where I placed the bag back on the bench next to the wheel.

Jacko told me later that when I was leaving *Daisy May* Lesley walked into the wheelhouse and asked where I'd gone. He told her that the Captain took that leather bag last night and he thought I'd gone to get it back.'

'This should be interesting,' she said to Jacko.

I saw Les take Lesley's breakfast to her cabin, with my cup full of coffee on the tray, then Les brought our breakfast and two cups of coffee into the wheelhouse.

'Thank you, Les.'

He looked at me. 'I will miss Lesley Boss; I'll miss her.'

I walked up to her door and knocked. A voice said, 'Come.' I opened the door and looked straight at her.

'While I am still the captain on this vessel, you will get back into the galley and do your part!' I turned around and walked out back to the wheelhouse. She did as I had asked. Les opened the half stable door and ushered her in. He raised his arm in the air as a salute. Jacko punched me on the shoulder. I saw Lesley pouring out coffee for the crew. She was talking to them and making sure they were all well fed.

I looked at the leather satchel on the bench. I picked up Colin's pipe, all his papers, his tin box, and put them all inside and buckled the flap. I put it on my bunk. I saw Ted and Michael talking to the two men in white coats. Ted shook both their hands. Michael just nodded at them. Then they walked back down the gangplank. One of them had given Ted a piece of paper, and he walked into the wheelhouse.

'Skipper, this is for Lesley.' He grinned at me. 'Or should I say, Miss Johnson?' He returned to put the hatch covers back on and lashed them down.

The Captain of the Port walked back up the gangplank; two men walked behind him carrying boxes. A woman was walking behind them. She was about five foot four, dressed in a very smart business suit and wearing a hat with a small feather in it, she was carrying a briefcase. The

Captain looked at me with a severe look. 'I do have permission to come on board, don't I?'

'As long as you keep your light fingers in your pockets.'

His eyes flashed at me with that arrogance. The two men put the small boxes on the bench. Lesley stepped forward and put her hand out to greet the woman.

'Good morning, Mrs Evans.' They shook hands.

'Good morning, Commander Johnson.'

Lesley replied, 'I think it's best we talk in my cabin.'

'I think so, too,' replied Mrs Evans. They both disappeared.

Captain Williams had a scowl on this face as they both walked off.

'We have the pay for your crew. As you are aware, this is now a Navy vessel.'

I raised my eyebrows. This was money, can't argue with that. The crew were assembled, and each one was paid off. I noticed them walking off with their envelopes, looking very pleased with themselves. Jacko was standing there very excited, but there wasn't an envelope for him.

'Where is Jacko's envelope?'

'Oh, we don't have any records of him. He does not exist. He doesn't have a birth certificate or any papers.'

'Just a minute,' I replied, and went into my cabin, brought out the two envelopes and handed them to Jacko.

'Show him your papers.' Jacko looked at me, puzzled. 'The first one is a birth certificate.' Jacko opened it, and unfolded the piece of paper and read it. His eyes met mine; I could see they were filled with emotion.

'Bill, Mum has used my real name, my Aboriginal tribal name!'

'Give it to the man.'

Still looking at my face, he handed over the birth certificate. The captain read it and gave it to his clerk.

'Now the other envelope, Jacko.' Jacko opened it, read it, and he stared at me again.

'What does this mean?'

'It means you are an Australian citizen. You are somebody besides being my brother. Our Mum made sure of that.' A cheeky grin came all over his face. He looked at the captain.

'Would you like me to give this to your clerk? Would you like me to do it?'

The captain reached out, took the document, and handed it to his clerk. The clerk read it, jotted down some notes in his notebook, and then gave the papers back to Jacko. He turned to the Captain and put his hand out, palm up. The Captain looked annoyed and embarrassed, but he knew there was no way out. He put his hand in his inside pocket, took out another envelope and handed it to his clerk, who gave it to Jacko. Jacko had that silly grin on his face and said a few funny words in his language. He turned to face me.

'No, no, no.'

He knew I'd clenched my fist and my elbow had come up slightly ready to strike out. He stepped in front of me. 'Hold it back. Let the Gidgee take care of him.'

The Captain walked out of the wheelhouse back to the gangplank. The two clerks were grinning. One of them said, 'Oh, that was beautiful. Any time you could do that again, we would love to be there.'

They both put their hands out and shook mine, and they slapped Jacko on the back. Jacko very carefully put the papers back in the envelopes. He stared at me very briefly, turned and walked away. I knew he needed time to be himself, back in the desert, totally free.

Lesley and Mrs Evans walked out of Lesley's cabin and saw the two clerks about to leave. 'Excuse me, gentlemen, may we have a word with you? My name is Mrs Evans.' Both of them saluted Lesley; Lesley saluted back.

'At ease, gentlemen. Perhaps we could walk to the stern?' I saw Lesley and Mrs Evans talking to the clerks at the stern, but I could not work out what they were saying. The two men kept nodding their heads as though they agreed with whatever was said. Mrs Evans shook both their hands. They saluted Lesley and left. Both women walked into the wheelhouse. I gave Lesley the envelope which was given to Ted from the men in the white jackets to say that the hold was clean. She read it and then handed it to Mrs Evans, who also read it and looked at Lesley.

'Well, it appears she is clean. That's put my mind at ease.' Lesley said.

I thought to myself, they have cleaned the hull. There is no debris or rubbish left to *put her mind at ease?* That doesn't make any sense.

'Well, Captain, could I ask everybody to leave the wheelhouse?' Ted and Michael nodded and walked out.

'Captain, my name is Jackie. May I call you, William?'

'You may.'

'I believe that is the Australian way. There is so much you don't know, all will be explained to you in due course. Firstly, this vessel is owned by the British Navy. We bought her in Melbourne, Australia. The crew also belongs to the British Navy, although they didn't realise this when they signed the documents. Every British Naval ship has two captains so that the ship is never without a captain. You have been under the command of Commander Johnson.' She gestured to Lesley.

Then Lesley spoke. '*Daisy May* will be tied up to those posts you can see in the centre of the harbour. Les and Jacko will stay on board as caretakers; I think that is the best place for them.' Just then, Cat stood up. 'I beg your pardon and Cat.' Cat sat back down. Jackie stared at Cat briefly and shook her head. 'Young Jarrett, however, will be going to the Naval Academy in Dartmouth.'

Then Mrs Evans said, 'William, you and I are going to London.' She looked at her watch, smiled and added, 'But not before I've had a cup of tea and some of those sticky buns that Lesley's been telling me about.' And to my total surprise, Les came in with a silver tray loaded with beautiful cups and saucers and a teapot covered with a towel. Sticky buns and jam? I shook my head. Is this what it's all about? Sticky buns and jam with cups of tea?

'But William there is one small thing that I would ask of you. You have a young man by the name of Trevor Evans on board. He is my sister's son. She migrated from England to Australia. I haven't seen her since. We've written to each other, and I would like to see my nephew if I may.'

'First of all, Jackie, you say we are going to London. Who are you?'

She looked at me very thoughtfully and glanced at Lesley.

'Well, you have the right to have one question answered. I belong to and am attached to MI5, which is one step higher than the Army or the Navy. You have important work to do in London.'

'Excuse me for a moment, Jackie.' I walked out of the wheelhouse.

'Michael, where is Trevor?'

'He is sitting on the bow.'

'Jacko could you go and get him and take him into the wheelhouse, please. Ted, where is Jarrett?'

'He is below with his notebook. He has never seen *Daisy May* empty.'

'Could you please ask him to come up. Then get the crew together. Jarrett, get yourself cleaned up. Jacko will trim your hair and give you my razor. Better still, he'll shave you. Put on those fancy duds you had on when you came on board. Get all your gear together. Bigger things are brewing for you, lad.'

The crew gathered around. 'Well, lads, *Daisy May* now belongs to the British Navy, and so do you!' There was a murmur amongst them. I paused. I had trouble getting my breath. I had not deceived them, but I was the Captain. '*Daisy May* will be tied up; she will be permanently moored. Jacko and Les,' I had a small grin, 'and Cat will stay on board as caretakers. The rest of you have duties elsewhere. So stow your gear and be prepared to leave.'

I stood there for a moment, looking around at the crew. 'Good luck to you all. I am going to miss you, but I hope we can meet again in the future.' I stood to attention and saluted them. They all saluted back.

Lesley walked up to Ted, spoke to him briefly, and I went back into my wheelhouse. Trevor and Jackie were talking with their mouths full of sticky buns.

'Captain, I'm going to see my dad. He's in Portsmouth, wherever that is.'

I put my hand on his shoulder. 'Then don't forget to wipe the jam and sugar off your mouth before you leave.'

I walked into my cabin and slid the door closed. Then I froze. Jacko. I can't leave Jacko. Then I remembered his words, '*I will always be with you. Just call me when you need me. I'll be there looking over the horizon for you.*' I sat down on my bunk, put my hands in my lap and then I heard that voice again. '*Stop worrying young William; I'll take care of him until you come back.*' I shook my head and stood up. I put everything I wanted into my haversack, went through my drawers, picked up my telescope and Walter Wright's.

On deck, I walked up to Ted and thrust the telescope into his chest. 'This was Walter Wright's. Take care of it, Ted.' He looked me straight in the eyes and nodded.

Lesley and Jackie were standing at the gangplank. Michael handed Lesley a beautiful pair of gloves made of sail canvas. They had lines stitched into them and were elbow length. When exposed, you could see *Daisy May* embroidered on them with very intricate stitches.

'Thank you, Michael. I will cherish these forever.' She just stood there for a moment staring into his eyes, then she said, 'Michael I have some vital work for you to do in the future. We will train you, and then you will be teaching others to understand the sea and the winds, and to know what the sea is telling you.' She shook his hand. 'Thank you, Michael.' Then she repeated in a softer voice, full of compassion, 'Thank you, Michael.'

Les was standing there with a bag of food which he handed to her. She choked back her emotions. She put her hand in her pocket and brought out an envelope. 'If you ever need me, Les, this is where you can reach me. Please don't hesitate to call.' She kissed him gently on his nose, put her finger up to his moustache and gently touched it.

She turned to Ted. 'Captain Coe. We will be working together shortly. I have the utmost respect for you. You are one hell of a professional.' She shook his hand.

Jacko was leaning against the baulk works to one side of the gangplank. She stood there looking at him for a moment. He winked at her. She slowly walked up to him 'When we were playing chess you got into my mind, you learned my darkest secrets, you know who I am, I couldn't hide it from you, but you have kept it a secret from the others, you understand.'

Jacko looked at her very gravely; his face changed. 'I am the keeper of secrets. I am the Peacemaker; you and I are as one.' Then his face returned to normal, and he had that silly grin. Lesley stood there looking at him. He winkled at Lesley again.

'You look after yourself Gidgee. I will wait for you. I'll be here when you're tired and worn out. *Daisy May* and I will take care of you.'

She could not contain herself. She put her arms out and walked over and cuddled Jacko. Tears flowed down her cheeks. 'You funny, spooky, beautiful little puppy.' She suddenly stamped her foot on the deck, shook him and shouted out, 'You look after yourself, or you'll answer to me. Do you hear me?' Her voice dropped a little softer, 'Do you hear me?'

'I hear you, Gidgee, I hear you.'

She turned and started to walk down the gangplank. She stopped abruptly, turned around, and for just a few moments looked deeply into my eyes. She stood straight to attention and saluted me. She said, 'Captain William Farquhar.'

I found my throat had locked up with emotion, and I couldn't say anything; I just gently bowed my head to her in respect. Lesley then turned and walked down the gangplank, saying to herself, *I must now be Commander Johnson and leave my emotions on board Daisy May.* But the tears would not stop.

Jarrett, who was carrying Lesley's bags, stopped and looked around at the crew, and put his hand up in the air. He shook hands with Ted and Michael. Les gave him a bag of sticky buns and slapped him on the shoulder.

Jacko quietly said to him, 'For a green boy, you turned out alright. You are now a man; walk tall.'

Jarrett replied, 'Thanks, Jacko, thanks.'

They were on the wharf. Mrs Evans walked down the gangplank in front of me. Jacko and I put our right hands up, both palms together.

'As one, Jacko.'

'As one, Bill. I will be flying high above you, watching, and I'll be sitting on the stump of a tree waiting.'

I walked down the gangplank. I didn't look back. My world had been turned upside down.

CHAPTER 18

Two cars were waiting on the wharf. Lesley and Jarrett got into one and Mrs Evans and I got into the other. The two vehicles went their separate ways. We went across on the ferry and drove to Exeter, and there we boarded a train for London. We had a compartment to ourselves. Mrs Evans got a notepad out of her briefcase and then started to ask me questions. Questions about commanding a ship and the problems that you face with the vessel you are in command.

'Captain Jack Fox. What are your opinions of this man?'

I hesitated. Why would she ask me these questions? Who exactly is she? I had asked this question before. I knew she worked for MI5, but what exactly does she do for MI5, what is her position?

'I have known Captain Jack Fox for a long time. I have always found him extremely reliable and trustworthy; his word is his word. He can play politics on board his vessel. He knows how to put every man to the right task at sea; he knows every one of his crew, every individual, inside out. He can make quick decisions because he's already prepared them in his mind. He expects everybody else to snap to it when he gives his commands, and that is what they do. That is why I believe his crew is still alive today.'

I thought of when we were going down the South Channel in Port Phillip Bay. He had seen my predicament and had prepared for it. I added, 'He is a man that will prepare himself to assist others in their command. He is a Captain; he will put the responsibilities of his command first. In short, he has my total respect.'

Mrs Evans took a deep sigh. 'This is war! We can't support little puppies that have been born with the golden spoons in their mouths. Mummy and Daddy in high places in society who have bought their positions and places, and use their political influence to further their children. We must have men and women who have grown up with the hard knocks, who know the rules of survival and command. Captain Jack Fox, with the burns he has received on his arm, with his age, and the experience of the pain of the loss of *The Castle*, will be an excellent man to take command of Britannia Royal Naval College (BRNC), commonly known as Dartmouth. He is going to play a significant part in helping us with this war.'

'I think you have made an excellent choice,' I replied.

I found myself thinking of Jacko. We used to sit on the stump of a tree, looking up into the sky, watching the eagles soar, wishing we could fly high. I awoke with a hand on my knee.

'Captain, we are just drawing into London.'

I was still weary and tired. I wanted to shut out the world for just a little bit longer. A man walked into our compartment. 'May I take your bag, sir?'

'Yes, but I will take the leather one.'

Everything outside was dark. There were no lights anywhere. We were ushered into a car, and eventually, we pulled up outside a hotel. A man opened the car door.

Mrs Evans said, 'Captain, there will soon be a lot of people fussing over you. Just do as they ask, have patience with them, trust them. I will see you in the morning. Good night Captain.'

'Good night, Mrs Evans.'

I was taken into a hotel room which was beautifully furnished. I put my hands on the bed and pushed gently. Then I looked at the floor. The bed is too soft; the floor is too hard. I'll sleep on the bed. There was hot coffee on the table, so I poured myself a cup and walked into the bathroom. A bath! Hot and cold running water! I'll make good use of that.

There was a knock at the door, and it woke me with a start. 'Good morning, sir. Breakfast! Sir, if there is anything I can get you, please call me.'

'There is! Do you have a mug?' I winked at him. 'I have been at sea all my life.'

He chuckled to himself. 'I perfectly understand sir; I'll find one.'

'Thank you.'

He went to walk back out of the door but stopped. 'It's nice to have a real person in the room sir.' With that said he left the room.

Then another man walked into my room with a woman. 'Excuse me, sir; we're here to cut your hair and trim your beard. May we, sir?'

I took a deep breath, the only person who ever cut my hair was Jacko, and I trimmed my beard. I thought of Jack Fox, Lesley and his beard. I hope he never hears of this. 'Yes, you may.'

Then yet another man, very neatly dressed with shiny shoes and an overcoat over his arm entered. 'Sir, I'm here to take you to be fitted for a uniform. I remembered Mrs Evans' words, '*Just do as they ask; have patience with them.*' Next thing I knew I was wearing a British Naval

Captain's uniform with all the trimmings. The salesman gave me a brand new pair of shoes.

The gentleman with me stepped forward. 'No, no, this gentleman is an Australian. Give him the appropriate pair of shoes.' The salesman then produced a pair of lace-up boots. I was a lot happier.

'We will forward the rest of your items to the hotel, sir.'

I just raised my eyebrows and shook my head slowly. 'Thank you very much. I would appreciate that.' I liked this man; he had a fluffy personality, but he was very professional.

My companion said, 'Well, Captain, the fun has finished. I'm afraid I've got to take you to meet some politicians. Please follow me.'

I sat in a beautiful chauffeur-driven Bentley; the back seat was so soft and comfortable. Am I dreaming? When am I going to wake up? One day at sea fighting a gale, trying to protect *Daisy May* and my crew, next, I'm here, sitting in luxury. It's crazy; it doesn't make any sense. Nothing makes any sense.

The car pulled up, the door opened. We got out and walked up the wide, imposing steps. I glanced around and saw tall buildings, a beautiful park, people everywhere. I felt lost and felt hot, although it was a cold day. I wanted to take my tie off and undo my top button. Suddenly we were in a lift, and the man with me handed the man at the lift some documents. He read them and looked at me. He was studying me. I noticed when he handed the papers back, my photo was attached. When did they get my photo? We were again ushered into a lift, but this time the lift went down instead of up. It went down, down, down, then abruptly stopped. The doors opened, two British Army men were there, fully armed. The man with me handed them the papers. They studied both of us. One said, 'Thank you, gentlemen' and handed the papers back. We were shown into a waiting room.

'Where are we?'

'All in due course, Captain, all in good time.'

'Good morning, Captain Farquhar.' The voice was familiar. I turned around sharply, and there was Mrs Evans.

'You're looking very smart, Captain, but I suppose you're feeling very uncomfortable.'

'Yes, I am Mrs Evans, yes, I am.'

'Well, we've got time for a cup of tea before they can see us if you would like to walk this way.' She turned to the gentleman who had brought me here. 'Thank you. That other matter we talked about, would you attend to it, please? I don't know where you will send him. Just make sure he's well out of the way!'

The man walked away briskly. She smiled at me with a devious sly smile. 'Captain, I don't think anybody will try to keep Jacko's money in the future.' She gave me that look, '*Don't mess with my people!*' I drank my coffee as she briefly talked to others. Then another familiar voice behind me made me freeze. My mind raced forward, a friend, a friend, I'm not alone, a friend! I turned around sharply, nearly spilling my coffee and stared directly into her eyes. I felt frozen in time. I remembered our talks, our chess games, the laughter, Les, Jacko, Ted, and Michael, the flour on her face, the tears.

'Good morning, Captain Farquhar.'

I didn't have any words, they were there, but they wouldn't come out of my mouth. Why? Because they were not the words, I could say here. Not in this place.

'Good morning, good morning.'

She turned and glanced at Mrs Evans. Mrs Evans glanced back and nodded. 'Would you follow me please, Captain?' A uniformed officer with a sidearm at his side opened the door. Lesley walked in, Mrs Evans and I followed. There was a man behind a desk. He was standing with his knuckles resting on the desk, his head down, reading documents. He grunted to himself, picked up his cigar, he drew in on the cigar, and blue smoke went everywhere.

A gruff voice boomed out, 'Gentlemen, I am satisfied that you have chosen the right man for Dartmouth.' He picked up his pen and signed the document. 'So, you will have him here next month once his arm has healed?'

'Yes, sir.'

'Good, good. Thank you, gentlemen.' Two men picked up the papers and walked out of the office. Still looking at the papers on his desk, he picked up a whisky glass and took two sips and then replaced it on the bureau. He drew back on his cigar once again, blue smoke curling all around him. He looked up and stared straight at me as if he wasn't seeing me.

Lesley stepped forward. 'May I present Captain William Farquhar?'

A grin came all over his face. 'So we deceived them, didn't we Bill? We played the game and won, thanks to you and your crew and the *Daisy May*. And *Daisy May* has woven a spell on you, hasn't she Lesley?'

'Yes, she did,' Lesley replied.

'Well Lesley, she wove a spell on me many years ago. I was a reporter then, and I wrote an article on her. I must find it again one day,' he said looking at me.

'Captain Farquhar, your cargo. This information does not leave this room. I repeat, this does not leave this room. Your shipment was a nuclear powder, commonly known as yellowcake. I do not fully understand it, but what I do know is that it can create heat to create steam to drive turbines for ships, for power stations and it also can be used in the medical world. Or, and I say this with the most profound respect, create a bomb that could end the war. The Germans, as far as we know, do not realise we already have it. They may have their suspicions, but not any proof. But I'm quite sure they'll get it shortly.' He chuckled to himself and then looked straight at Lesley. 'Then the chess game will have to change, won't it, Lesley?'

He looked straight at her. How did he know about the chess game with Jacko? However, he did know. Nevertheless, this was Winston

Churchill, one of the greatest politicians. He had to have an insight into nature itself, the same as Jacko.

'Captain William Farquhar, it is my honour sir to award you this medal in gratitude for your services.'

There were three boxes on his desk. He picked up one, took the medal out of the box, walked over to me and pinned it on my uniform. 'All the time you wear this uniform, wear this medal. It gives you total command.' He shook my hand, a firm handshake. 'Three vessels were carrying this cargo, one was *The Castle*.' He paused. 'There was another.' He picked up one of the medals, 'Mrs Evans, could you please see that his daughter gets this medal?'

He sat down at his desk. 'Thank you. Thank you.' We had been dismissed.

Back in the foyer, Lesley put her hand out. 'Goodbye, Captain and good luck.' She turned and walked off.

Mrs Evans put her hand out. 'Goodbye, Captain. You will be picked up at your hotel at 9 am. Good luck, Captain, good luck.'

I felt I was in a whirlpool of people where I did not belong and was entirely out of place.

My escort said, 'Sir, could I save you and get you out of here and back to your hotel?'

'Yes, you can. Let's go.'

He stood for a few moments, staring at the medal. 'There are very few of those medals, sir. May I be the first to congratulate you?'

'Thank you, but I don't know what all the fuss is about.' I leaned slightly towards him. 'I don't understand it.'

'Well, Captain, in the next month it will all be explained to you, but first of all, let's leave here before people start to ask too many questions. When they see that medal, their jealousy will be unbelievable.'

The lift brought us back up onto the ground floor. 'Would you like coffee, Captain?'

'Yes, I would.'

'Follow me, sir.'

'Before I follow you, would you please call me, Bill?'

'Ah, yes, you're Australian! My name is James.'

'Very pleased to meet you, James.' We sat down at a small table in a coffee shop, and James ordered coffee.

'Bill, there is a car waiting for you and the man driving the car will be your valet. He will look after all your needs; anything you want, he will get for you. You have the afternoon to yourself, so if there is anywhere you would like to go or anything you would like to see, tell him. But please, keep him informed of your whereabouts at all times.' He tapped me lightly on the arm. 'You are treasured, you know. But please don't call me James when there are others around; it's not the done thing you know.'

Next minute I was on the footpath and the car door opened for me. 'Good morning, sir.' It was just an average car, but the back seat was very comfortable. I saw a small compartment in it, with alcohol and a writing tray pinned up against the back seat.

'Where to sir?'

I put my hand on my leather, satchel. 'The Bank of England.'

'Excellent sir.' Just then, Big Ben struck noon. 'I hope it keeps striking sir throughout the war. It is England.'

When I arrived at the Bank of England, I spoke to a young man behind the counter.

'I've come in for a safety deposit box.'

'Do you have your papers and your security deposit number, sir?'

I handed my papers and numbers to him, and after handing the papers back to me, he gave a note to another gentleman. 'If you would like to follow this man sir.'

We went through a couple of security doors into a lovely room with a small table in the centre. 'If you could wait here, please, sir.' He returned with a box. I looked at him, puzzled. 'If you'd beg my pardon, sir, have you ever opened a safety deposit box before?

'No, I haven't.'

'You have a key sir. I will leave you here and when you have finished, please lock the box back up and take the key with you. Just knock on the door or press that buzzer. Thank you, sir'. He left the room.

I opened the box and stood staring at the contents. There were two bundles of £5 notes, a small tin and some documents. I opened the tin box and found inside a piece of folded paper. I carefully opened the paper and found four beautifully cut diamonds; they were the size of a fingernail. I just stared at them, and the £5 notes. *Well, well, Colin. You were quite a rich man!* I folded the paper back up and returned the diamonds to the safe deposit box. I put all the documents in my leather satchel then locked the safety deposit box and pressed the buzzer by the door.

Back at my hotel, I found parcels of clothing: underclothes, spare boots, shirts, and suits, and a white raincoat with a belt that tied up around the waist and a big floppy collar and big pockets. The valet stood there for a moment. 'Sir, they do not have your overcoat yet, so they have given you this raincoat.'

'We haven't been formally introduced. My name is Captain William Farquhar, and you are?'

'Mervyn Nelis, sir.'

'Well, Mervyn, when we are alone, my name is Bill, and you are Mervyn.' I put my hand out and shook his hand. 'Where are you from?'

'Australia, Bill.' He had sadness in his voice. ' And I'm too far away from home.'

'So explain to me why you're here and your role with me.'

He gave me a cheeky grin. 'They told me you were sharp, and she told me you could see over the horizon, so you're not easily fooled! I'm in high profile security. In other words; I am your bodyguard. That's my expertise. I've been all over the world, China, Japan, Asia and many other places.'

'I'm happy to have you on board.' I tapped him lightly on his arm.

'I've got the adjoining room, so knock, bang, or call me, and I'll be here. There is a menu on the table, but I'd suggest rump steak, eggs, and chips.'

'Could we make that for two Mervyn?'

'I'll order it now, Bill.'

I took the papers out of my bag. Documents, stocks, and bonds? I knew what stocks and bonds meant. Now that I have them in my hand, what do I do with them? There was a title to an estate, a manor house with six farms and a row of cottages. There were two envelopes; one of which was addressed to me. I opened the envelope.

Bill, I have made you the executor of my estate, which I have left in trust to my sister'. It is rightfully hers. The money and diamonds are yours. The stocks and bonds are my sister's. Fair sailing, my son.

It was signed by Colin. The other envelope contained addresses of solicitors and additional information I needed to know to enable me to carry out his wishes.

The next morning Mervyn appeared with my breakfast. 'Good morning, Bill. We have to leave here by 8:30 am. I reckon you've got a busy day.'

Soon I was in the foyer of another large city building. I was ushered into a large room with big paintings of ships and naval men adorning the walls. Admiral Nelson seemed to take the limelight. There was a large table in the centre with chairs around it. There were six other men in the room; we were all dressed in the same uniform. The door opened from the far end, and a woman walked through it. I was taken entirely by surprise. It was Lesley! I felt my chest tighten. To me, she represented *Daisy May*, Jacko, Ted, Michael and Les.

'If you would all be seated at the table, gentlemen.'

We all took a chair and sat down. A large folder was put down in front of us. 'Gentlemen, the Commander-in-chief will be with you shortly. When he enters, please stand and sit down only when he does.'

The big doors opened, and a man walked in and went to the only vacant chair. We all stood. 'Good morning, gentlemen. Please sit down. My name is Cunningham. You gentlemen will answer to me and only to me. I answer to Winston Churchill and only Winston Churchill. That we must establish first. Do we have that clear gentleman?' We all acknowledged by a nod of the head.

'You gentlemen are the best, the very best that we could find. In this war, we must have men of the sea, not puppy dogs, in command of our naval vessels. You are all now commanders, and you will go from here to have further briefings. Gentlemen on the vessels you will be assigned to, there will be men with a range of expertise to assist you in your command. Are there any questions, gentlemen?' I shook my head. I felt I just had to move with the tide and play the game.

'Commander Johnson will brief you on where you will be tomorrow. Good morning gentlemen.' He turned to walk out of the door, stopped, and looked straight at me 'Ninety-one days! Remarkable Captain, remarkable.' He walked back out of the door.

Lesley stood talking for half an hour. 'Gentlemen, you have the rest of the day to yourselves. You will be taken to another location tomorrow. You will be staying at that location for approximately three weeks. Good morning gentlemen.'

Her eyes briefly met mine, but she just nodded. Nobody else would have noticed. I stood frozen for a few minutes; then she was gone.

A trolley was brought in with tea, coffee, biscuits and cake. We all introduced ourselves to each other.

Nevertheless, I couldn't get her out of mind. I was confused enough, but seeing her made it even harder. But in a different sense seeing her made things better.

'Mervyn, do we have the car all day?'

'Yes, Bill, we do.'

'I need to visit some people. Here is the address, and it's at a place called Edenbridge.'

'Yes, you go down through Oxted; it is on the way to Hever Castle in Kent.'

'Could we go there today and still be back in time?'

'Yes, we can, but let me phone in first.'

We were on our way. It was late afternoon by the time we arrived. We drove through large open gates and up to a grand old manor house in beautiful English gardens. As I walked up to the front door, it opened, and a lady and gentleman stopped in the doorway.

'Good afternoon. My name is Captain William Farquhar.'

The woman's hand went up to her mouth, and she gave a small gasp. The man put out his hand to shake mine. 'Please come in, Captain.' I was taken into a comfortable lounge with a log fire.

'I wonder whether my colleague could join us?'

'Certainly, yes, yes.'

Mervyn came into the lounge. 'A cup of tea, Captain?'

'I would prefer coffee if you don't mind.' I turned to the lady. 'May I call you, Jenny?'

'Yes, you may.'

I found myself biting my lip. 'I'm afraid that I have some bad news for you, Jenny. Your brother Colin passed away some months ago, in the latter part of September.' I could see the pain in her eyes.

'He wrote to us earlier in the year and said he was having troubles with his chest, so we were prepared.'

'We buried him at sea where he wanted to be.'

'Thank you, Captain.'

'Colin asked me to leave these papers with you. They are the papers to this estate and some stocks and bonds. I have to sort this out with the solicitors.' I took out the title to the estate, the stocks and bonds, plus some photos and I spread the title out on the table. 'This is your estate.' They both studied it for a while.

'No, this farm is not ours; we don't own these cottages.'

'But this title says you do own it. Has Colin sold this farm and these buildings, do you know?' My mind was racing, why didn't they know about the other farm and the cottages? Country estates in the early days usually had cottages provided for their workers.

'No, we don't.'

Mervyn's voice broke in. 'Excuse me; perhaps we could check with the titles office in London before you go to the solicitor's office.'

'Good suggestion, Mervyn. It was Colin's will; I will leave the stocks and bonds with you and delve into this a bit deeper.'

'Thank you, Captain; we would appreciate that. I think you would carry a bit more weight than we do. We were so glad to hear that Colin found his son Terry and that they made friends. That is something Colin desperately wanted.'

'Say that again? He found his son Terry?'

'Oh, yes, in one of those far eastern ports.'

I thought to myself you cunning old fox, is that why you got him on board? I could never understand the relationship you had with him. I'd always wondered what made him take off to sea.

'Our father had arranged a marriage for Colin, it didn't go too well, all sorts of kerfuffles. Colin had a mistress, and she became pregnant by him and had a son. She died, and our family took Terry in, making out he was Colin's legitimate son. Colin could not take it and disappeared. Then we learned he was on the *Daisy May*; occasionally we would receive letters from him. When father and mother died, the estate went to him because he was the only son.'

'Well, Jenny, if I can take these papers with me, I will try to sort it all out.'

We said our goodbyes. It was a slow trip back to London. We were stopped several times by security, but when they saw my uniform, they didn't ask any more questions.

Back at the hotel, I went through the folder which was put in front of me at the meeting that morning. I looked at my watch; it was 2 am. I wasn't used to looking through documents like this, so I had to read them several times.

Early next morning Mervyn was at the door with my breakfast. 'You're up early Mervyn.'

'Yes, Bill, it was a good morning for a run. The parks and gardens here in London offer good running tracks.'

I laughed. 'You're a greater man than I am.'

Soon we were on our way to our next location. My mind was racing ahead again. Why didn't they know about the other farm and the houses? Country estates in the early days had cottages for their workers. *Beware of the finicky winds in your sails, be prepared!* I needed to ask sensitive questions of the right people.

Before I knew what was happening, we were at a high-security gate, and Mervyn was handing his papers to the guard. The guard looked at his clipboard, then looked at me. He gave me a salute. I saluted back.

'Thank you, Mr Nelis; you may proceed to Building Number 22.' The guard grinned to Mervyn then smiled at me. 'She'll be right cobber,' and put his thumb in the air, giving me the Australian salute. I raised my thumb back.

'Where are you from?' I asked the guard.

'Perth, sir.'

'Hang in there; you'll get home one day.' I could see the sadness in his eyes as he stood back and saluted. I gave him the Australian salute again.

Over the next three weeks I received training in how to command others; their roles and duties; their positions and the chain of command above me. How I was to enter and leave ports, and how I was to communicate the codes that would constantly change. I kept saying to myself, *Get to know them, the numbers, the letters; how my orders were to be initiated.* The three weeks went past very quickly.

We were all once again sitting in the same conference room, talking among ourselves. The door opened, and Admiral Cunningham walked in. He seemed more relaxed, more at ease with us. We all stood up.

'Please, please, gentlemen, sit down. It has been a hard three weeks for you all. Commodore Johnson will give you your orders, the name of your battleship, what time you are to be at her location and the names of your officers.' His voice became stern. 'Gentlemen, let me remind you, on your command, you are God. You rule with an iron fist! Nobody questions your orders; they will be obeyed instantly.' His voice softened again. 'We know the high burden that we are now going to place upon you; it will be a heavy weight upon your shoulders. Gentlemen, may God go with you, he will be the only friend in your command. Now, gentlemen, I would be very proud if I could have tea and coffee with you and meet you all as individuals.'

Tea, coffee, biscuits, and cakes were brought in on trays. Admiral Cunningham chatted with us all. He put one hand on my shoulder and shook my hand with the other. 'William, we left you in a confusing world, for which I must apologise. The submarine, the gunboat, and what happened to them. One of our submarines was following you at all times.' I thought of Jacko's words, '*Big fish following us, Boss*'. 'The submarine captain did a remarkable job of protecting you. Commodore Johnson told me about your brother and his extraordinary abilities but also said that we would destroy him if we brought him into the war so we will leave him to look after *Daisy May*.'

'Thank you; I very much appreciate that.'

'But who knows William, his abilities might come into good use in the future.'

'Sir, there is a regiment of Australian soldiers guarding the area we were just in, but they were wearing British uniforms. It puzzles me.'

He studied me for a few moments. 'Commander William Farquhar,' and he tapped my medal with his finger, 'this medal you are wearing, in some respects, it is above my command. Use it as you will.' He gave me a small grin. 'Yes, it is a bit disrespectful to Australia.' He briefly looked at his watch. Commodore Lesley Johnson appeared at the door; he nodded to her.

He called out in a loud voice, 'Gentlemen, I will look forward to meeting you all in the future.' He slightly bowed his head. 'May God go with you.' He turned and walked out of the room.

Lesley's voice broke in. 'Gentlemen, If I may have your attention, please?' We all turned to face her. A gentleman dressed in naval uniform carrying a box stood beside her. What alarmed me was that the gentleman was wearing a sidearm, and it was Mervyn Nelis. 'Gentlemen in these satchels are the documents you will require for your command, including the name of your ship and the information you need to know before boarding her, including the names of your officers who you will meet tomorrow. You have another appointment at a different location tomorrow, and then you will be given three days' leave. Gentlemen, the rest of the day is yours.'

We were given our satchels. Each had our name embossed on the front. I stood staring at my name: *Commander William Farquhar*. Then it hit me. My stomach seemed to turn upside down. I don't want this. This war! It is the world gone mad! The universe is trying to maim, to kill, to destroy itself; it is hell! I am to come face to face with the devil, and they want me to destroy him. I walked outside and sat down on a bench under a beautiful maple tree. I had tears in my eyes. *Where are you, Jacko? Where are you Daisy May? Lesley, I need you. Jacko, I need you.*

I looked up at the sky and saw there a beautiful big bird. Was it an eagle or another breed of big bird? To me, it was Jacko. *I see you, Jacko, I see you.* I didn't notice Lesley walk up behind me and sit down on the bench alongside me.

'Hello, Bill.' She put her hand on my arm. 'I've missed you, Jacko and *Daisy May*. I feel lost.'

I felt something swell up from deep down inside me. 'Yes, Lesley, I am also lost. We fear the future; we don't want to be there. But I know we both have to face it, because if we run from it, then we lose control. We are strong; we will stand, face it and beat it'.

'Yes, Bill, we will. If you give me a letter to Jacko, I will make sure that he gets it, and he will get my letter as well.'

'Thank you, Lesley.' We stood up and just looked at each other. We did not say goodbye; we just turned and went back to our responsibilities.

I returned to the office of the Commander of the Base. The desk clerk stood to attention.

'May I help you, sir?'

'Yes, I would like to speak with the officer in charge.'

'Yes, sir. You are?'

'Commander William Farquhar.'

He picked up the phone. 'Commander William Farquhar to see you, sir.' The door opened abruptly, a man stepped out and saluted me.

'Captain James at your service, sir.'

I walked into his office with both my hands behind my back. 'Captain James, in our position of command, we have to make decisions and hopefully the right choices. In certain circumstances, we have to be respectful to those we have under our command. If you are given Australian soldiers, it is very disrespectful to Australia to put them in British uniforms. Do you understand what I am saying?'

'Sir, this is a British base. This is England.'

I tapped the medal on my collar. 'Do you want to argue with me?'

'No, sir.'

'So Captain James, we do not need to discuss this any further do we? Good morning Captain!' I turned and walked out of the office.

Captain James's office door had been left open. As I walked out the clerk had a big smile on his face.

'Where do you come from?' I asked him.

'Coober Pedy, sir.' I put my thumb in the air; he did the same.

'Don't worry lad; we'll get you back home one day.'

'Yes, sir'.

'And I'd like to have a beer with you when we do. See you at the bar.'

I went back to my quarters, opened the satchel and browsed through my papers. My command is a British destroyer. A dreadnought, with heavy armour plate. It is designed to take a pounding and has a top speed of thirty-six knots. I read it again and again, thirty-six knots! If *Daisy May* ever did eight knots in a strong tide, I would have been surprised. But thirty-six knots? There was information on the size of the guns and small arms, all sorts of information which I knew I'd have to see to understand. I turned to my crew list.

First Officer Captain William Code. I felt myself shrink into the chair. I put both hands on my face; I felt myself scream out inside, *I am not alone! I am not alone; I still have him with me.* Navigational Officer: Captain Jarrett Collins. I slapped my hands on the table. *You arrogant little sod. Your father will be so proud, of you, and your mother will have to understand you are her son, Captain Collins.* Other officers included gunnery officer, chief engineer and one or two others. I went back to the engineer's name: Freddie Lees. I wonder. Structural Engineer: David Eagles. I wondered why so many Australians were guarding this base and working in its administration. Mervyn. What's he doing here? How far do his duties go? Back to those loose ends again.

I glanced at Colin's title again. Six farms and some cottages. That is what the title says, but they say they only own five farms. I went through the rest of the papers Colin had left me. In pencil down one side of a document he had written,

Check the local church boy; they have all the information you require. Beware of Slippery Jack.'

Beware of Slippery Jack? Who or what is Slippery Jack? I've read that name somewhere. I read through the rest of the papers. The lawyer who handles the will and documents for Colin's family is Jack Whitehead! So the church is a key to Jack Whitehead. The church is in the local village. I need to go to the church first. I have to have a plan.

The next day I went to meet my future crew. Everybody in the room stood to attention. Commodore Johnson was standing to one side of the room. I thought to myself. 'You're enjoying this, aren't you? Get your ego in check! This is not going to be fun.'

'Good morning, Commodore Johnson. Good morning gentlemen. Please be seated.' My eyes caught Ted's. 'Captain Edward Coe, would you stand alongside me, please?' Ted moved to stand at my right side. 'Gentlemen, I am in command. What you must understand first is that my second-in-command is Captain Edward Coe. When Captain Edward Coe gives an order, it will be carried out at once. If any of you question that order, I will slam the door on you so hard you will not be able to stand for a month. We are at war, and the lives of the crew and the welfare of our vessel will depend on teamwork. Those crew members who are working under you must also understand this. I expect all of you to perform your duties to make your team understand this. Gentlemen, you are my officers, and I demand of you the very best you can do. Fail me, and our vessel will lie at the bottom of the sea with all her crew. I'll leave that to your imagination. Gentlemen stand at ease and get to know each other; If you have a problem, talk to Captain Coe. You will have access to me any time you wish through Captain Coe.'

I walked down between the men shaking their hands. 'Welcome aboard. Welcome aboard.' Jarrett was standing there trying to keep a straight face. I took his hand and shook it, but I placed my other hand on top of his and stood straight. 'You have my permission to come on board, Mr Collins. I will write to your father and let him know his son is more than a man. Thank you, Mr Collins.'

I turned to the next man. 'Welcome on board, Mr Lees. Proud to have you come on board.'

'Mr Eagles, they tell me you're an incredibly good man with tapestry. Hope to see some of it on board.'

I walked back up to the front of the room and stood in front of them. 'Gentlemen, I will see you all on board, but before you leave, I have a strict rule—no alcohol on board, and no drugs of any type. I will keel-haul any man I find who has brought anything of that type on board. I will check the length of the vessel.' They all nodded. I stood to attention, bowed slightly to them. 'Gentlemen, I will see you all on board.' I turned to Captain Coe. 'You have my permission to dismiss them.'

I turned and walked over to Commodore Johnson. 'I would very much like to return to London this afternoon. I will leave the letter we spoke of on the table in my room.'

'Thank you, Commander; I'll have your car ready for you, sir.'

'Thank you.'

I went back to my quarters, packed my things, sat down, and wrote to Jacko. I told him about the crazy world I was tied up with. I told him how I was sorting Colin's business out, and I wrote of *Daisy May* and said that my old boson was doing well. I knew I could not mention his name.

Seen your chess mate, still playing the game well. I know you are with me. I was sitting under the tree and saw you flying high. I will call on you again shortly. May you have cool breezes and fresh water.

I signed it *William*, folded up the letter, and put it into an envelope and placed it on the table. I put my hand on top of the message and thought of Jacko, *Daisy May* and Les. There was a knock at the door.

'Your car, sir.'

I picked up my leather satchel and the bag containing my documents. At the gatehouse, the guard was wearing an Australian uniform. He spoke to the driver.

'Your papers, sir.'

He studied them and started to hand them back. 'This envelope is yours, sir. One of my men is a tinsmith and makes jewellery. We would be very proud if you wear this, sir.'

I opened the envelope. In it was a tie pin made from gold. Embossed on the badge were the words, Commander Farquhar, Australian.

I glanced up at the man. 'I would be very proud to wear this.' The man stood back, saluted and opened the barrier. We drove through. I pinned the tie pin on top of my medal and said to myself, *Yes, I will wear this with pride.*

It was quite late when we arrived back at the hotel. I asked the driver to have the car waiting at 8 am and went to my room and started to order room service. There was a knock at the door, and Mervyn walked in.

'Make that for two people, and we will have steak, egg and chips, with coffee in mugs.' I turned to Mervyn. 'I want to go back to Edenbridge and go to the local church. From there, I should be able to get some information on Colin's family. Then I'll have to sort this out with the family lawyer, a Jack Whitehead.'

'Do you still want to go to the Title's Office, Bill?'

'Yes, I'll have to do that.'

Mervyn commented, 'You look tired, Bill.'

'Yes, I am. A good night's sleep is what I need. See you in the morning.'

The following morning we had a good breakfast. I thought a lot could happen in the next couple of days and I might need some clean clothes. What do I have to put them in? I looked at my leather satchel, I needed that; Colin's papers were in it. My naval bag with other documents in it? I took them out and folded them neatly in an envelope. Now, where shall I put them? I pulled out a drawer from the dressing table. The drawer had runners on either side and a plywood base. I put the papers on the plywood base and closed the drawer, then pulled the drawer open and closed it again. If anyone were to open the drawer, they wouldn't see the papers. I picked up my underclothes, socks and a clean shirt, and put them in my naval bag.

Mervyn had the car ready at 8 am. I noticed him looking at my two bags. We arrived at the church. It was a beautiful old English Church. Its age fascinated me; we didn't have anything like this in Australia. We walked into the foyer of the church, and the reverend came to meet us.

'Welcome gentlemen. I am Reverend Ted Bailey. How may I help you?'

'Good morning, Reverend. I am Captain Farquhar, my friend here is Mr Nelis. I am after some information, and I am hoping that you can help me.'

The Reverend smiled at us. 'Yes, yes, please come into the vestry. I am free today. We used to have bell ringing practice at this time, but due to the war, we are unable to have it anymore.'

I spread out the will and documents on the table. He read through them.

'Yes, I remember. I was a very young clergyman then, and this was my first funeral service. You never forget your first funeral and the circumstances surrounding it. We buried Mary's mother alongside her daughter many years ago. I liked Colin, but I didn't like Mary's brother, Jack Whitehead.

Well, you want some information, don't you? Colin and Mary were friends at school; they did everything together. Everyone thought they would one day be married. Unfortunately, Colin's father had arranged a marriage for Colin with a high society lady. Her father was high up in the military and would help Colin's career in the future. Despite this, Colin and Mary kept seeing each other, even though Jack Whitehead made it very hard for them. And Colin's father was not a man to tangle with either. Mary became pregnant, and it was decided by all, including the Church

Council, that the baby should be given to Colin's wife and, to save the reputation of the family, the child would be christened under her name.

We don't fully understand why Mary died. Colin was shattered. The only real friend he had was his sister; she took care of him, but then Colin's father died suddenly, and Colin inherited the estate.

I have all the papers here in the vestry. I will get them for you in a moment. But first of all please let me explain to you that Colin had given Mary's mother the right to live in one of the farms for the remainder of her life and that any profits made by selling agricultural products go directly to her. She was to pay all rates and taxes. Mary's mother was to receive the rent from four of the cottages; the church was to collect the rent from the other two. However, the cottages were to remain the property of the estate, and Mary's son Jack Whitehead was to look after its affairs. But, I believe Jack Whitehead thinks that he owns both the farm and the cottages. As a Minister of the church, I should be not saying this, but if Slippery Jack could manipulate things, he would, and he did. Now, I will go and get those papers for you. I would very much appreciate you returning them to me after you have finished with them.'

Mervyn and I went back to the car and sat for a few moments taking in the beautiful English countryside: the soft green of the trees; the freshness in the grass; the gentleness of nature in a country village where everything seems to be typical, as it has done for hundreds of years.

'Mervyn, let's go and look at those cottages.'

We drove the short distance to where the cottages were. From the outside, they all appeared to be in good condition. I fell in love with all of them. To me, they represented England with their thatched roofs and their whitewashed walls. They seemed to have been like that for hundreds of years. This is undoubtedly England.

'Let's go to the manor house and let them know what we have found.'

I knocked on the imposing front door. Colin's sister opened the door, and a beautiful big smile came over her face. She dragged me into the house and called out to Mervyn. 'Come in! Come in!' She ushered us into the large country kitchen then went out the back door and called to her husband. We all sat around the big table, and I explained everything that we had found.

'So, the six farms and four cottages all belong to you. It was Colin's agreement with you, or I should say, his mother-in-law. It all ended when she died, so now somebody owes you a fair bit of rent. However, I feel that you would be better to let this go; it would become too complicated. I do need to put this Jack Whitehead back in his place. I will be seeing him tomorrow.'

Colin's sister asked, 'Would you like to stay with us today? Maybe you could have a look at the estate and perhaps relax. You do look tired. We are very grateful to you for what you have done. We are farmers at heart but we only barely scrape by with our overhead expenses. We cannot do everything ourselves, so we have to employ people. Four of the cottages are accommodation for some of our workers. Six farms is a lot of work for my husband and me. Why don't you stay the night and I can cook a roast dinner?' I saw Mervyn's eyes light up.

'Yes, I think we would both very much enjoy that, and we could head back up to London in the morning.' Mervyn asked to make the necessary phone call.

'That will be okay, Mervyn. You report in and let them know we will be in London first thing in the morning and that we will be going to HM Land Registry titles solicitor's office. Then I would like to be on board my command a day early to get things straight in my mind before the crew comes on board.'

Mervyn stood to attention. 'Yes, sir.'

'Now, we can both relax, can't we?'

'Yes, Bill.'

I enjoyed walking around the estate, meeting the people. I kept thinking of Colin; this is where he grew up. This is where his world was shattered, through the greed and selfishness of others. The beauty of this estate with the small river which flows through it, its wildlife and history, this is something Australia would never have. This is England., But Australia too has a beauty that England can never have. One only needed to look at the paintings by Arthur Streeton and many others who have captured the beauty of Australia.

Mervyn and I set off for London in the morning, but he didn't go back the same way as we had come. We pulled into the car park of a hotel called *The White Bear*.

'There is somebody who wants to see you, Bill, before you go back to London. If you would like to go to the hotel, she will be there waiting for you.'

There she was, sitting in the corner by the window, Mrs Evans.

'Good morning, Jackie.'

'Good morning, William, please sit down. I have ordered coffee for you – in a mug.'

'Thank you,' I replied. In my mind, I was ready for this lady, and I was getting in first.

'And what can I do for you, Jackie?'

'Straight to the point William.'

'That is how we play the game,' I replied

'Yes, William, yes. You are having a meeting today with the solicitor Jack Whitehead.'

'That is correct.'

'I would like you to do something for me. This packet of cigarettes?' Her eyes flitted around the room, quick and sharp. The waiter was coming with coffee. 'Put them down on the table.' The waiter nodded and disappeared. 'On this packet here, you will notice there is a small black switch. If you turn the switch towards the edge of the pack, then a recorder is switched on to record sound when you are in Mr Whitehead's office. Place this where no-one can see it, but where the cleaner can find it.'

I stared at her and looked down at the cigarette packet. 'I will do this for you, but I want Mervyn Nelis!'

Her eyes widened, her face became hard and cold, then she grinned at me. 'You drive a hard bargain. Lesley said you play a good game of chess. He's yours, but the game isn't over yet, William.'

I took a sip of my coffee. 'Could you answer something for me?'

'Depends on what it is William.'

'Why do you have Australians guarding your secret base?

'Yes, I heard what you did, William. Winston thought it was most amusing; didn't stop laughing for quite some time. The Australians we chose for the base come from what you call The Outback; they know nothing of the politics in Europe. They have no allegiance to any foreign powers. They are extremely hard-working and trustworthy. They work as a team without anybody training them. To my mind, they are the best men for the job!'

'Is that why you chose *Daisy May*?'

'Yes, but might I say *Daisy May*, her captain, and her crew were remarkable. We will never find another *Daisy May*.' A small grin came all over her face. 'But we still do have the *Daisy May*.' I thought to myself, have you moved another chess piece on the board? 'Good morning, William.' She stood up and walked out of the hotel, got into a small car and disappeared. She invited me here, and I end up paying the bill!

I picked up the cigarette packet and put it into my pocket. I noticed a waiter behind the bar looking at me. I got up, walked over to the bar and paid my bill and asked for a box of matches. My world had changed. Now I thought that I couldn't trust anybody or anything, even the waiter behind the bar. I remembered Jacko's words, '*Go back to the desert Bill, to survive.*'

Mervyn had trouble parking the car, so I walked the half block to HM Land Registry. It was now raining heavily and quite cold. I put on my raincoat and lifted the big collar around my head. I presented my papers at the Registry, and a clerk brought me the information I needed. I chuckled to myself when I saw how old the title was. All the information was there: who had given the land to whom; who had created the estate; who had built the manor house; who was now the owner; whose name the estate was in; an inventory of all the buildings, the roads, the ground upon which the church is built, and the age of the church. However, the full title was in Colin's name and still owned by Colin's family. I thanked the clerk and went outside. Mervyn was waiting for me in the foyer. The rain had become more substantial, and I appreciated my heavy white raincoat.

We then went to the office of Jack Whitehead, the solicitor.

'Sir, may I take the other bag? You won't need that one, will you?' It annoyed me that Mervyn had called me 'sir', but I did realise that in public it had to be that way.

'No, I won't Mervyn.'

I handed him the bag and spoke to a young lady sitting at a desk in the foyer.

'I have an appointment with Mr Jack Whitehead. My name is William Farquhar.'

'Thank you, sir. If you would like to take the lift to the fifth floor, it is Room 525.'

I found Room 525 with the name Mr Jack Whitehead, Solicitor and a few other fancy titles. I didn't knock but walked straight in and went up to the young lady sitting at a desk.

'My name is William Farquhar; I have an appointment.'

She picked up the phone. 'There is a William Farquhar here to see you.' She looked up at me and said, 'Sir if you'd like to go through that door, Mr Whitehead will be with you shortly.'

The room was quite large with big windows and a large desk, in front of which were leather chairs. There was also an old impressive-looking couch, where I sat down. I remembered the cigarette packet in my inside pocket. I reached in to the pocket, found the switch and turned it on. Before I removed it from my pocket to place it on the arm of the couch, I heard Colin's voice in my head, *'They could be watching you, boy; they could be watching you!'* so I deliberately put the box of matches on top of the packet. I took the documents that I had received from the church out of my satchel and browsed through them. A man came through a small door to one side of me. I could smell him before I saw him, first the cigar, then the body odour, indeed not very pleasing to my nostrils. I didn't look up, just continued browsing through the documents.

A voice boomed out. 'Come on, man, who are you?'

I moved my eyes to one side and glanced up at him, an overweight man, suit too tight, incredibly arrogant.

'I am Captain William Farquhar. I am here to sort out the will of one of my crew, Boson Colin Garland, who died on my vessel and was laid to rest at sea.'

'Yes, yes. Colin shirked all his responsibilities and left us in a mess. I need his death certificate.'

I stood up and handed him the document. 'This is his death certificate, witnessed and signed by members of my crew and me.' I gave him the paper.

'These witnesses are just nobodies.'

In frustration and annoyance, I informed him, 'One is Captain Ted Coe of Her Majesty's Navy. The other signature is Commander Lesley Johnson. I'm sorry, but I don't have the Prime Minister's signature!'

'You don't have to be sarcastic!' He stood studying me for a moment. 'Yes, you are the captain of a sailing vessel that is well past its time.'

I grinned to myself but kept a stone face; this was going to be amusing. I was hot in this room; it was sticky and clammy. I slipped my raincoat off of my shoulders; half folded it, laid it on top of the cigarette packet and matches and turned to face Mr Whitehead. 'Now, perhaps we could get down to business.'

He stood there stunned, his eyes widened. They flicked up and down my uniform.

'Yes, yes, yes, sir. If I could get you to sign these documents, we will sort everything out.' He picked up the three papers from his desk and walked around to the other side of the desk, placed the first one down in front of me and handed me a pen. 'It's just a lot of legal mumbo-jumbo; all you need to do is sign this paper to release your responsibility.'

I sat down on the couch, slightly moving my overcoat. I knew that the cigarette packet had slid down onto the floor. I read the document. Whitehead's eyes had not left me. It was as if I had asked him to climb to the top of the mast in a stiff breeze. I read and re-read the document. I looked up and looked straight into his eyes.

'You do not own the farm, the four cottages or the land on which the church is. It belongs to the estate.'

'No, no, they belonged to my mother, so now they belong to me.'

I handed him the document from the church. I saw the anger rise in him, and sweat started to pour from his forehead. He threw the paper back at me.

'This is a note from the Land Registry. The title is still in the family name. You do not own any part of the estate, not to mention the money you have collected for years from the farm and the cottages, which is not your right to keep.'

He sat back down in the seat with a slump.

'So if we were to talk about his son, Terry.'

He stood up straight again and slammed his hand on the desk. 'Terry is dead; he died somewhere overseas.'

'No, Terry is alive. He is an officer in the British Navy. He was a member of my crew.'

He walked around his desk and out of his office, slamming the door. He was gone a good fifteen minutes or so. I stood up and slid the cigarette packet and the matches under the couch with my foot. I walked over to the window and put my hands behind my back and peered out of the window. The rain was falling even harder. I thought to myself, *Daisy May would have enjoyed this on her rigging in the Indian Ocean. We would have filled our water barrels.*

The door opened again, and Whitehead walked back in. 'Well, we had better wind up our business.'

'Yes.' I walked back to my leather satchel and took out another document. 'If you would like to sign this on behalf of the family. It releases you from any responsibility to the family, and they will no longer require your services.' I picked up the pen and signed the document. 'If you would please sign here, and here, and here on the document.'

He stood staring at me for a moment; I handed him the pen. 'By the way, I believe Terry will not require any of the money plus interest, that you owe him. He thinks that you have done the honourable thing.'

He snatched the pen from me and signed both documents. I gave him one and put the other back in my leather satchel. 'I don't think we have any more business, do we Jack Whitehead, or, as Colin would say, "Slippery Jack!"' I turned and walked out of his office.

Mervyn sat on a seat in the foyer, watching an overweight man who was smoking a cigar and breathing very heavily; the man was talking to the woman behind the reception desk. Mervyn didn't know that it was Slippery Jack.

The man looked up and studied Mervyn. He noticed the bag Mervyn had on his lap and was puzzled. He'd seen one of these bags before and suddenly he remembered where. He spoke with the woman again, and she answered him very quickly. Mervyn noticed them talking and look-ing at him. The man disappeared into the lift, but he returned a few minutes later, went back to the reception desk, spoke with the woman and disappeared again into the lift.

The woman smiled at Mervyn, but he didn't like the smile. She got up from her desk and walked through another door. Mervyn thought to himself, *I don't like this; something is wrong. Maybe I'm just overreacting!* A few minutes passed, and three men walked in through the main door, just ordinary looking men. They may have been workers. They started arguing among themselves; pushing and shoving each other. One of the men landed in Mervyn's lap. Mervyn's unique skills went into action, and he protected himself but the bag slipped off of his shoulders, and before he could think, one of the men had snatched it.

As Mervyn ran to grab the bag, he was king-hit on the back of his head and knocked flat to the ground. He rolled over onto his back and bounced back up onto his feet, and chased the man. A car was waiting for the men with a passenger side window open. The man threw the bag into the car, and it sped off. The three very professional men disappeared. Mervyn slumped back and sat on the footpath. He felt very dizzy, but the rain seemed to revive him. He shook his head and the pain at the back of his neck made him groan.

A voice from behind annoyed him, 'Now, now young man, had a bit too much to drink, have we?'

I walked back into the foyer. Where was Mervyn? The young woman was coming back to her desk. 'Have you seen the man who came in with me?'

'No, sir, I haven't.'

I had my raincoat over my arm and went through the front door. There was Mervyn with a policeman.

'Is there something wrong, constable?' I asked.

The constable spun around, noticing my uniform. 'Sir, this man was lying on the footpath.'

'I'll take care of him, constable.'

'Right, you are sir.' He gave a small salute and walked off.

'What happened Mervyn?'

'I was set up. I should have seen it coming. Three men got your naval bags and your papers.'

'Let's go back to the hotel, Mervyn.'

'Yes, sir.'

Mrs Evans sat at her desk; her glasses on the end of her nose as she was looking through some documents. Her phone rang. She picked up the receiver, and the person at the other end gave her the appropriate password. She paused for a moment.

The voice on the phone said, 'Yes, ma'am, we followed them to the solicitor's office. He had his leather satchel and the naval bag. We saw three men go into the foyer, one came out and threw the naval bag into a waiting car. We followed that car to Number Six. We are at Number Six now.'

Mrs Evans thought for a minute. 'Give them fifteen minutes, then use all the men who are on surveillance at Number Six and retrieve the bag and wait there for me.'

Mervyn was in no condition to drive, so I hailed a taxi. Once we got back to the hotel, Mervyn said he had to make a phone call.

'Just before you do Mervyn.' I pulled out the drawer and took the documents out. He slumped back onto the bed.

'Thank God for that. You might have saved my arse yet!'

While Mervyn made his phone call, I rolled up some towels and put them under his legs and either side of his head.

'I'll be right Boss. Just let me rest for a moment.'

An hour and a half later, there was a knock at the door. I opened the door, and there was Jackie Evans along with a man carrying a doctor's bag. She was also carrying my bag.

Not one to mince words, she asked, 'Where is he?'

'In the other room,' I replied.

The doctor went straight in to see Mervyn. He examined his eyes and asked him, 'How many fingers am I holding up?'

'Three, sir.'

'Sit up. Now stand up, bend down, and touch your toes.' He examined the back of Mervyn's neck. 'Turn your head from side to side.' The Doctor picked up his bag and walked back to where we were. 'He'll be all right; be a bit sore for a while.' Mrs Evans asked him if Mervyn would be able to perform his duties. 'Yes, he is a very fit individual.' The doctor left the room, closing the door behind him.

'Well, William Farquhar, I don't know what to say. You placed the recorder in exactly the right place, and we received the information we wanted. But the documents in this bag were precious to others, and they thought that they had them. We have been keeping surveillance on this individual for quite some time. He is one of those who plays the game from both sides of the fence, for his selfish interest and the interest of those higher up the chain. That information we received from his conversation on the phone and the two individuals who desperately wanted to read those documents of yours.' She paused and shook her head. 'And they only got your dirty washing!' She handed me the bag. 'You are a remarkable man, Mr Nelis, all that just for dirty washing. Well done, Mr Nelis.' She gave him that smile with her eyes and left. I walked into his room and put my hand on his shoulder.

'I don't think Jack Whitehead will be giving us any more trouble. Steak, eggs and chips, Mervyn?'

'Yes, please, Boss.'

The next day we headed down to the naval dockyards. At the entrance we were advised where we needed to go. I had to fill in many documents, ask questions and talk to other officers, but my mind kept slipping. *Where are you, Jacko? Are you safe? Are you with Daisy May, looking after her? I don't belong here. I don't belong here, and there isn't any wind in my sails.*

CHAPTER 19

I stood on the wharf looking at a big iron monster towering above me. I slowly walked from one end of it to the other. The bow loomed up in front of me, and the anchor was three times bigger than me. I walked back to the gangplank. Mervyn was standing there, waiting. I stood staring at him for a moment; my mind just couldn't put things together. I couldn't relate to this monster of a ship.

Mervyn stood to attention. 'Sir, do you wish to stay on board tonight or stay in a hotel?' I had trouble sorting it out in my mind. I wanted to get away, but I was in command; I was entirely in control of this vessel. Cunningham said I was God. Is it bigger than I am? No, I am in command.

'I will be staying on board from now on Mr Nelis.'

I turned and walked up the gangplank, and when I got to the top, the crew were there to greet me, saluting, blowing their whistles.

'Thank you, gentlemen. Captain Coe, to the bridge.'

I turned and looked down at the wharf, and there was Mervyn at the bottom of the gangplank. I nodded to him; he nodded back. I was leaving the world behind, and he had been a part of that world. I entered the bridge.

'Captain Coe, would you ask everyone to exit the bridge except yourself and the technical officer?'

'Yes, sir.'

'Now, let's go through everything on the bridge. Do we have the right man for the wheel?'

Ted's voice came back in a whisper. 'No, we don't!' I turned around and looked at him. 'Yes. We have three naval officers, all highly trained sir,' he said.

'Keep them sharp, Captain Coe and teach them to see over the horizon.'

'Yes sir, yes,' he replied.

'Now, take me on tour right through the vessel.'

At that moment I was not interested in her guns. I wanted to see the engine room, to see what powered her. Captain Coe presented me to the Chief Engineer.

'Mr Lees, we have met before.'

'Yes, sir.'

'So we should get an understanding right from the start, Mr Lees.' His head went slightly backwards. 'This is your world. I do not understand everything here, I will not interfere with your world, but I will depend on you to give me everything you have got when I need it.'

'Yes, sir.'

'Walk to one side with me, Mr Lees.' He followed me. I turned my back to the others. 'How much speed can you give me Mr Lees?'

'The record is thirty-six knots in her sea trials. She did reach forty knots, but this hadn't been noted in her records'.

'If we were doing thirty-six knots, and I asked for *hard astern* what would happen?'

'She handled it in her sea trial. She performed everything flawlessly; she only snapped one bolt in her turbines.'

'How many bolts in the turbine?'

'One hundred and ninety four,' he replied.

'Thank you, Mr Lees. That burn heal up all right?'

'Yes, sir, thank you.'

'Thank you, Mr Lees.' I winked at him. 'If you see me here lost, tactfully show me the right way.'

He chuckled. 'Yes, sir, but I have the same problem!'

'To the bridge, gentlemen.'

I walked up to the comfortable chair. *This is my chair*, I thought to myself, *I'll have to get one of these for Daisy May. I'll have to get two because I know Jacko will want one.*

The time passed quickly; we found ourselves in several battles. The gun crew performed admirably. I enjoyed working with Jarrett. He was quick and switched on; he gave me exactly what I wanted without fuss. I kept his father up to date with his progress, but I didn't tell Jarrett.

We returned to our home port for minor repairs, fuel, food and shelter. When I received my new crew list manifest, two of the crew members' names struck me: Trevor Evans, Australian and Mervyn Nelis, Australian. I walked back out onto the bridge from my cabin.

'Mr Coe!' I handed him the piece of paper. 'Could you have these two gentlemen report to me?' His eyes flickered up and met mine.

'Yes, sir, indeed. Sir, a Commodore Johnson is coming on board with three others. Top secret sir.' *Would Ted be privileged to this information?* 'Do not pipe her on board. Bring her and the others straight to my quarters.'

'Excuse me, sir. Nelis and Evans are here sir.'

I saw Trevor's face and his eyes.

'Stand to attention.' Mr Coe's voice boomed out.

I put my hand out and placed it on Trevor's shoulder. 'This is war, Evans. What was before is now in the past. Perform your tasks well and make your mother proud. Mr Nelis, it doesn't exactly say you're one of my crew?'

'Permission to speak sir. I have a letter for you, sir.'

I read the letter he handed me. 'You have further orders for me, Mr Nelis?'

'Yes, sir.' He put his hand into his inner pocket and brought out another large envelope. I read the document and gave it to Mr Coe.

'Get ready to leave port as soon as Commodore Johnson is on board. Mr Coe, the message that she was coming on board was in code?'

'Yes, sir.'

A truck turned up on the wharf, and the stores were being loaded on board. Darkness had just started to fall, another truck came, and four people boarded. The gangplank was raised, and we were on our way.

I read through my orders, wrote down the coordinates, longitude, latitude and degrees. I handed this information to Jarrett.

'Plot this course and discuss it with nobody. Do it in four stages. Give the first part to the helmsman.'

'Yes, sir.'

I went back to my cabin. Commodore Johnson and the others were waiting for me.

'Good evening, Commodore Johnson.'

'Good evening, Captain.'

I studied Reno, then looked straight at Dominic. I considered him then turned to Philip.

'Why do you bring these vagabonds on my ship?' I shook hands with each one of them. 'Welcome aboard, gentlemen. Please, be seated.'

I picked up my telephone. 'Ask Mr Coe to come to my quarters please and bring some coffee. Thank you.' I got my documents out again and browsed through them. There was a knock on the door, and Mr Coe walked in. He looked at the three men, shook their hands with pride and turned to me and shook his head.

'You let them on board? What is the Navy coming to?'

He turned to Lesley. 'Good to see you on board, ma'am.'

'It's nice to see you, Captain Coe. I've missed you.' She became serious again. 'We will be meeting a submarine. You have the coordinates, sir.'

'Yes, it's already been taken care of sir. The equipment that was brought on board will be transferred to that submarine, and we will board that submarine. Are there any questions, gentlemen?'

'Not that we can think of at the moment.'

'Mervyn is going with you, also?'

'Yes, he is.'

Commodore Johnson grinned at me. 'A lady friend of mine said she would keep her promise.' She glanced at Mervyn. 'Could I invite you to a game of chess, sir?'

'Ma'am, I would certainly enjoy that, but I think we will play the game on the bridge.'

'You will arrange things, Mr Coe, please.'

'I certainly will. Ma'am, I certainly will, but before I go, could you please tell me where Michael is?'

He had tears in his eyes, and I had tears in mine. Commodore Johnson smiled at both of us.

'At the moment, he will be working with about two hundred women, making all sorts of things out of canvas – hammocks, tents, canopies for trucks, whatever is needed for the war.'

Mr Coe just shook his head. 'Two hundred women, all to himself.'

'Yes, I'm sorry to tell you, all to himself!'

Ted turned to me. 'Permission to return to the bridge, sir. It isn't good to see a grown man cry.'

'You have my permission, Mr Coe.'

We saw three flashes from the submarine and we signalled back. One of our tenders* was already fully loaded and was lowered into the water. There were five of them on board. The tender disappeared into the darkness, returning half an hour later. We were on our way.

The chessboard was still on the bridge; I felt pain deep inside me. *Look after her Jacko; take good care of her.*

Five days later, in the early hours of the morning, there were three flashes and the tender was sent off into the darkness again. It returned, and once again we were heading back to our port at thirty knots, but in a zigzag pattern, an unpredictable route.

'All on board?'

'Yes, sir, but not in very good condition. They are in the surgery, sir.'

Commodore Johnson had a bullet graze on her forehead, and one of the others had a bullet wound on his arm. The others had cuts and abrasions.

'Very good. Thank you.'

---

* A ship's tender, usually referred to as a tender, is a boat, or a larger ship used to service or support other boats or ships, generally by transporting people or supplies to and from shore or another ship. Smaller boats may also have tenders, usually called dinghy

Mr Coe commented as he walked past me, 'She's all right skipper.'

I picked up my coffee cup; it had my name printed on the front. I said to one of the sailors on the bridge, 'Fill this with fresh coffee, add two sugars and give it to Commodore Johnson with my compliments. She is in the surgery.'

The next day I went into the surgery. 'Good morning, doctor; how are your patients?'

He gestured to me with his head to move to a more private place.

'They are all quite traumatised. The bullet wound on Commodore Johnson's head isn't dangerous. I have stitched it. I don't think it will leave much of a scar. The bullet wound on Reno's arm, however, will need further attention when we can get him ashore. The others will need rest. Mervyn is the problem. He wants to exercise; he wants to make sure he keeps fit. I have sedated Commodore Johnson as she needs rest. Wherever they've been, it must have been hell.'

I walked back up the passageway, and on my way to the bridge, a young seaman was standing to attention. I acknowledged his salute, then realised who he was.

'Whisky, young man?'

His head bent slightly forward, and I grinned. 'Young man, what I don't see, I don't know!' I put my hand on his shoulder, 'You're one of Jack's crew lad; just stick with me.'

I knew after seeing Lesley, my emotions were in turmoil, and he was a part of *Daisy May*; he was mine. I continued to the bridge.

When we docked two ambulances were waiting for us, and the fuel barge came alongside. Stores were loaded on board.

'Excuse me, sir, there is a gentleman who wishes to speak with you. He is at the gangplank. He said his name is Terry.'

'He has my permission to come on board. Bring him straight to my day quarters.'

There was a knock at the door.

'Come!' In walked Terry, in a naval officer's uniform. I gritted my teeth, trying to keep my emotions in check. I shook his hand. 'It is good to see you, Terry.

'Good to see you, sir'.

'So, what are they doing with you, Terry?'

'I am training junior ranks. When they've finished all their courses, they are sent to me, and I do my bit. I would love to bring them on board the *Daisy May* and finish their training there.'

I fetched the leather satchel and put Colin's papers on the desk.

'I was speaking with your aunt about you; she would like to meet you and get to know you. She doesn't have any children of her own, and they need help. These papers here are now yours. Colin was your father, I know how much you meant to him and the pain he must have gone through leaving you behind. I will leave all of this with you, Terry. I think you have a future in life where you are needed, and Colin's dreams will have been fulfilled.'

There was a knock at the door and in walked Ted. He glanced at Terry, and they shook hands, arms around their shoulders, just shaking each other.

Ted said, 'Terry, you look good in that uniform! It is funny what happens when you clean a man up, but I prefer you as you were.'

Ted turned to me. 'Sir, there are two politicians and their families wanting to come on board to meet you in about half an hour.'

'The fuel barge has finished fuelling, and all our stores are on board. Terry, here are your papers. Good luck.'

'And good luck to you, sir'. And with that, Terry left the ship.

'Get the gangplank stowed Mr Coe and cast off. I have my orders; they don't mention politicians, their families or damn photographers.'

As we were pulling away from the wharf, three cars pulled up. I stood on the bridge wing, watching them, then turned and went back into the bridge.

'Mr Coe, ask the number one gunnery officer to come to the briefing room'.

'Gentlemen, we will shortly be joining a convoy heading to a secret location. We will then be releasing a barrage of gunfire before the invasion force lands ashore. Fire three rounds from the heavy guns and make sure everything is as it should be. Check your small arms fire also, as we expect to be attacked by aircraft. Gentlemen, you have your orders. We will be in the thick of the war. Mr Coe, assemble the whole crew on deck.'

I looked down on the gathered crew. 'Good morning, men. I don't often see all of you on deck. You have performed your duties well on this ship. I am extremely proud of you all, and I am very proud to be your Captain. However, now we are going into battle to protect our shore troops. Do not question orders, work as a team and protect each other. I have asked the padre to say a few words.'

I put my hands together on my lap and bent my head, but I didn't hear the padre's words. I only felt fear. *I've got to protect them all, but I fear I am going to lose some of them. However, I am not going to lose this ship.*

I had the bosun dismiss the crew. I went back to the bridge.

We were soon in a convoy sailing parallel to the coast, fighting off aircraft with all of our small arms fire clacks, clacking away. I was watching

Jarrett for the exact coordinates and checking my watch. The second hand was ticking away; fifteen seconds to go. All our guns were facing ashore, and everyone was on edge. I had a lump in my throat, and I knew my arm was shaking.

'Stand by! Fire!'

Everything on the ship erupted. The ship's hull shook and vibrated. You could smell the cordite and hear the boom, boom, boom of the guns. I could hear bullets from the overhead aircraft striking the metal on her upper decks. I saw a bombshell hit her deck, bounce and explode. It must have come in at a right angle, as the bounce made it explode ten metres high in the air. Pieces of the deck, a lifeboat but more importantly and to my great sorrow, some of the men, were shattered to pieces. The attack didn't stop; it just went on and on relentlessly. Then, I looked at my watch.

'Ceasefire.'

Everything went silent, but for the occasional small arms fire. I saw an aircraft on fire spiral and then cartwheel into the water and disappear. We went back out to sea, licking our wounds.

'How many men did we lose Mr Coe?'

'Twenty six, sir.'

'How many injured?'

'Forty, sir.'

I stood with the rest of the crew, watching silently as one by one; the bodies slid into the sea. Twenty six young men in their prime, lives wasted, and for what? For the greed of others, a thirst for power and control down through the ages. They have fought for freedom.

I went back into my day cabin and sat. Inside I was screaming. I cried for the twenty six young men. I thumped my fist on my desk. There was a knock at the door, and I thought, *Go away, go away and leave me alone*, but I could not ignore it.

'Come.' Ted and Jarrett walked in.

'We thought you might need some friends at the moment, Bill.'

I stared at them for a moment.

'Yes, I do. Sit down with me for a moment. You know, in a raging storm with *Daisy May*, or when we thought pirates were coming too close, I thought we had troubles. I figured we had problems with the eye of the needle, but they were not like this. Thank you both for your support, but now I have a battleship to command. Gentlemen, let's go back to our duties.'

We went back up onto the bridge. The structural engineer Mr Eagles was waiting for me.

'One aerial bomb struck the port side midships, but there is no structural damage. There is a dent in the deck, but it is watertight. The handrail is missing and one lifeboat. There are small dents and scratches from flying bullets. It is remarkable sir that was the only damage.

'Thank you, Mr Eagles. A report from the gunnery officer?'

'Yes, sir. Three small machine guns were out of action but have now been replaced. Permission to test them, sir.'

'You have my permission but first advise the crew; some of them are quite traumatised by what we have been through. Mr Coe, have you the fuel report?'

He handed me the report. 'We need refuelling. Request a fuel tanker to meet us at sea.'

'Thank you, Mr Coe.'

Early the next morning the fuel barge arrived on our port side.

'We've had a request for permission for three to board sir.'

'They have my permission.' It is fascinating to watch refuelling at sea and to watch personnel being transferred from one ship to another.

'Commodore Johnson and two others on board, sir.'

'Bring them to my day cabin, and would you bring us some coffee, please?'

Seated in my cabin, I rose when my visitors arrived. 'Commodore Johnson, we have the pleasure again. Dominic, Mervyn, please be seated.'

Lesley handed me her documents. I read them through. 'Another short holiday?'

'You could say that, sir.'

'If you would inform the quartermaster, he will give you all of these items.'

Once again, they were picked up by a submarine.

Seven days later, we picked them up again. Lesley was suffering from severe hypothermia. Dominic had some burns and was also suffering hypothermia. Apart from a few scratches and bruises, Mervyn was all right.

We headed back to port and refuelled, rearmed, resupplied and went back to sea. We were back in convoy protecting merchant ships. Then we were sent on to a beach-head, and we were again firing our guns onto the beach. After that my orders were to find a particular merchant ship supplying German submarines.

It was one of those calm mornings; the air was thick and humid.

'Sir, battleship to the stern.'

I grabbed my binoculars, went out onto the wing, and raised them to the horizon, but they kept fogging up. The air was too thick and humid. Ted handed me his telescope, Walter Wright's telescope. I slapped him on the shoulder, clear and sharp.

'There is the destroyer Mr Coe. She is bigger than us, and her guns are bigger.'

I handed him the telescope, he looked through it then gave it back to me. I focused on the destroyer again. Then I saw the flashes from her forward guns. Has she got our range?

I shouted out, 'Engine room! Full speed ahead!'

I felt the hull underneath me surge. Then I heard the hissing of the shell right on our stern. A column of water shot straight up into the air. A few moments later there was an eruption of water, boiling and bubbling to our port side then another column of water rose up in the air, water boiling and hissing once again.

I shouted out, 'Helmsman, ten degrees to port. We've got a big problem, Mr Coe.'

I shouted out again. 'Navigation Officer! Our bearings?' A voice inside me was screaming out, *Jacko I need you. I am in trouble. She is bigger than us, and she can outgun us. Jacko, help!!*

'Bearings, sir.' He gave me the bearings and the coordinates. I knew where I was; this was one place on the chart I would never forget. Then I felt it; I felt what Jacko felt when on *Daisy May* and the fog was rolling in. I slapped Ted on the shoulder and pointed to our starboard.

'Helmsman, starboard twenty degrees.'

Another two columns of water shot up into the air right on our stern. I ran back into the chart room, and Jarrett put his finger right on the spot.

I said to Jarrett. 'Good man!'

I went back into the bridge and picked up the intercom to the engine room. 'Give us all the speed you can provide us with; all the speed! Helmsman another fifteen degrees to starboard that is thirty-five degrees to starboard.'

The other officers on the bridge just stared at me, but Ted knew what I was doing.

Ted's voice was low and calm, 'Now gentlemen back to your duties; work as a team.'

Another two shells burst to our port.

Ted shouted out, 'She's doing it, sir!'

Ted could not contain himself. He gave me a slight thump with his shoulder. 'She has altered course to starboard to cut us off.'

We started to slide into the fog bank and another two columns of water shot up in front of our bow and water sprayed all over our decks. 'She is still trying to cut us off.'

My inner voice was saying, *Keep her coming Jacko, keep her coming. Don't let her alter course.* We were now in the fog bank.

'Helmsman, port forty degrees.'

'Port forty degrees sir.'

'Half speed, Mr Coe!' I shouted.

I went out onto the wing to listen. Then we heard it. The large destroyer was sliding up onto the sandbank travelling at least thirty-five knots or more. With all that tonnage behind her, we could hear her big props screaming out of the water. She was now fast on the sandbank and wouldn't be giving us any more trouble.

Mr Coe said. 'What a beautiful job, Skipper!'

'Yes. Now let's get out of here. She still has her big guns. Mr Coe, I have never liked these coordinates, but one could change one's mind. Give us thirty knots.'

We slid out of the fog bank, out into open water. I was thinking, *Thank you, Jacko, thank you. I may be at sea, but you will always be playing the game in the desert: to survive. The fog bank and the sandbank that is nature, that is you. I wonder what the captain of that destroyer is doing—banging his head against the wall?*

'Sir received a message; a U-boat is working at these coordinates.'

'Mr Collins set a course for those coordinates and work out the time we would arrive.'

'Early hours of the morning. 6 am sir.'

'Mr Collins, if the submarine was travelling at eight knots, where would they be now?'

He drew a circle with the compass, and we both studied the ring.

'Mr Collins, if they were low on fuel and torpedoes, where do you think they would be if a supply ship were to meet them?'

'I would think, sir; it would be about here.' He put his finger on a point in the circle.

'I believe the supply ship would come from here.' He tapped his finger on a seaport on the chart. 'This is the only port which could supply them with torpedoes, so this would be the course.'

'Mr Collins set a course for those coordinates and give it to Mr Coe. Then, Mr Collins, I will take two hours rest.'

While I was resting in my cabin, the phone rang.

'Mr Lees here, sir. We have a small vibration in the port side prop shaft. I don't know where it is coming from, but I need to shut that shaft down.'

I thought for a few moments. 'Go ahead, Mr Lees, but stand by the starboard prop shaft. We are in submarine territory, and they could give us a fish at any time.'

'Yes, sir.'

I went back onto the bridge. 'I don't like this situation, Mr Collins. Get the quartermaster to work and get everybody on deck with binoculars. Why does everything happen at the wrong time and in the wrong place?' I gritted my teeth in frustration.

'Sir torpedo! Starboard forward!'

My mind clicked into action.

'Full speed ahead or she will get us on the stern! Hard astern! Starboard prop shaft! Helmsman! Hard to starboard!'

The helmsman faltered; his mind was confused. I slammed my shoulder into his, knocking him sideways and spun the wheel hard to starboard. We watched a torpedo slide past us, not thirty feet from our bow.

I kept the wheel to starboard and shouted out, 'Ten revolutions on the starboard prop shaft.'

I grabbed the helmsman by his shoulders and wrenched him to his feet.

'That will not happen again, will it? Sharpen yourself up, lad! Be prepared for the unpredictable! This is a warship, not a toy!'

I stopped myself. I was taking my frustrations out on this young lad; a lad too young to be at war, too young for the responsibility we had thrust upon him.

'Yes, young man. It frightened the hell out of me too,' I said softly.

My mind kicked back into action again. Why didn't they send a pattern of torpedoes? I would have expected that. I noticed a seaman with his binoculars down, talking to the man next to him.

'Get those binoculars to your eyes! Sharpen up! Either that submarine is out of torpedoes, or he has one left. Sharpen up on the starboard side! Expect another torpedo!'

They must have known I would have trouble if the torpedo came in at that angle. I drew some lines on a piece of paper. If the last torpedo came in at that perspective, then the next torpedo would also come in at that angle. I picked up the intercom.

'Mr Lees, when I command it, I want full power to the stern on both props. Standby for my orders.'

'Sir, torpedo starboard side midships.'

'Hard, astern! Full power!'

We felt the deck vibrate underneath us; we felt our props cavitating in the water. Ted turned up alongside me, and we both watched the torpedo. We had full power astern, but was it fast enough? Seconds turned into minutes; everything was in slow motion.

'Hard to starboard.'

The helmsman reacted instantly. Then with relief, we watched the torpedo pass in front of our bow.

'All, stop! Gunnery officer stand by all guns!'

'Mr Collins, you have the coordinates for the origin of those torpedoes. Where is the sub?'

Mr Collins did some quick calculations then handed me the piece of paper.

'No, Mr Collins! Give it to the gunnery officer! Pound those coordinates with everything we've got!'

All our guns erupted. Approximately a mile away, plumes of water rose high in the air. Then one of the lookouts shouted, 'Submarine surfacing sir!'

Has she still got a torpedo? I don't know.

'Keep firing!'

I snatched a pair of binoculars and focused them on the plumes of water. I could see the submarine. Then I saw one of our shells hit the bow of the submarine. There was one powerful explosion. For a blast that big, she must have had another torpedo on board. The submarine disappeared below the surface.

I shouted out in frustration, 'Cease firing and let's get out of here! Mr Coe, let's go and find that supply ship.' I picked up the intercom. 'Mr Lees, give me half an hour, and we will reduce speed.'

'Sir, I believe we have a problem with the prop on the port side. That last explosion was a little bit too close for comfort, and now the prop is out of balance. In an emergency, we could probably use it...'

'Thank you, Mr Lees. Mr Coe, keep the crew on deck. We might find ourselves with another fish. Then could you please go and get some rest, Mr Coe? You have been on duty for more than twenty hours.'

I went back to my day cabin and closed the door. I looked at my hands; they were shaking. That was so bloody close; so bloody close. I nearly lost her. Snap to it, Bill; get it together.

I walked back into the chart room. I noticed young Jarrett, he had lost his puppy fat. He was now a good looking young man, six foot two with blue eyes and his hair cropped short. His mother would not recognise him! His body had become hard; he most certainly was now a man. I felt a deep sense of pride as if he was my son also.

'Mr Collins if we looked at the coordinates of that submarine and the directions of the first and second torpedoes, where would the submarine have been?'

'I've already worked that out, sir. Here it is on the chart.'

I thought to myself, *You had better sharpen up Bill. He is one step in front of you, but that's my lad!*

'So Mr Collins, the nearest place for a supply ship to leave port with supplies for a submarine would be where?'

'Here, sir. This is the only fuel depot in range, so if we plotted a course for the supply ship so that they could meet here.'

Mr Collins placed his finger on the chart to where the supply ship would be and pointed to the map again. 'That submarine was there, so if it were to rendezvous with the supply ship, this would be its course. If the submarine was travelling at eight knots, this is the approximate time they would meet.'

Jarrett hunched his shoulders and tightened his lips. 'Quite possibly, sir.'

'Well it's a plan. Mr Coe, we are looking for a cargo vessel somewhere here. I believe we interrupted your sleep, I do apologise, a few more hours would do you the world of good Mr Coe.'

'I accept your apology, sir.' He winked at me and disappeared.

I sat down in my comfortable chair on the bridge with my hands around my coffee mug; it was warm and comforting. I looked down at my mug and thought, *Where are you, Lesley? What danger have they put you in now? Are you somewhere safe? Not knowing is the greatest pain to me.* My mind snapped back to the present.

'Sir, cargo vessel here.'

'Ask Mr Coe to report to the bridge. Mr Collins give me her course.'

I picked up the intercom. 'Mr Lees, can I have the full power of both props?'

'Yes, sir. And we will monitor the port prop shaft.'

'Thank you, Mr Lees.' I glanced at Jarrett.

'East six degrees, sir.'

The helmsman shouted out, 'East six degrees, sir.'

'Helmsman, you have certainly sharpened up! But I am the Captain; I give the orders.'

'Yes, sir.'

'East, fifteen degrees.'

'East fifteen degrees, sir.'

'I want to be broadside to that cargo vessel so that we can bear all our guns on her if she has a submarine loading alongside her. Mr Coe, we need to keep a sharp lookout for enemy ships that might be guarding her. Engine room! Full power both props.'

She came alive underneath us. We could feel the power surging through her. The salt spray was being thrown over the top of her as her bow plunged into the swell. I wondered if she had ever travelled at this speed with all guns to port. Well, we were going to find out.

'Mr Coe, bring all our guns to bear on that vessel. Fire when ready.'

Everything erupted again. Black and blue smoke swelled into the sky; the smell of cordite was everywhere. The ship was vibrating from the forces being thrust upon her.

'Keep firing!'

There was another round of gunfire. I could see plumes of water go high into the air around the cargo vessel. I could see two submarines tied up alongside her, and there were two more on the other side. Then there was a powerful explosion, and a ball of flames shot up six or seven hundred feet into the air. Then there were more explosions.

'Keep firing! I want those submarines!'

My mind went to *The Castle* and all the other old tramp steamers that had been sunk, the hospital ships and so many others. We did a full sweep around her, coming back facing north.

'Half speed and keep your guns trained on her.'

The guns were now trained on our starboard side. There was one submarine still afloat. I could see men on the deck guns.

'Commence, firing!'

Another volley of gunfire from our guns and the submarine was shattered to pieces. 'Cease fire! Pick up any survivors Mr Coe.'

Twelve survivors were found.

'Engine room, sir.'

'Yes, Mr Lees?'

'Sir, Mr Eagles and I believe that we have lost a blade on our prop port side.'

'Shut it down, Mr Lees. I know we carry a spare prop on board, but we can't change it while we are at sea.'

We were now very vulnerable. How could I send a message to command without the enemy knowing?

'Send this message to command: *Hands are on the top of my head.* Mr Collins give us the course for England, and could you give this to the helmsman please.'

'Yes, sir.'

Ted just grinned at me. I put my hands on the helmsman's shoulders, 'Once when I was your age and the helmsman, I had not been watching the compass. It was ten degrees out. I sat for two days at the top of the mast!'

Ted burst out laughing. 'I remember it well. Walter Wright had some strict rules and watching the compass was one of them.'

I shook the helmsman's shoulder. 'But that was many years ago.'

I went down to the infirmary. 'How are those survivors doc?'

'Two of them are quite seriously injured. The others will survive all right. However, they all have signs of malnutrition. They seem to be happy that they are on board this vessel. I think that for them, the nightmare has finished. If you look at their eyes, their hair and the colour of their skin, they have been starved of clean, fresh air for too long.'

He hesitated and then said, 'They are too young. They never wanted this. I don't believe that they will ever get over it, physically or mentally. Do we have anyone on board who speaks German? One of them does speak good English.'

'I will talk to them. Which one speaks English?'

The doctor gestured to a weary and dirty young man seated on a lower bunk.

I faced him. 'Bring your men to attention.'

He spoke some words in German, and they all stood to attention.

'Good afternoon, gentlemen.'

The young German man addressed his crew, 'Guten tag männer.'

He repeated my words in German as I spoke.

'I am the Captain of this vessel. As seamen we respect you. You have done your part; you have carried out your duty. If you need anything, please inform my officers, and we will do everything in our power to make you comfortable.'

I paused for a moment, dropped my severe look and grinned. 'But gentlemen, unfortunately, we do not have any women on board.' I raised my shoulders slightly, lifting my hands in the air. I saw them relax, and a grin came over their faces. 'Gentlemen!' I saluted them and left. Yes, they were too young even to know why they were fighting in a war.

The doctor looked at me with a grave expression. 'I don't understand Skipper. We fight to protect England, and you fight to protect Australia. But they don't fight for Germany. They fight for one man. They would destroy their country for one man. I can't get my head around that.'

I put my hand on his shoulder and glanced back at the young men.

'Yes, Doc, it is total madness. Will we ever understand? I don't think so.'

I returned to the bridge, and I was handed a piece of paper.

'Message from Command, sir.'

I read the paper and gave it to Ted. I put my finger on the small tag of my shirt. Australia.

'Mr Collins, plot a course to take her to her home port.' My eyes met Ted's, and we said a thousand words without saying a single one.

We tied up at the wharf and I went ashore. I handed in my report and was given an envelope. I opened it and read it, but it didn't make any sense.

Walk through the office and go through the blue door.

I hesitated, but I opened the door and went through.

A man dressed rather neatly was standing there waiting for me. He showed me a document. 'MI5 sir. If you would care to come with me, quietly and discreetly.'

We got into a car and went through the security gates with no fuss. An hour later, we pulled into the driveway of a big country estate. I was ushered through the front door into a large office.

'I will get you some coffee, sir and something to eat.'

'Thank you. I'd appreciate that.'

I stood looking out of the window at the beautiful lawns and trees and a rose garden. One moment at sea in turmoil; the next, I am looking out of this window at a beautiful garden. Nothing makes any sense. It never seems to make sense. The door opened, and a young woman carrying a tray of coffee and sandwiches came in. I stood staring at her.

'Excuse me, sir, is something wrong?'

I chuckled to myself. 'No, no. I look at you, and everything is alright. I've been at war where nothing makes any sense, but you put everything back into perspective.'

She looked at me puzzled and left the room. I drank the coffee and ate the sandwiches. There was a knock at the door, a man and woman entered. I had met this gentleman before, in London, at the Admiralty and the woman I recognised immediately.

The man spoke first.

'Good afternoon, Captain Farquhar.'

'Good afternoon, sir. Good afternoon Mrs Evans.'

'You destroyed one fuelling vessel and four submarines in one blow! Remarkable Commander Farquhar.'

'We couldn't get that German destroyer.'

'But you did put it up on the sandbank. I wonder if the Germans love you as much as we do.'

I was still wondering just who this man was and what his position was. Was he in MI5 – or MI6? Would I ever know?

'Mrs Evans, you have not brought me here to talk small talk. Not under these circumstances.'

She took a deep breath and turned to her colleague.

'Could you bring me a cup of tea please and some of those lovely sandwiches?'

'Yes, ma'am.'

'Well, William, you have knowledge that we do not. We'd like you to decipher his message for us.'

She took out some papers from her briefcase and put them on the table. She took a notepad and pencil and laid them on the table also. Her tea and sandwiches were brought in by the young woman. Jackie Evans reached out and took her hand.

'This is my daughter Deanna.'

Turning to her daughter, she said, 'I would like you to meet this most remarkable man. His name is William Farquhar. He brought Trevor from Australia.'

Deanna gave me the most beautiful smile. 'I would never have met my cousin if it wasn't for you. He is marvellous and wonderful. I wish my father could have met him before he died.'

'I found him on the train when he was coming to Melbourne looking for work, and now he is an excellent seaman. What makes me even more proud is that he is one of my crew.'

'Yes, I am very proud of him as well.'

'Thank you, my dear. Now, we have some work to do.' Deanna disappeared through the door. 'Excellent sandwiches. My husband could eat a whole plate of these to himself.'

I thought to myself, *She is stalling. Nobody knows where I am; this is all small-talk!*

'Let's stop the small talk. What do you want?'

She stared at me. I could see the strained look on her face. Her eyes looked like they'd seen the devil and now come face to face with him. She handed me some documents. I read them and looked up at her. I was shivering and shaking; tears welled up in my eyes. I could not speak. I wanted to shake her by the neck.

I heard my voice yelling. I was out of control. 'What have you done? What have you done? Where is he? Where is he?'

I heard myself saying, 'If, if, if you, you…' Then I got myself back under control. Mrs Evans lowered her head and looked at her lap.

She sobbed in a whisper, 'I hate this war. I hate it!'

She looked up at me. 'So you understand what those documents mean?'

'Understand is not the word. We're going back to the channel people. Their minds work differently from ours. Jacko is with Lesley, and he is with one other.'

'Yes, it is Mervyn. Let me explain it to you. This is a crucial part of the war. If the Germans can create a nuclear bomb, we are finished, obliterated. Every time we send our people in, somehow the Germans know our codes. We've used Native American, Welsh, Scottish, Samoan yet they seem to know all these languages. Lesley informed us there is a language which very few people know. And you are one who knows, and you've just proved it. I need your help; humanity needs your help. Could you decipher this for us, please?'

I looked once again at the document.

'Jacko comes from an ancient people, and they say his language has disappeared. But it has not. In Aboriginal, he's of the Channel people. In his tongue, he is *koa gunna Yanda*, and they are his people. His father was an elder, and now Jacko has taken his father's place. His mind works differently from ours. His mind is more alert, sharper, more complex. He does not want to possess or control; he wants to be at one with all *Gidgee*. That is what it is called. It is *good wood, good water, good place, good people*. It is the language of the Indigenous people of Queensland, the land where rivers flow in good times and are life itself. Now, let me read this and think. I know that now I must put my logical mind to one side and use my senses. He will talk to me.'

I sat down in front of the window and stared at the trees. I had a pencil and paper with me. Then I heard, no, I sensed Jacko; his energy was with me. I drew a snake on the piece of paper: a burning sun, a cross on the bend, trees and mountains. Then I knew what he was saying; what was written on the paper.

'I need a cup of coffee, please.'

The young woman brought in coffee and tea; I saw the coffee was in a mug.

'William, where did you go? You were staring into nowhere. I waved my hands in front of your eyes, but nothing happened!'

'I went back to the desert; back to the Diamantina River; to the channel country. Now, let me explain to you on this piece of paper. This snake is a river. It has two bends in it, then tapers out. What you are looking for is here on the cross. There is water here also. It could be a big pond or a big lake, but it gives life. To what, I do not know, and I don't believe he knows either, but where the cross is, is the burning sun. There are mountains to one side, which feed the river. At the head of the snake, there is the sea. Does that make any sense to you?'

'It certainly does now; we know where the plant is.'

Mrs Evans looked at me more seriously. 'We want them all out, so this is my plan. We cannot send in a steel vessel. It has to be a particular type of wooden vessel – a vessel like *Daisy May*. I want you to go in there and get them out.'

'I will need my crew – Ted, Jarrett, Michael and Terry. And any other members of the crew I can get, but I also want...' Her eyes widened. 'You took Jacko, and you did not have the right. He belongs to Mum and me. Now I want Trevor. I want him because he's one of the best seamen we've got. Now you can feel *my* pain.'

I could see the hardness in her face; a face that knows duty comes first. She stared at me for a few moments.

'This is top secret. Most of your crew are already on board the *Daisy May*; Jack Fox is looking after that. You have not left your battleship, and nobody knows *Daisy May* is leaving port at one in the morning. I will have your location and the rest of the information you require. If you would take your uniform off, you will be given back your ordinary clothes. We had a lot of trouble making them smell right. Thank you for your assistance.'

She looked at me; I could see her start to buckle. 'William, Lesley is mine, and she's also yours. Jacko is yours. Trevor is mine. Mervyn belongs to both of us. Bring them home safely.'

She turned, picked up her briefcase, snatched the drawing and disappeared through the door.

I sat down in front of the window again and looked at the trees, the lawns and the garden. I retreated into my mind; it was as though Jacko was there alongside me. He always used to say, *'Your senses are a knowing; you just know if something is right, is wrong, is hot or cold, is good or bad.'* It was protection against the elements.

Mrs Evans knocked on the door of another office and went in. The man sitting at the desk put his cigar down in the ashtray.

'Well, Jackie, what does he say?'

'Yes, Winnie, he understands. And he is infuriated with me for using Jacko, the Aborigine. But he translated everything into this drawing. Captain Farquhar sat down in front of the window and appeared to go into a hypnotic state. The information he gave me leaves me a little lost. He said that the snake, to an Aborigine, is the River of Life. In the desert, you have a burning sun. I believe this might be the nuclear power plant. The circles mean water surrounded by tall trees. We know that there is a big church here with a cross on the top of it. Could this be the power plant? The snow-covered mountains? That could be where they get their heavy water.'

He stared at her for a few moments and then said, 'Get him anything he needs; use all our resources.'

He picked up his cigar and drew deeply on it, letting the blue smoke drift from his lungs. Mrs Evans left and went back into the office where Bill was waiting.

'Captain Farquhar, we need to get our people out now. We have very little time. We have to destroy that plant as quickly as possible. Is there anything you need?'

'Yes. A doctor – a whole medical team.'

'Why do you need them?'

'I just know that I need them.'

'Where do I get them?'

'Get the doctor off my ship. He is on leave while the ship is being repaired.'

'You've got him. Let's get you to Dartmouth.'

Ten days later everyone was boarding *Daisy May*. Les was there waiting for them, tears flowing down his cheeks. He shook their hands and embraced them with great love and affection. When he came face to face with me, his arms went down to his sides, and he stood there sobbing.

'They took him, Bill; they took him. I could not stop them; I don't know where they've taken him.'

I put my arms around him. 'He's looking after Lesley. He is with Lesley, and now we're going to get them and bring them home.'

I slapped Les on the back and ushered him towards the galley. 'Now I need coffee and sticky buns. Where we're going, it's going to be cold, and we will need hot food. Ted, Michael, Terry, get her ready for sea. We will not be using the motor. We will be leaving port silently so extinguish all lights, and I want no smoke from your chimney Les. Doctor, give them a hand where you can.'

Foxy walked up to me and handed me an envelope.

'Here's the cargo manifest. You've got sixty ton, enough to keep *Daisy May* down in a good sea. She is still going to toss and roll a bit though. The bundles with the blue on them are for the fishermen; they are general stores, no weapons. Good luck. There will not be any fair winds where you're going, but I wish I were going with you.'

He slapped me on the shoulder and disappeared over the side. Then his head popped back up again, and he shouted out to Ted and Michael, 'You two take care of each other, or you'll answer to me!' And with that, he disappeared again.

'We have an outgoing tide. Ted, slip her moorings; let's get her to sea,' I said.

I went into the wheelhouse and put my hands on the wheel. I thought, *I'm home, Daisy May. I'm home, and we're going to get Jacko and*

Lesley and a man you haven't met as yet. But I will introduce him to you, Daisy May.

My eyes drifted to the opposite end of the bench, there he was, sitting, watching me. He slowly stood up and stretched, then he walked alongside the bench and stood in front of me. I reached out my hand; he gently rested his head against it. He seemed to get some comfort from my hand.

'You miss him, don't you Cat? I miss him too.'

Soon we were out in the Channel. I swung her to port and Ted, and Michael came into the wheelhouse. I thought to myself, *Where are you, Jacko? Are you safe, Jacko?*

CHAPTER 20

Michael put his hand on Ted's shoulder. 'How are you going, Ted?'

Ted nudged me with his shoulder, and a big grin came over his face.

'You ask me how I'm going? All I've been saying is *Yes sir*, *No sir*, *Straight away sir*, *I will take care of that sir*, *Three bags full sir*. And you? You've had two hundred young women all to yourself! Making all those fancy bits and pieces.'

'Sorry, Ted, but somebody had to do it. Do you realise what a demand it's been on this body of mine? I might never recover!'

I didn't realise how much I had missed them. Oh, God, how I had missed them. 'When you have finished whining, could you please ask Jarrett to come in?'

Ted turned to Michael, 'He said *please*! He hasn't used that word in two years. We are back home again.'

Then Jarrett walked in.

'Jarrett, you have some new naval charts for us?'

'Yes, sir.'

'Jarrett, while we are on *Daisy May*, do not salute me or call me sir.'

'Yes, Skipper.'

'We are going to Norway to rescue Lesley and another man by the name of Mervyn Nelis. Then I am going to kick Jacko's backside from the bow to the stern and back again!'

I felt the frustration rise in me again. I said to myself, *Get yourself under control!*

'Well, Jarrett, did you get to meet Princess Elizabeth?'

'Yes, yes I did, when I was in London. The Queen and Princess Elizabeth were walking through the streets talking to people. The Queen was saying how Buckingham Palace had received a few direct hits. Their warmth and compassion, the way they were with the people, giving them encouragement for the future, I will never forget it.

When we were coming back to Devon we stopped at a small country village with thatched roof cottages and a good English Pub; nobody told me to duck as you go through the door, those low beams! God, do they hurt! It must have taken half an hour before the pain in my forehead went, so we had a few ales.' He looked at me and grinned. 'So we had a few soft drinks. The barman said that Princess Elizabeth would be in the village talking to the people and the girls from the Land Army. They need the girls to keep working the land to feed the people of London. I was standing in the crowd waiting, when people started cheering and waving, and there she was talking to the village people. When she got to me, she had such a warm, friendly voice. She asked me "What is your name?"

I replied "Jarrett Collins ma'am". "Where are you from Jarrett?" I answered "Australia, ma'am". She studied me for a few moments. "You didn't come, by chance, to England in a sailing vessel?" She took me totally by surprise, how could she know that? She smiled at me with a gentle smile and a knowing look in her eyes. "Yes, ma'am, I did". She then put her hand out and touched my arm and said "One day I will come to Australia, and if I have a son I would like him to finish his education in Australia. Australia has something special you cannot find anywhere else in the world; perhaps we might meet again". She nodded at me and moved on.

'Bill, she touched me! How could she know I came to England in a sailing vessel?'

'Her Royal Highness has one or two relations in the Admiralty.' I winked at him. 'You are a good looking man; I don't think that would have gone unnoticed.' I slapped him on the shoulder.

Jarrett, Latitude 60° Longitude 5°. That is approximately the destination. I want to sail up the coast of England into the North Sea, sail inside Dogger Bank then on to Wick in Scotland. If we have any trouble, we can call into Aberdeen, but only if we have problems. Later on to Kirkwall and the Orkney Islands before heading directly to Latitude 60° Norway.

There is a trench under the sea off Norway, the Norwegian Trench, and they tell me that this is where the submarines hide. There is an inlet or a cove near there where some old sailing vessels are moored. They are out of commission, they're useless, but we can hide there until we pick up our passengers. Then we need to get back to the Orkney Islands, and from there they will be flown back home.

Jarrett, plot us a course and try and find us a place to hide where the submarines can't follow us. The reason why the *Daisy May* has been picked for this job is that she isn't made of steel and therefore cannot be picked up on their new radar. Any questions?'

They all shook their heads. 'Let's get every bit of canvas on her. Michael, could you ask the doctor and his team to see me, please?'

The doctor walked in with two others.

'How are you, doctor?'

'Confused!' He turned slightly and put his hand on the shoulder of the man behind him. 'I believe you know Timothy.'

'Hello, Timothy.' I shook hands with him. 'Good to have you on board.'

I glanced at the next man, and I was a little bit shocked and surprised. 'He' was a 'she'.

'May I introduce you? Doctor Vera Henderson.'

I know my eyes slightly narrowed because there was something wrong. I felt a warning; a knowing. I put my hand out and shook her hand; it was firm and strong.

'It's nice to meet you, William Farquhar. I have read quite a bit about you. We have a mutual friend, and we both found your dirty washing to be most amusing!'

So, she is MI6.

'You are a medical doctor?' I asked her.

'Yes, I am. Please call me Mrs Henderson.'

'If you would take the single cabin and introduce yourself to our cook and advise him of what you require. He will look after you well. Now, do you all know why you're here?'

Jarrett's voice broke in, 'Excuse me, Captain, the course?'

'Good man Jarrett. Could you take the wheel for a few moments?'

'Yes, Skipper.'

Mrs Henderson had walked up to Cat and was rubbing her finger up and down his neck. Cat didn't move. He just let her do it. Very unusual!

'Well, we've got to pick up some individuals who are imperative to the British Government. The information they have is precious. Their health and well-being are most important, that is why you're here. I would suggest you find a suitable spot on *Daisy May* that you could use to take care of them. In the cargo hold, you will find a bundle with red markings. It has everything you require, but do not open it until I tell you. We wouldn't want anybody to get the wrong impression if they should come on board. Do you have anything to add to that Mrs Henderson?'

'No, Captain. I think you have covered everything.'

'Please make yourselves comfortable. *Daisy May* might bounce around a little, but a full cargo holds her down in a swell. You've probably noticed her Plimsoll line sits well out of the water. If you have any questions I can help you with, please talk to me in private. Thank you.'

I noticed Michael and young Trevor talking together. Michael was a big brother again, but now Trevor had grown up. He had lost his innocence, and not in the right way, only time will tell. A voice behind me made me smile. It was Terry.

'Morning, Skipper.'

'Morning, Terry. You got to meet your aunt and uncle?'

'Yes, Skipper, I did. I got to see them, and it was something I can't explain, having a family. After the war, they want me to manage the farms. They said the farms would be mine because they don't have any children of their own. They were my father's. I have a lot to thank you for. You have given me back something I thought I had lost.'

'No, I think that shifty old man, Colin, had it all worked out a long time ago.' I thought to myself, *Sneaky old sod.*

'I have a cargo of sixty tonnes. Part of that load we will deliver to our destination; it is food and medical supplies. It will have blue markings on it. When we get to our destination I want it off this vessel as soon as possible. So just before we arrive make sure it's sorted and ready to go. What we are going to offload to, or where, I'm not sure, so be prepared. Thanks, Terry.'

I was standing alone at the stern wondering why MI6 would be on board. Did I worry them by asking for a medical team? I knew that I needed one. If Lesley were severely injured or died before we could get her back to England, they would not have the information they required. I believe that is why MI6 is on board. I felt a cold shiver go through me, and I repeated those words, *if she is severely injured or died.*

I felt the deck move under my feet. Something was wrong. *Daisy May* doesn't like this. She only has sixty tonnes of cargo, not the two hundred tonnes she was built for. I walked back to my cabin and got out her papers. They showed all of her riggings and had a diagram of her hull which was designed to carry passengers and cargo and to give passengers the smoothest ride possible. *Daisy May* was a barque sailing clipper, high sided, built for comfort and to keep the water off her decks. The hull was designed for the trough between the waves. We were in the North Sea now, and the troughs between the waves were different heights. *Daisy May* sat high in the water. If we were fully loaded, we would have been drawing eleven feet from the Plimsoll line. Now we were drawing only eight feet. I read the architects' and engineers' reports and their suggestions.

I called in Michael and Ted. '*Daisy May* feels wrong to me. I've been going through her paperwork, and I think we've got too much sail on her. So much we could drive her mast down through the deck. I want to keep her bow down in the water, but I need all the steerage we can get. Leave the flying jib on but take the outer jib and inner jibs off. Take off her fore-royal and topgallant and take off the main mast, the main royal, the main gallant and her mainsail. We will leave the mizzen mast. Let's see how she reacts now.'

Les brought me in a cup of coffee, in my mug, and some sticky buns.

'Les, I've missed your cooking, and I've missed your sticky buns. I've missed you too!'

I looked down at my mug of coffee; his eyes followed mine.

'Will they be all right Skipper?'

'Hopefully, Les. Jacko told me *Yes* but things are *not good*. What he means by *not good* I don't know. I do know that in his mind, he is distraught. I tried to tell him that we're coming.'

'Lesley came on board late one night to talk to Jacko for a few moments. Before I could do anything, they had gone.'

'It's not your fault, Les. It is far bigger than you or me. Why don't you take Mrs Henderson some of your coffee and sticky buns?'

'She has already asked me for some Skipper.'

'Word gets around Les, doesn't it?'

We were well into the North Sea. The wind cut straight through our clothes, and everybody was trying to keep warm. We got the occasional wave over the bow, that didn't help matters very much. It certainly wasn't a perfect location for a sailing vessel. We were passing the entrance to Edinburgh and St Andrews, and we would shortly be passing Aberdeen. A Spitfire flew in low towards us. He moved his wings up and down three times; I stood with my three fingers in the air. He banked sharply and headed back towards land.

Suddenly I felt that there was somebody behind me. I turned around sharply, and there was Mrs Henderson. 'You remember your signals well, Captain.'

I replied, 'There are some things you never forget Mrs Henderson. They remind you of people you are very fond of.'

'Yes. I believe you carry a coffee mug.'

She turned and walked away. I thought, *She knows how to put you in your place, doesn't she?* I went back into the wheelhouse, and she was there.

'Jarrett, I'll take my watch now.'

'Right Skipper.' He went to the galley.

'I hear you play a good game of chess, William.'

'If I am William, you are Vera.'

'What's good for the goose, is good for the gander William. The chessboard?'

Darkness had fallen, and we altered course for Latitude 60°.

Ted's voice behind me said, 'Here we come, Jacko. Skipper, that wind is cold.'

'Ted, would you and Michael start up the motor? Just warm it up a little.'

'I might sit on top of it Skipper to get warm.'

'Why didn't I think of that, Ted?' And why didn't I keep my mouth shut? He was gone like a flash.

Daylight was breaking over the water, and there was a drizzle of rain. The First Officer on the German submarine ordered the periscope to be raised. He peered through the looking glass and, to his total surprise, he saw an old sailing vessel. He turned to the man behind him.

'Klaus, get the Captain.'

'Yes, sir.'

'Captain, we have a surprise,' and he gestured to the periscope.

The Captain peered through the periscope, studying the old sailing vessel. He turned and studied his First Officer.

'We only have two torpedoes, and the deck gun is out of action. Do I waste a torpedo on an old sailing vessel that doesn't have any cargo? It is harmless. I need those two torpedoes for a bigger prize.'

'How do you know it doesn't have any cargo, sir?'

'I did my apprenticeship on a sailing vessel. See how high the Plimsoll line is out of the water? Look at how high she sits out of the water. Does she fly a flag? No, she doesn't belong to anybody. We will not waste our time. Down, periscope.'

However, he did not record this encounter in his logbook.

'Skipper, Trevor says he can see land.'

I picked up my telescope and trained it on the horizon. I grinned to myself; I felt very proud of the lad.

'Trevor is doing all right Jarrett. Check your figures with mine. According to both of us, we are where we should be. Let's get a little bit closer to shore so that we can see the land better.'

As we got closer we could see the high snow-capped mountains. We were looking for an entrance to the fjord, and according to my instructions, a square patch of green land should appear and below that a small outcrop of rock. On the highest rock, there would be a small pile of rocks. Michael's voice cut in.

'There is the entrance to the fjord! And there is your pile of rocks.'

'Ted, Michael, stow all her sails. Make her look abandoned and start that motor up.'

On the battleship, I could see everything, but now I was having trouble seeing over *Daisy May*'s bow. It was very frustrating.

'All right. Do you see the rock? The big one coming down to the water? We have two hundred feet under our keel. There should be a small rowing boat there to meet us.'

'Small rowing boat. Port side. Two people in the boat, sir.'

My crew have sharpened up.

'Bring them on board.'

Two were on board the rowing boat, but only one came through the hatch. The other rowed back to where he had come from.

'Ted, could you ask the doctor to set up his surgery?'

The man who had come through the hatch was small, and as he walked into the wheelhouse, he spoke. But the voice didn't fit. It was a young girl! Just then, Mrs Henderson's voice boomed out.

'Hello, Margaret, how are you?'

'Very well, thank you, ma'am.'

'We thought we had lost you.'

'No, ma'am, still here,' she replied.

'You are looking very tired Margaret.'

'Yes, ma'am.'

'I think that we had better get you out of here. You have done a remarkable job for us. You are one of the very few left.'

'I would very much appreciate that ma'am.'

The girl was nearly in tears. What has she seen? What has she done? How far have they pushed her?

She turned to me very, very serious.

'Captain, follow the shoreline as closely as you can. You have deep water. You will find a small opening just around that bend. It is very narrow but tie up alongside the third vessel. Any aircraft flying above will have trouble noticing you there because of the high mountains either side of us. We don't know whether the Germans know how many vessels are there.'

'Trevor, take this young lady to Les and feed her.'

'Yes, sir.'

'Trevor on this vessel, I am just the Skipper.'

I put my thumb in the air. The young lady looked at me and then looked at Trevor with a puzzled expression. Trevor winked at her.

'He's really God!'

Ted burst out laughing. Then we saw the small opening to the fjord. I thought to myself, *We haven't got any paint to scratch off*, but she squeezed through just nicely. I noticed Terry and a few others putting packages on the deck. Good, they're on the ball. We tied up alongside the third vessel. She had been a magnificent ship in her day, but now she'd been left here to rot. Two men appeared on deck, one with a bandage around his head. The other had his hand bandaged. They took the mooring lines.

'Doc, I think you better go on board first.'

The doctor and his assistant went over the side, directly onto the deck. They went down below, and I could not wait any more, I was over the side and on to the deck of the other vessel. Then I heard that familiar voice.

'Took your time, didn't you?'

I spun around. There he was, the cocky little sod. I took a pace towards him, and I was shaking my finger in his face, but the words wouldn't come out of my mouth. Tears poured down my cheeks.

'I will deal with you later.'

He did one of those little dances back and forth on those feet, swinging his hips, his arms swinging loosely by his sides and said in a mocking voice, 'I will deal with you later.'

I went below and found three crude beds. Lesley was in one. Mervyn and another woman were on the other beds. Others were lying on the deck.

'How is she Doc?'

'I don't know for sure yet, but I think she's in a bad way. Can we get her on board *Daisy May*?'

'Yes, of course.'

Mervyn's arm was in a makeshift sling.

The doctor said, 'He's got two bullet wounds in the shoulder.'

Michael had a boson's chair and a litter* over the side waiting. Within twenty minutes everybody was on board *Daisy May* and supplies were being offloaded. We had six extra on board, and the young girl was the seventh.

Cat was sitting on the baulk works by the hatch. He was making a funny sound in his throat as though he was crying. Jacko stepped on

---

* A litter is a stretcher or basket designed to be used where there are obstacles to movement or other hazards: for example, in confined spaces, on slopes, in wooded terrain. Typically it is shaped to accommodate an adult in a face up position and it is used in search and rescue operations.

board, and he and Cat just stood staring at each other. We all watched them as Jacko walked over and picked up Cat in his arms. Then he walked over to Les with tears flowing. Jacko put his head into Les's chest.

'They shouldn't have done that to Gidgee; not Gidgee. Mervyn carried Gidgee for twenty miles with bullets in him. I knew *Daisy May* would come and get us. Bill told me he was coming.' Then Jacko shook himself, and a big smile came all over his face. 'I'm hungry, Les. I'm starving!' Les hugged him tightly.

'So is Cat Jacko. He hasn't eaten since you left.'

Les grabbed Jacko by the scruff of his neck and said, 'You need a bath and some clean clothes. Then I might give you a good thrashing. You've worried the life out of me!' Laughing, they went off into the galley.

I turned to the doctor. 'Well, Doc, we are in your hands. We've lost part of our cargo, so when we get out to sea, it is going to be rough. *Daisy May* is going to pitch and roll, and we have three hours until the turn of the tide.'

'Well, Skipper, we will start operating now. We need to get those bullets out of Mervyn. I think one has gone straight through, but I don't know yet. The other is underneath his armpit. Mrs Johnson has been severely beaten. I believe she has water in her lungs, and that is our biggest health concern. However, I also fear that mentally she's gone over the edge. She will need professional help to bring her back.' He then turned and left.

Jacko was in the wheelhouse, his mouth stuffed with sticky buns. Margaret walked in and stood, studying me. She looked at Jacko. 'You said he was your brother?'

With a mouth full, he replied, 'Yes, he is. Oh, I see what's puzzling you. They ran out of paint. They only had white, and that's why he wears a black stubble on his chin.'

I shook my head at him. 'To think I was worried about you. Alright, you two, what happened?'

Margaret spoke first. 'I was sent here with two others because we are Norwegian and they wanted people who understood the language. The other two have gone.' She went silent. Jacko put his hand on her shoulder.

'We thought we had found what we were looking for. It was heavily guarded, and we made contact with our people inside. Then things went horribly wrong. The Germans arrested many of our people, and I have not seen them since. Mrs Johnson turned up with Mervyn and,' she added with a smile, 'this freaky little man here.'

Jacko stuffed another sticky bun in his mouth. Margaret continued, 'But we did get all the information we required. The plant was here to produce nuclear power, and we found out the stage of its development. This information was relayed back in Jacko's language, but a particular individual in our group could not keep his mouth shut, and Lesley was arrested along with some of our other people. This lovable, kind, and beautiful soul and that extraordinary man, Mervyn Nelis, got Lesley out along with some of our people. We still don't believe they got them out. This freaky little man is nature itself. He seemed to know things we did not know. When the Germans thought we were there, we were here. When they thought we were here, we were there. I don't know how he did it. If he is your brother, what magic gifts do you have?'

'I hope they are very confused young lady, at least for another three days.'

'Jacko tells me you're a high ranking officer in the British Navy.'

'I'm just another Australian doing my part.'

'Well, I certainly want to meet some more Australians.'

With that, Jacko's voice boomed out some true blue, fair dinkum words. 'Some like me that eat grubs, we've got wombats, possums, snakes, all sorts of grubs and we got politicians, they're a funny mob.'

The doctor came to the door. 'We've taken care of Mervyn or should I say he's taken care of us? No morphine for him, get on with the job. And he signed the papers. Only time will tell for Mrs Johnson.'

'Put Mrs Johnson in my cabin. I think she would be more comfortable in there,' I said.

'She's all yours.'

'What about the other three?'

The doc replied, 'One lost all his fingernails on the one hand and had some bruises. One has got two broken ribs, and I believe a fractured arm and one of his eyes is badly damaged. The third one has internal injuries, but he is made of steel. I've just got to keep him quiet until we can get him back for more medical attention. Thank you, Skipper.'

'No, Doc, thank you!'

Mrs Henderson turned up at the wheelhouse door.

'Captain, could I suggest we make great haste now? If they decide to do something with that plant, we don't want to be here!'

'I will take your advice, Mrs Henderson. Ted, let's get on our way. Cast off. It will be dark in an hour, and it is overcast and drizzly, which is just what we need.'

Soon we were back at sea.

'Ted! Michael! Rig the same combination of sails as we had before entering the fjord. Jarrett, plot our course home.'

The swell was coming in from our stern starboard quarter, and *Daisy May* seemed to be quite happy.

'Jarrett, take the wheel.'

This was the first opportunity I had to see Lesley. I went to my cabin. Cat was curled up on her feet, keeping them warm. Les was holding one of her hands, Jacko was holding the other.

'How is she?'

Les replied, 'She seems to be asleep Skipper.'

Her eyes slightly opened and in a whisper asked, 'Where am I?'

'You are on board *Daisy May*; here in my cabin with Les, Jacko and Cat.'

She closed her eyes and seemed to drift into a more gentle sleep. I left my cabin and walked to the stern of *Daisy May*, standing where Colin used to stand. I spoke aloud, 'She will be all right, Colin; she'll be all right now. *Daisy May* will take care of her. We will get her home.' I bit my lip; there was blood in my mouth. I cursed myself, *Idiot! That will do no good*. I noticed the swell had changed; it was now coming from our starboard side, and *Daisy May* didn't like it.

'Ted! Michael! Take the foremast upper topsail off her and the mizzen topmast staysail; that should take the pressure off her.'

Once again, the second-in-command of the German submarine ordered the periscope up. He looked through the lens, going in a full arc, then stopped abruptly. There was something on the horizon – a strange shape, a square? He could not quite work out what he was seeing. He switched to a higher magnification, but a series of waves blocked his view. There it was again, looking sharper and brighter but then it disappeared. Then it came back again. The young officer was confused.

'Periscope down.'

He did not want to disturb the Captain unnecessarily, as he had been up for many hours; they'd all been at sea for many days and were weary. He flipped through the logbook but found no answers there. He walked to the Captain's quarters, hesitated, then decided to delay and get a cup of coffee. Once he had finished his coffee, he returned to the Captain's quarters and knocked on the door.

'Come.'

'Captain, there is something I cannot explain on the horizon. I do not know what it is.'

The Captain looked annoyed. He had orders to stay at sea, and he wanted to see his wife and children desperately.

'Well, well, what is it?'

'I think you should look, sir.' They both went to the periscope.

'Up, periscope.'

The Captain scanned the horizon, but couldn't see anything; he turned to his first officer. 'You have been at sea too long; you see things. Down, periscope.' He went back to his cabin.

Daybreak had come. It was a beautiful day with clear blue skies, but still cold and windy. *Daisy May*'s sails had been lashed to the yardarms making her invisible to prying eyes.

They heard the motor of a Spitfire as it flew towards *Daisy May*. It repeated the same three movements with its wings, Bill raised three fingers into the air – but with both hands, making sure the Spitfire understood. Then, it was gone. Mrs Henderson appeared.

'Well, Captain, they've got the message! All they need now is my report.'

'We should be there in the early hours of the morning; with no real cargo on board I cannot push her.'

Lesley was now sitting up in bed. Somehow the freshness of the sea air had cleared her lungs and she had stopped coughing. She said the pain had gone from her chest and she could sleep soundly. I don't know what the doctor had given her, but it was undoubtedly a good sedative.

Mervyn walked into the wheelhouse. 'I like your *Daisy May* sir and your crew.' I felt a small pain in my heart; he had carried Lesley for twenty miles with two bullets in him.

'Mervyn don't ever call me sir again. You call me by my name, which is Bill Farquhar. Whenever you are on the bridge of my ship, my name is Bill.'

'Well, I've still got to get you to sign some papers for me.'

'I will do that anytime, Mervyn.'

'I have studied human beings all my life, Bill. I've had to know how they are going to move, how they are going to react, their weaknesses, their strengths, whether they will move quickly or slowly. However, your Jacko is like no other man I have ever met, he moves so fast, he blends in with the surroundings, he is there, but he's not there. He had the Germans totally confused; he didn't carry a firearm or even a knife. I would like to spend more time with him in the future. How would you explain him, Bill?'

I laughed. 'I cannot explain him. Jacko is an Aborigine, he is of the Channel people from the Diamantina River, the only person who understood him was our mum. She loved him so dearly.'

'Well, Bill, he certainly gives me something to think about. I will sit with Lesley for a while; then I must rest again.'

Early the next morning we were in the Shetland Islands, we were tying up to the wharf, we towered above the small fishing boats, people came down to the dock to see us, I don't think they saw too many strangers. A military car came down to the dock; three men got out, all dressed in uniform.

'Jacko, there's a friend of yours down there.'

'I've got no friends here, skipper.'

'You remember Captain Williams, the man who didn't want to pay you? Well, there he is. Jackie said she'd take care of him, and she did.'

An officer started to walk up the gangplank. Captain Williams walked behind him, another man, carrying a clipboard, walked behind them. 'Permission to come on board, Sir.'

'You have my permission.' I put my hand out and shook his hand.

'Captain James, I am the Captain of the Port.'

'Captain James, Captain Williams does not have my permission to come on board *Daisy May*.' He looked at me, confused. 'Now Captain James, I believe you have an aircraft waiting.'

'Yes, Sir, we do. I have been told to give you every assistance I can, our priority is to get these injured people on a plane, and away, he turned to his transport clerk.

'Yes, Sir.'

He looked over the side to Captain Williams. 'Get five more thermoses, tea and coffee on board that plane, have her ready to take off instantly.'

'You've had trouble with that man Captain?' I asked.

'Yes, we have. Somebody has given him orders to fly back on that plane, and I'm very pleased to get rid of him.'

I watched Lesley being carried out on a stretcher; I just nodded to her, and her beautiful smile came back. 'Thank you, *Daisy May*, thank you.'

'Any time Commander Johnson, anytime,' and I saluted her. Then she was gone down the gangplank.

'Captain James, I don't think there's any more room on the plane is there?'

He replied. 'Come to think of it; there isn't.'

'I do have room on *Daisy May* if you still wish to carry out your orders.'

'I would be most grateful Captain if you could help me carry out my orders.'

'It will be my pleasure, Captain James.'

I could not understand how orders had come for Captain Williams to fly out on that plane, as this aircraft was top secret, no-one was supposed to know about it.

'Mrs Henderson, would you have a minute please, Captain Williams was flying back on your plane, I don't know whether I'm speaking out of turn, but it seems a bit odd to me.'

Her face became severe; you could see her mind racing ahead 'Who sent that order?' Her words were sharp.

'I don't know. Captain James just told me he was given the orders, we believe there is not enough room on that plane, so I suggested he came back with me.'

She stood staring at me for a few moments. 'Yes, William, there is something wrong, and it smells! However, it may answer some questions for us, you only have to find one link in the chain, and then you can trace it backwards or forwards. He doesn't know your rank does he?'

'No, I don't think so.'

'And he doesn't know who I am, so keep him on board. I will take care of him when you return.'

I saw Mervyn and Jacko saying their goodbyes. There was a deep friendship there, a special bond, Mrs Henderson nodded to me, the other men and the doctor were gone as quickly as they had arrived.

Captain James returned to the *Daisy May*. 'I've arranged transport for you and your men to go and have a hot shower and anything else they require. The locals want to entertain you with a bit of a dance and dinner tonight, would that be all right?'

'I don't see why not, our job is done. We do have supplies on board for you, and they tell me you have some items to go back, to give me cargo. I need one hundred tonnes.'

'Strictly confidentially Captain Farquhar, the locals make exquisite jumpers and jackets, they need to get them to London to be able to sell them.'

'Captain James, I need a cargo, but I also need an address of where to take them.'

'That will be arranged Captain, the local people here are the best you can find, and they need a little help.'

'It will be a pleasure.'

On the second day, we were ready to set sail. I thought Trevor had found himself a girlfriend, and his heart was a little bit broken, but who knows what the future might bring. Ted and Michael both had lovely headaches. The rest of the crew were quite content. Jacko had performed his usual dances and tricks and was the centre of attention. We had an excellent cargo so that I could get full sail on *Daisy May* again. Captain James had said his goodbyes, and Captain Williams turned up with his kitbag, totally confused.

'Ted, could you get Captain Williams some suitable clothes? Stow that uniform away, we're not supposed to be a military vessel.'

'Well Captain Farquhar, I hope you have a safe voyage home, for some reason we've got a significant amount of aircraft coming in to refuel, so I must go.'

Jacko raised his eyebrows and gave me that knowing look. We both knew it was to refuel the bombers that were going to destroy the nuclear plant. We shook hands, Captain James disappeared down the gangplank, and Michael was already taking the gangplank on board. Then I heard Michael's voice. 'Come on, Cat, or we will leave you behind.' There was the Cat, a little thinner, tufts of fur missing, but he was quite content. We had a pleasant, uneventful voyage back.

CHAPTER 21

We had to be a little careful sailing past the mouth of the Thames, what with sandbanks and the Thames barges carrying cargoes of hay, cargo so big a man would have to stand on the bow directing the helmsman. They were relying on the tide to take them up the Thames. But it was the Dover Strait that concerned me the most. It is very narrow, and there is no room to tack back and forth. Also, the tides and winds are very unpredictable. I don't think any seamen fully understand the forces here, so they play the game cautiously.

However, as a jockey would say, *'Give a horse its head!'* and so I let *Daisy May* go. We didn't have to tack once; she was a perfect lady. Just before Dartmouth, I ordered all her sails to be stripped off and stowed below to make her appear as though she had never left port. The little tug was waiting for us. Darkness had fallen, and *Daisy May* slipped silently up the Channel. Soon we were tied up between the two posts. Had *Daisy May* left, or had she been here all the time? We hope that's what people would wonder. Foxy's naval tender pulled alongside, and he came on board.

'You keep late hours, Bill.'

'Come into the wheelhouse, Foxy.'

Foxy punched Jacko on the arm. 'You caused a few problems. Jacko, it's good to see you back.'

'Foxy, I've got Captain Williams on board.'

'Yes, I know, just let him go ashore. We have cars waiting for all of you if you could leave as soon as possible.'

'Foxy, we've got a few packages to go to London. They are jumpers, jackets, scarves, and hats from the people at the top end of Scotland, to give them a bit of income. Can you handle that for us?'

'Jacko and I will take care of it.'

The doctor found himself back in the car that had picked him up. It delivered him back to the pub. He was dressed in the same clothes he had left in.

'Doctor, your wife and children are waiting for you. Remember, this did not happen. You never left that pub!' The man got back into the car and drove off. The doctor stood staring into the darkness.

I was back in the big country house; my uniform neatly laid out on the bed. As I put one of my fingers on the small badge that said 'Australia' I thought, *Perhaps one day Mum, perhaps one day your boys will come home.*

There was a knock at the door.

'Come in.'

A neatly dressed man stepped into the room.

'I wonder if you could come down to the conference room, sir.'

I followed him down the stairs into the familiar big conference room. Jackie Evans was sitting there, sipping a cup of tea.

'Good afternoon, William.'

'Good afternoon, Mrs Evans.'

'Well, the project worked out extremely well, and you gave us a little bonus. Some people in our society believe that they are far above others and for their own personal interests like to play on both sides of the fence. The gentleman you brought back with you is one of those. Or should I say he has become a pawn for his family?' She then added bitterly, 'We will take care of him. More importantly, we do not have any more problems in Norway. We have destroyed the site. We want to thank you and your crew.' She paused for a moment, 'But you do know it will always be top secret?'

'Mrs Evans, there is only one thing I would ask.'

'What is it, William?'

'Sell *Daisy May* to me when this war has ended.'

She stared at me for a few moments. '*Daisy May* is a British Naval Vessel. I will have to discuss this with my superiors. For now, we have to get you back to your command.'

I couldn't help it; I had to ask, 'Where is Lesley?'

A small smile came over her face. 'I understand William. She's resting in a quiet place. We have pushed her far enough. We will take her to a place where she will be happy and content. I promised you and Mervyn, and I will keep my promise.'

The car went through the dock gates; the guards did not stop it. I walked through a blue door. An officer greeted me.

'Good Evening, Captain. We have all the papers here ready for you to sign: her seaworthy certificates, engineers' reports, and your orders. Your crew are all on board, sir. Here are their signed papers.'

I just stood there, staring blankly into nowhere for a few moments, then I shook my head. 'Yes, yes, where is the pen?'

'Here, sir.'

After that everything seemed to be a blur. We were back out to sea and I was sitting on the bridge.

'Sir?'

I turned to face the man alongside me. 'Orders from Command.' Mr Collins handed me a piece of paper. I read it and plotted the course.

'Give this to the helmsman Mr Collins.' I put my hand on his shoulder. 'Thank you, Jarrett.'

'We have a new security officer on board, sir. Would you like to meet with him now?'

'Yes, I would.'

'I believe he is with Mr Coe.'

Mr Coe and the new security officer stepped onto the bridge. I thought to myself, *She kept her promise!*

'Sir, may I introduce you to Mr Mervyn Nelis, Chief Security Officer.'

'You seem very familiar to me, Mr Nelis. Have we met before?'

A big smile came over his face, and he stuttered a little as he said, 'I don't recollect sir. I don't think we have.'

'How is your arm, Mervyn?'

'You must be psychic sir! There's nothing wrong with my arm; just two little holes that are mending well.'

'I wish we had a woman on board so that you could keep fit carrying her around. Welcome on board, Mr Nelis.'

'Thank you, sir.'

Three weeks passed. We saw many aircraft in the sky, rescued the crew from an American bomber which crashed into the sea and then we were ordered back to port.

'Sir, a woman and three men are coming on board. One of them has handcuffs on.'

'Bring them to my cabin, Mr Coe.'

'Sir, we have met the man with the handcuffs before Dartmouth.'

There was a knock at the door.

'Come in.'

Mr Coe opened the cabin door. Mrs Evans, Captain Williams and another man wearing side arms entered.

'Captain, I have taken the liberty of asking Mr Nelis to wait outside the cabin door.'

I glanced at Mrs Evans.

'Mr Coe, ask him to come in, please. Mrs Evans, a pleasure to see you again.'

'Likewise, Captain Farquhar. May I suggest that you take Mr Williams somewhere safe and secure. This gentleman will stay with him.'

Mervyn nodded. 'Yes, ma'am'. The three men walked out of the cabin door.

'Ted, could you please arrange for a cup of tea for Mrs Evans? Earl Grey tea, milk and sugar, preferably sugar lumps.' Ted disappeared.

'Now, what are you up to Jackie, and what do you want me to do?'

'You have a good memory, William, and you are very suspicious. I get the impression you don't trust me.'

'You are right Jackie.'

'We found our friend Mr Williams has been passing information on to somebody in our high command, and he has also been giving that information to our good friend Mr Hitler.' She grinned mischievously. 'So we have suggested to Mr Hitler that our good friend Mr Williams knows more about our nuclear capabilities and their advancement in this area than anybody else. So now our good friend Mrs Henderson has arranged for us to bargain. We give them a spy, and we get back one of ours. A nice little swap.'

Just then, there was a knock at the door. Ted walked in with a steward carrying a tray of tea and biscuits.

Mrs Evans spoke, 'Stay Ted. You are soon going to meet up with another vessel, a fishing trawler. They will exchange our friend for their friend, and you can bring our friend back here. William be careful; they are becoming very desperate. Now I must go. Here are your orders and papers with all the information you will need. Oh, yes, by the way, I spoke to my superiors about you buying *Daisy May* when the war is over. They said yes. We will work out the details later. Good afternoon gentlemen.'

'Good afternoon, Mrs Evans. Mr Coe, ask Mr Nelis to report to me.'

When Mervyn came in, I explained everything to him and read through my orders.

'Navigational Officer, Mr Collins report to me, please.

'We are going to meet a fishing trawler here.' I pointed to a spot on the map. 'This is the course and the suggested speed so that we can reach them on time. Thank you, Mr Collins. Mr Coe, let's get her on her way. Cast off.'

We were back at sea again. I went to the doctor's office.

'How are you, Doc?'

'Still, a little bit dazed and confused by the little holiday you took me on. Like all holidays, you wonder if it was all just a dream or something else.'

I shook my head. 'Well, Doc, we have another little adventure for you. We will be picking somebody up.'

His face went serious. 'We have picked up people before, and they've been in quite a bad way.'

'Yes, Doc, I know, but I thought I had better prepare you. We are doing a prisoner exchange. We have a man in the brig and I don't want him doing anything silly, so please keep an eye on him for me. Is Mr Nelis' shoulder all right now?'

'Yes, it's going quite well.' He frowned at me. 'How is she?'

'They tell me she's all right. I get the impression that mentally, she's had enough.'

'Yes, I can quite understand.'

Two days later we were out at sea again.

'Sir! There is a fishing trawler!'

I picked up my binoculars. 'Trawler, be damned! She is a spy ship! See the wires in her rigging? Long distance communications radio. Mr Coe, let's keep inside of her, so we're in between her and land. Too close into shore for a submarine so if they want to give us a torpedo, they will sink their craft as well.'

We flashed Morse code with our light, and they gave us Morse code back; all nice and cosy. We exchanged our passengers. The captain on the fishing boat gave me a salute. It was from one captain to another; a sign of respect. I realised he did not want to be here either.

'Mr Coe, full speed ahead to starboard.'

I looked at my watch. Eight degrees hard to port; another eight degrees hard to starboard. Then we saw them. Three torpedoes. But the submarine captain's timing was wrong. He thought I was going to be predictable and not keep a steady pattern, and so he had wasted three torpedoes. Now we knew where he was, and our speed put us out of his range.

'Sir, the doctor wishes to speak with you on the intercom.'

'Yes, Doc, how can I help you?'

'Would you have a moment to come down to the infirmary, sir?'

The way he said it, I didn't hesitate.

'Yes, Doc, I will be straight down. Mr Coe, take command.'

When I walked into the infirmary, I saw a young lady, half sitting up but strapped down to the bench. I gasped and said in frustration, 'Margaret, we get you out of one frying pan, and you jump into another!'

I walked up to her and pulled her head into my chest.

'What have they done to you, you beautiful, courageous soul? I would have thought Norway was enough for you. How is she Doc?'

'She is very dehydrated. I think she's been kept awake for long hours. They have given her drugs as you can see from her eyes and the colour of her skin and hair. I think she's been beaten. When she came in, she was very, very lethargic and I was apprehensive. Captain, when we returned from Norway, did you see any relationship between Margaret and Trevor?'

'No, I was too busy. But I did see them talking together.'

'Well, as I said, I was apprehensive for her future. Then Trevor turned up, and when she saw him, the light came back into her eyes and the colour of her skin changed. I recalled Lesley's reaction when you were with her in the cabin.'

'We assign Trevor to you, and I'm sure you'll put him to good use when you feel the time is right. Put Margaret in the Visitor's Cabin.'

I went back onto the bridge.

'Signal to Command. Three fingers.'

I was sitting at my desk in my cabin, going through my logbook reports and other documents, getting all my paperwork in order. There was a knock at the door, and Margaret came in. She was like a breath of fresh air.

'It's good to see you up and about.'

She smiled. 'The doctor doesn't know. I was in the other cabin.'

'Would you like a cup of tea, Margaret?'

'No, thank you, Captain. That's all Trevor seems to do; one cup of tea after another. He's so sweet and kind.'

I chuckled. 'We are talking about the same Trevor?'

I saw her eyes flicker to the sketch of *Daisy May* on the wall. 'Where is *Daisy May* now, Captain?'

'As far as I know, Dartmouth in Devon. And Jacko? I pray he is with *Daisy May* and that Lesley is safe.'

'It was so good to see Mervyn. You exchanged me for a German spy?'

'You realise Margaret, I know nothing, but yes, I think somebody in High Command in the British system is in a little bit of trouble with the German High Command.'

'Captain, I also know nothing, but I told them what they wanted to hear. They desperately wanted their men. We don't know anything, do we, Captain?' She walked over to me and put her arms around my neck and hugged me. 'Thank you for looking after me. I think I had better get back to my cabin before Trevor misses me.' And with that, she was gone.

The phone rang. 'Yes? What is it?'

'Captain, there is a heavily coded message for you from Command.'

'Bring it to my cabin.'

I read through the document and picked up the phone. 'Mr Coe, would you ask Mr Nelis and Mr Collins to come to my cabin?'

The British submarine captain was sitting at his desk looking at the picture of his wife and children. He was feeling weary and homesick. Suddenly he felt a vibration go through the submarine and he then heard a loud squealing noise. In a few seconds, he was standing at his command post.

'All Stop. Damage Report. Up Periscope.'

There were no ships in sight and no floating objects.

A voice behind him said, 'Sir, Damage Report.'

'Yes.'

'Something between the prop shaft and the mechanical workings in the gearbox has let go.'

'Do we still have power generators and air tanks?'

'Yes, sir.'

'How bad is it? Do we still have propulsion forward and astern?'

'Yes, sir, but for how long I do not know.'

The Captain studied his chart. 'This is where that German destroyer went aground on the sandbanks. If we can get in between one of those sandbanks at the right depth, we could hide until I can find out what we can do. But give us snorkel depth for oxygen.'

Bill studied the papers briefly again.

'Jarrett, do you remember these coordinates?' I tapped my finger on the piece of paper.

'Yes, sir. That is where the destroyer went aground.'

'On the same bank, well partly, there is a British submarine. They want us to rescue the crew and scuttle the submarine.' Ted gave a little whistle and raised his eyebrows. 'Yes, Ted, dangerous waters. We don't know who is lurking there. They must think I like those sandbanks. Mervyn I nearly wrecked *Daisy May* on those sandbanks, and we lured a German destroyer onto them. The German captain had to wait for high tide. He slewed his destroyer back and forth, using his props to blast the sand away, and when they returned to their home port, they found that they had wrecked the hull. It was so badly twisted that she could not return to sea; They stripped her. I don't like things in threes. OK, gentlemen, let's get on our way.'

Early in the morning of the second day we reached our coordinates.

'Mr Coe, I do not want to stop. I don't want to give anybody a target so have two boats ready, both with a bag of incendiary bombs. Get everybody you can spare on deck with binoculars. We are looking for periscopes and aircraft. If a German pilot spotted us and they get above that submarine, they will be able to see her. Man all guns.'

The ship's sirens went off. 'Man your stations! This is not a drill! This is not a drill!'

The captain of the British submarine ordered periscope up. He spotted the British Navy ship.

'Prepare to surface.'

The sand had pushed itself up alongside the submarine wedging it tightly. There was a hissing sound, and bubbling and gurgling, but the submarine did not move.

'Give me more pressure in her tanks, Number One.'

They all watched the gauge rise; then it touched the red. They all waited for the Captain to give the order, but the Captain kept staring at the gauge. They felt the submarine shudder.

A voice said, 'We could damage her tanks sir', but the Captain did not answer him. The submarine slowly moved more and more, until finally, she popped to the surface. Everybody sighed with relief. One man had sweat pouring from his forehead and was wiping it with a rag.

'Let's see if we can go astern Number One.'

'Yes, sir, slow astern.'

They could hear the cracking and tearing sound from her mechanical workings.

'Everybody on deck! Leave all your belongings behind.'

'Sir periscope port side. He is right in the middle of the same sandbank.'

'Prepare the rescue boats. Mr Coe do not launch them until we are sure it's her.'

We made three passes in a zigzag pattern; then we saw her come to the surface, slowly, coming astern. All the crew cheered.

'Go ahead, Mr Coe, let's pick them up!'

The crew, already on the submarine's deck listened to the strange noises coming from their vessel. Suddenly there was one almighty crack and its gearbox split in two.

'All, stop! Shut everything down.'

The captain felt great sadness. 'We've been together for a long time. I have hated you and cursed you, but now I find myself in love with you. You have served us well.' He went into his cabin, picked up the pictures of his wife and children, his logbook and letters and walked out. He climbed the ladder into the waiting rescue boat and then turned and saluted his submarine.

The two bags of incendiary bombs were placed in the submarine, and as the captain went onto the bridge of the destroyer, there were two loud thuds. The submarine shook. Nobody said a word as they watched her slowly slip into the water and disappear.

'Mr Coe, let's get on our way. Captain, if you would come to my quarters along with your First Officer.'

Once settled in my quarters, I said, 'Please sit down gentlemen. Rest assured we will get you and your crew home. We are now heading straight back home. I'm happy that you haven't lost any of your crew.'

'Have you had any news of the war?'

'No, we haven't.'

'I have heard that Germany is in a mess. The Russians and Americans are nearly in Berlin. France has been liberated, but it is at the cost of many lives on both sides.'

I noticed his First Officer looking at the picture of *Daisy May*.

'The name of that sailing vessel is *Daisy May*.' They both stared at it for a while. 'Where did you get this sketch, sir?'

'One of my crew sketched it and gave it to me a long time ago.'

The submarine captain turned and stared at me for a few moments. 'We followed the *Daisy May* at the beginning of the war, from Cape Town to Britain.'

I was puzzled, but I was smiling inside. I thought to myself, *So you were the big fish following us.* I grinned and said, 'You did a beautiful job on the submarine, and that torpedo boat was great. A wonderful job! I would say three fingers.'

They both stood staring at me. 'Now, Captain, you have us a little bit confused.'

I felt a deep sense of pride. 'I am the captain of the *Daisy May*.'

'Well, I'll be damned! Where is *Daisy May* now?'

'She is tied up in a harbour, safe and secure.'

'She was a nightmare; a phantom! One minute she was there, the next she was gone. We worked out that if we stayed on the same course, she would always come back.'

The First Officer asked me, 'What was your cargo, Captain?'

'Wool bales and muttonbird oil. That's what it looked like to me, and that is what was on my shopping list.' I touched my nose with my finger. 'It was certainly something valuable. I want to thank you and your crew for looking after us.'

'Who was the man sitting on top of the wheelhouse?'

'That was Jacko.'

'We always believed he could see us; he spooked the whole crew.'

I laughed. 'Jacko spooks everybody.'

'One day I was watching him through the periscope, I turned to high magnification, he had blankets over his head and shoulders, and he seemed to be staring straight at me. He slowly raised his right arm; it appeared that he was pointing straight at me. A cold shiver went down my spine as I've never experienced before. There was a breeze in the submarine which I couldn't explain, it wasn't just me who had this experience, and others had felt it too. I yelled out down periscope, and it had vanished.'

I laughed. 'He spooks everyone, he even spooked me many years ago, but that's Jacko.'

'The man who jumped overboard and hit one of the lifeboats?'

'We believe he was a German spy. He is the one the torpedo boat wanted. But of course, history will say the *Daisy May* did not exist, and you did not follow her!'

We arrived back in port. Mrs Evans was on the wharf waiting for Margaret. I stood on the bridge, staring down at them. Margaret looked up and waved goodbye. Mrs Evans just nodded her head, and they were gone.

Soon we were back out patrolling again. I was sitting in my chair on the bridge when the radio officer brought me a piece of paper. He was grinning and yet I thought he was going to cry at the same time. I read the sheet of paper. I read it again and again.

'Mr Coe, could you give me the intercom, please?'

I grasped the intercom in my shaking hands and said, 'Now hear this, now hear this! Germany has surrendered. Germany has surrendered. The war is over. I repeat, the war is over!'

We played the British National Anthem, and everybody stood to attention. When the anthem had finished, I softly sang Waltzing Matilda to myself.

Over the next few months, we recovered troops from strange places and returned them to Britain. We helped with the clean-up operation or acted as a messenger ship.

When we returned to port and were tied up alongside many other navy vessels, my battleship was just one of many. She faded into them and seemed to disappear. Soon I was back in the barracks where I had started, and along with other sea captains, we were debriefed. I was one of many. Was it a dream? Did it happen? Or was it just a frightening nightmare?

CHAPTER 22

I was content because I now had everything I had ever wanted.

A voice startled me, 'Captain Farquhar, you have been ordered back to London. There is a car waiting for you, sir.'

And there I was, back in that same hotel room as before.

'You have an appointment at nine o'clock, sir. The car will be here for you in the morning.'

London was a mess with bombed and burned out buildings; I asked the driver to stop the car. I got out and leaned on the mudguard. What I saw made me smile. Big Ben was still there, standing tall and straight, defiantly ringing his bells. The Houses of Parliament and Tower Bridge, there as they've always been through time. I could see the drawbridge opening to let a vessel pass underneath it. The Thames seemed to be flowing as it always did. I could see the Tower of London, where so many people over the centuries had lost their heads. Even one spy was executed there during the war. I walked around for a bit and saw that Paddington and Victoria Stations were as busy as ever. People were putting up their stalls, selling hot soup and food.

One elderly lady said to me 'Cuppa tea love?' She looked at my uniform, 'Captain, I hope you gave them buggers a bad time, we showed them a thing or two, didn't we?' Churchill was right 'Britons will never be slaves' I smiled as she scurried off to serve someone else.

There were horses and carts, men and women sorting out bricks, separating the good ones which could be reused, from the broken ones. Men with big dollies thumping rubble into holes in the road, others were laying bluestone cobbles. London was alive, she was defiant and proud, and she would not be beaten. The children of London had been protected. They were sent into the countryside, to farms and villages where they were safe from the bombings. And there, standing so proud was the majestic St. Paul's Cathedral, as though it had been protecting its city of London who was still here; she was alive, and she will return to her former self.

I got back into the car that had been slowly following me and tapped the driver on the shoulder. 'Right you are sir,' he said and we were on our way again.

I was waiting in the office at 9:05 the next morning. Mrs Evans and two gentlemen walked in. I stood up sharply and saluted the gentlemen with the cigars.

'No, no, William! Sit down! You did some remarkable work for us, and I appreciate you looking after our people from Scotland. It goes a long way with the voters you know. Would you consider staying on in the British Navy?'

'No, sir. I have seen enough, heard enough and experienced enough for one lifetime.'

'Yes, yes, I understand, So, you would like to buy the *Daisy May*?'

'Yes, sir, I would.'

'Then we will go hand in hand. I need the public's support. Do we sell her to you as salvage? Or as a seaworthy vessel with all the paperwork and engineers' certificates? However, the British Government needs to get food supplies to outlying ports. What if we give you a contract to deliver these supplies? We would give you *Daisy May*, but you will need to pay for all the expenses.' He did not wait for my reply. 'Trust me William and sign the papers.'

I did not hesitate. I signed the papers.

'Good man William! Good man!' He turned and walked towards the door, and as he left, I heard him say to the other gentleman, 'Well, it may get some votes yet.'

I turned to Jackie Evans. 'Where is Lesley?'

Jackie replied, 'She is where she is happiest. Lesley is where she can mend, and she has been there for some time. You will see her soon.' She put her hand out and said, 'Your clothes are in that bundle. Thank you, William, thank you. Very few men have your strength, courage, high principles and your unbending integrity. Goodbye William and I pray they never send you to war again.' She turned and walked out of the office.

Soon I was back on the train heading towards Devon, to Paignton in Torbay. It felt as if I was going back through a time tunnel, waking up after a dream. What did I have to show for it? I was back in my civilian clothes. I had the same swag that I had left with. But I did now have the leather satchel and in this satchel were some documents to say I had been awarded a medal. But at what price? There was also the clip with *Australia* on it. I reached into the leather satchel, took out my clip, and pinned it on my collar. I watched England slide past the window with its small villages and fields – not paddocks like in Australia. These fields were small and many shades of green, like a patchwork quilt.

I changed trains and before I knew it, I was back where I had once been, so long ago. I felt sad, and my soul felt as if it was a hundred years old. I was so very weary. As I walked down to the harbour, I noticed how busy the place was. Wherever you looked, people were putting things back together. I got to the harbour and looked for *Daisy May*. Then I saw her, and I was taken entirely by surprise. I had to blink several times. She was tied up at the wharf on the opposite side of the river. But she was not like the old *Daisy May*. Her hull was freshly painted a beautiful royal blue; her rigging masts were all freshly varnished, other bits and pieces were painted black and white. I stood staring at her; she was so beautiful.

A voice startled me, 'Are you coming on board the ferry?'

'Yes, yes.'

The man chuckled. 'She certainly looks a lady doesn't she?'

'Yes, she certainly does.'

'She did a great job bringing the boys home from across the Channel; all the other little boats as well. My wife and I are very proud of her. She brought our two boys back. When the war ended, we had no work but when a bit of money turned up out of nowhere, and with paint supplies left over from the war, we had enough to pay someone to paint her. It was our way of saying thank you. Do you know anything about her?'

'Just a little.'

I could not take my eyes off her. She was beautiful. Unfortunately though, as the ferry reached the other side of the river, a building blocked my view. I walked off the ferry, turned right between the shops and there she was again. I felt like running to her. The tears started to flow, and I had trouble seeing where I was going. I heard a voice within me cry, *Daisy, Daisy, Daisy May! I'm home!*

And there he was, sitting cross-legged on top of the wheelhouse. Cat was sitting next to him. Jacko slowly stood up like a ballet dancer and stood staring at me; I couldn't stop staring at him. A thousand unspoken words passed between us. At last, I walked up the gangplank. Cat was there waiting for me. Time had taken its toll on poor Cat. I put my swag and leather satchel down, went down on one knee and put my hand out to him and he jumped into my arms. As I held Cat my tears flowed. I had been away far too long.

Jacko picked up my swag, then the leather satchel. He stared at the satchel for a few moments; then his eyes caught mine. We both felt sadness. Then that cheeky grin stretched across his face and he did one of his little dances. He shouted at the top of his voice, 'Look what the Cat brought home this time!'

Les's head appeared out of the galley; Ted appeared out of the wheelhouse, Trevor came out of nowhere with Jarrett. They all started laughing and shouting. I embraced them all. Sticky buns, jam doughnuts and coffee, appeared from nowhere, as usual.

I flung my arms around Les. 'Have you been keeping well, my father?'

'Yes, my boy, I have.' His whole body seemed to be shaking. 'It's all over now, son; it's all over.'

Then I sensed her. I could smell her; I could feel her energy. I knew she was there and my body came alive; all my senses were sharpened. I turned around sharply and there she was. She was looking at me very seriously but with warmth also. I was frozen for a few moments. The war had taken its toll on her; she seemed to be a little shorter, a little thinner. Then I realised how much I loved her. I have never actually even held her. I have been around her but never held her. Instinctively I put my right hand out, my arm extended. I slowly walked up to her and put my arms gently around her. She pushed her head into my chest, and I gently squeezed her.

'Jackie told me she'd put you somewhere safe where you could mend. I know Jacko and Les would have looked after you well.'

She regained control of herself and said, 'Yes, like two fussy brothers; overprotective! I hope you're not going to be the same.'

'I've got bad news for you. I am going to be worse!' and I squeezed Lesley tightly. Then I heard another woman's voice.

'Don't I get any attention?'

I turned around, and there was Margaret. I embraced them both.

'Margaret, what are you doing on board *Daisy May*?'

'I'm with my husband.'

'Your husband?'

Trevor walked up alongside her.

'Well, that makes sense, doesn't it? You certainly didn't waste any time, did you?'

The next morning Captain Jack Fox approached *Daisy May* with another man who was wearing a fancy suit. But Foxy stopped him before they came on board. 'Before you go further, you must ask permission to come on board.'

The man raised his eyebrows and looked a little startled. 'I beg your pardon? Do you realise who I am?'

Foxy stood a little bit straighter. 'I know who you are, but Captain Farquhar is the captain of this vessel!' Foxy was grinning to himself '*I will put this cocky little sod in his place!*' The man looked annoyed.

'May I have permission to come on board?'

I looked at Foxy's eyes and that playful grin. 'Only if Captain Fox vouches for you.'

I saw the arrogance in the man. Foxy smiled at me. 'May I present Mr Ferris from the Ministry?'

I put my hand out to shake his hand, which was weak and clammy. 'Come into the wheelhouse.'

Ferris spread his papers out on the bench; he was enjoying his authority.

'If you would like to read these documents and the conditions.' There was a mocking arrogance in the way he said it. I read through the papers carefully. A lawyer had definitely put these documents together.

'Mr Ferris, if you would excuse me for a moment.'

I went through to my cabin, took out my bag of papers and my medal. I went back into the wheelhouse and placed the medal in front of Mr Ferris with a firm gesture.

'I have not yet been discharged from the Navy and those other papers I signed in front of Winston Churchill, so I would strongly suggest you put those documents right. I am quite sure Captain Fox will let you use his office. If you wish to argue with me…' and I tapped the medal with my finger. 'Put the conditions of sale as it is in my documents. Good morning. I expect to see you at three o'clock this afternoon.'

Mr Ferris scooped up the papers and disappeared down the gang-plank, but he must have heard Foxy and Jacko laughing.

Jacko said, 'Don't mess with an Aussie!'

Foxy picked up the medal and looked at me. 'Bill, I have one just like this, but I've never worn it.'

'Foxy, when I was presented with this, there was another one, but I never knew who it was for. Now I know, it was you!'

'Bill, I have been asked by Command to tidy up any loose ends. I've also been speaking to Mrs Evans, and she tells me that the *Daisy May* never left Melbourne, that she never came into Dartmouth. It will remain one of those secrets. As a consequence, the three lifeboats from *The Castle* have been moored up the river. According to our records, they don't exist, but the records do show there was a vessel moored here during the war. I have had one painted a Navy grey, and the number three painted on it. The records will show that it was moored here during the war on standby. The other two have been painted blue, and with the help of our lawyer friend, the papers will show they belong to the rowing club. There are only three of us who know the truth. Would you agree with that, Bill?'

I grinned at him, winked, and put my hand on his shoulder. 'What lifeboats Foxy?'

Foxy gave a deep sigh. 'What do we leave behind us to say we've been here?' He thought for a moment. 'I'm going to put a brass plaque in Number Three's hull, just two simple words – *The Castle*.'

'Then Foxy, could you do something for Jacko and me? On one of the rowing boats paint the name, *Diamantina* and on the other could you paint, *Heavens Above*'.

Foxy put his hand on my shoulder. 'Consider it done, Bill. Now, these papers are regarding your cargo which will arrive tomorrow; the first to arrive will be the last off. Nobody knows what your cargo is, or its destination and the fewer people know, the better, but I think food is more valuable than gold at the moment. We have many other stores here which are left over from the war. We are to equip you with any-thing you require, so a list would be very helpful.'

I could just make out what was written on the bottom of this docu-ment. It was in very scrawly handwriting: *Trust me*, And it was signed: *Cigar*.

I burst out laughing, 'I wonder whether he understood that I am an Australian, and therefore, I cannot vote for him.' The sly old fox. I gave him a salute.

Foxy looked at what I was reading and chuckled out loud. 'I get the picture. Not all of it, but most of it.'

I went through the shipping manifest. We were going to Aberdeen in Scotland then back around to Liverpool. My mind was going back to work. I was back on *Daisy May*, and I had to find my cargo to make money. If we went back to the Shetland Islands and picked up another shipment of handicrafts, that would help those people out and put some money in the bank. I explained my thoughts to Foxy.

'Bill, we have stores here we will not use that the people in the Shetland Islands could use. Can you give me a list of what you will need? I'll sort out the other.'

'OK, Foxy. I had better send a telegram to the Shetland Islands and make sure my new cargo will be ready.'

'Good idea, Bill.'

I knew I was home again. The game had changed. It was my game. The lawyer turned up again at precisely three o'clock. Foxy, Jacko and Ted came into the wheelhouse. I read through the documents.

'Jacko, sign here.'

I signed the papers. Ted and Foxy witnessed my signature and cosigned.

'Thank you, gentlemen. Jacko, you and I now own *Daisy May*. We have bought her from the British Government. We have been commissioned to deliver cargo to various ports so we will load our cargo tomorrow and leave at first light the following day. Ted have *Daisy May* prepared, but before you leave Ted, I have something to say. Please, wait.'

Foxy just looked at me. 'I'll book a restaurant for tonight.'

'We will look forward to that, Captain.'

Foxy and the lawyer left.

'Ted, from now on you will get your wage and a cut of the cargo as does Les. Jacko and I will pay for all the expenses.' We all shook hands.

'It's a deal. It's a deal.'

Lesley walked into the wheelhouse, and I put my arm around her. Jacko placed an envelope on the bench then put his watch in the leather pouch on top of that. I stared at the envelope. 'Where did you get that envelope, Jacko?' I noticed Ted looking at him thoughtfully.

'Well, they wanted *Daisy May* to pick up soldiers from across the Channel, but they didn't have a skipper that understood *Daisy May*. So, they said to me, "*If you can answer some questions we would like to use you to skipper the Daisy May.*" I answered all of their questions. They said that nobody had responded to those questions as quickly as I did. I don't think that they were impressed, but they had to admit that I was good because I didn't get any wrong – except when they talked about steam. I said I didn't like steam, so they gave me a question about *Daisy May* or any other sailing vessel. So now, I am a skipper!'

Ted's voice broke in, 'You wombat! You have a skipper's ticket!'

Jacko gave a little grin and a little dance. 'Would you like me to show it to you?'

'No, wombat. Just remember I am the second-in-command of this vessel. I got my skipper's ticket before you. Who taught you? Who put up with you? I'll tell you what, the first one up to the top of the main-mast wins.'

They both ran out of the wheelhouse, and suddenly they were on either side of the mainmast, climbing the rigging, shouting insults at each other. Jacko was quicker; he was younger, agiler and his body was a lot more flexible. He reached the very top of the mainmast laughing and shouting and doing his funny little dance with his legs wrapped around the mast. Ted was halfway up, panting, huffing and wheezing. He had lived a good life on board a battleship with plentiful food, but not the healthy food Les served.

I put my hands on top of my head and shouted out, 'What have they done to me? What have they done? I'm going to have to put up with this for years!'

Then I heard Lesley starting to laugh. Her laugh got more profound, and the tears began to flow down her cheeks. Ted, Les and Jacko were suddenly there, and I heard Les say, 'She's let go; she'll be all right now. She's let it all go, all the horror of war.' I put my arms around Lesley and held her tightly. I felt a pain deep within me, but the pain was for her. *Daisy May* was doing her magic trick.

Les put his hand on my shoulder. 'She will be all right; she will be fine.'

'Lesley, please come with me to the stern.'

I stood with both my hands on the baulk works railing, looking out over the stern. Lesley was standing alongside me. 'Lesley, I have never actually known many women. In my younger days I did go ashore and spend some time with women in ports. But when I became captain of the *Daisy May*, she came first. When we were leaving Port Phillip Bay and I saw you, I had a strange feeling inside that I could not understand.'

When you were working with the crew, talking with them, being a part of them; when you were working with Les in the galley, laughing, and chatting with flour all over your face, there was a longing inside of me that I'd shut out many years ago. You opened that door back up. I had trouble getting control of myself. Jacko kept telling me what it was when he called you "Gidgee", but I refused to listen to him. He tried to let me know there was a lot more to you, but again, I didn't hear. When you took command, I was confused. I kept thinking back to how you looked after Colin; the way you just did it, without question. I dwelt on the chess games, the long conversations we had in the night.

But when you walked down that gangplank, something inside of me broke, and I felt so alone. Then when I saw you at the Admiralty and the naval barracks, I just wanted to hold you tight. Every time you came back from a mission and you were hurt and bruised, I wanted to be there with you, to put things right, but I could not. When Mrs Evans gave me the documents and Jacko was telling me you were in trouble, big trouble, I was furious. Jacko was in danger. They had used him, and they were abusing him. But deep down I knew he was with you and he would protect you; no-one else could keep you safe as well as Jacko.

When I knew Mervyn was with you, I had a profound sense of relief. But when I saw you lying there on that crude bed, my heart broke, and I realised then that I loved you more than anything else in this world.'

I was crying, but I didn't care. I turned around and faced her. Lesley was also crying. 'Lesley, I need you so desperately in my life. I want to be a part of you.' I reached out and touched her face with the palm of my hand.

She reached up and pressed her hand to my face.

'Bill, when I first came on board *Daisy May*, I knew I was in love with you. I had never met a man like you. Every time I saw you, my heart would break. When I talked to Jacko, it was as if I was with you, but I felt as if I had betrayed you. And when I thought my life was finished, you were there.

'Jacko and my beautiful Les, along with Ted and Mervyn were there to protect me. When I knew I was back on board *Daisy May*, I knew I was safe.' Lesley started to sob; her whole body shook. I put both my arms around her and held her tight, and then I put my lips to hers and kissed her as gently as I could.

'Bill, I must tell you something first. I don't know whether you remember but we met on a Cattle station on the Diamantina River. My father was Frank Thompson. We first met on our house veranda, you had to take the mail into town for dad.'

I stared at her, my memory racing back through time. 'Yes, I remember. That was so long ago.'

'When I was playing chess with Jacko he somehow got into my mind and saw my deepest secrets. My dad died of a heart attack when I was fourteen years old. My sister and I were shattered, he was a real dad to us, he tried to prepare us for the hard life working and living on a Cattle station. He always talked to us; always explained everything.

'Dad had married an Aboriginal lady. She was the sweetest, kindest person you could ever meet. She never played politics with him, Dad idolised her, she was always there for him and she was my mum.'

The tears started to swell up in Lesley's eyes. The family in England and the officials in Australia decided that we would be better off in

England with one of my dad's sisters. My sister and I were educated here. My mother's name is on my birth certificate, but it doesn't say that she was an aboriginal. They tell me Mum went back to her people and died of a broken heart. Being with Jacko, his personality and his funny ways brings back memories of my mother.

In my heart I am very proud to say that I am half Aborigine and I'm going to have that put on my birth certificate. She was my mum and she belongs to me. I am very proud of her, she loved my dad, she loved me and she loved my sister. She loved us all, and I will always remember her arms around us telling us stories of the time before the time, before the time. Bill, tonight, I will show you how much I love you.' She pressed her body tight into mine.

Jacko, who was in the wheelhouse watching, gave one of his little dances and said in his language, with a small laugh, 'Who will be in command tonight? I think it will be Gidgee.'

Les lifted his apron and wiped the tears away from his eyes as he watched Bill and Lesley on the stern. He turned around and looked at his Aga stove and thought, 'I have never cooked a wedding cake on an Aga stove. What would I need? Eggs, flour, fruit, marzipan? Where do I get them?' He went looking for a suitable baking dish, and he giggled to himself, 'Which Captain would marry them?' This could be interesting.

That night we all went out to dinner with Foxy. We went to the local pub where they had an Irish band and a few girls dancing an Irish jig.

Trevor made us all laugh, he sat there mesmerised. If there had been flies in that pub Trevor would have swallowed them all. Margaret sat there looking at him with her arms intertwined with his. It was one of those special moments. Jacko could not contain himself. There he was dancing, but in his mind he was back in the desert, doing his little dance. Everyone was fascinated by the way he did it. I was so proud of my brother.

At eight o'clock the next morning the trucks started to arrive.

There was a crew of Navy men loading the cargo on board. Ted and the others were kept busy. Foxy and a little well-dressed man carrying a briefcase walked up the gangplank. Jacko noticed him and went and shook his hand; they seemed to be the best of friends. Jacko, with a big grin all over his face, slapped me on the shoulder. 'Skipper, this is Mr Dolan. He is my friend, and he is a solicitor.'

The man put his hand out and shook mine. 'Captain Farquhar, I have been commissioned to look after your insurance. I am very fond of this funny little man. He rescued my sons from across the Channel and brought them home. My wife and I owe him so much. Now Captain, if we can go into your wheelhouse?'

He spread the papers out on the bench. 'Before we start, I worked for a particular department during the war, and we have the same friend, so that makes this more complicated. *Daisy May* does not exist. She entered a port in Australia, but there are no records of her leaving. But, as you know, strange things happen in a war, so *Daisy May* is in somebody's imagination.' He tapped his nose with his finger.

'So, the question of her insurances. This cargo belongs to the British Government, they are the underwriters for it. *Daisy May* has a number painted on her bow, so she is still under the British Government, which means the government are the underwriters for *Daisy May*. Never remove the number on her bow. This figure must always remain. So, if you and Jacko would sign these papers, I would be a very proud man to know I did my part as one of many parents to say thank you to *Daisy May* for my sons.'

Jacko and I signed the papers. Mr Dolan stepped back and looked very seriously at Jacko. 'I will always be your friend. Call me at any time. Now I must go and call Mrs Evans.'

He looked at me with a warm smile on his face, winked at me, and touched his finger on his nose. 'You are just in somebody's imagination!' He turned and disappeared down *Daisy May*'s gangplank.

I saw Michael at the top of the gangplank stop and look Daisy up and down, looking up at her masts and rigging. A warm smile spread across his face. He walked into the wheelhouse. '*Daisy May* is certainly a lady Skipper; she's looking great.'

'How are you, Michael?'

'Doing well Skipper, doing well. I'm staying in England. I have met a lady, and we've got a small business in Devon, just down the road from here. There is a lot of good work here, so I have just come to say goodbye.'

Ted, Jacko and Les were standing in the wheelhouse door. Ted spoke first.

'I suppose if you work with two hundred women, one must get you in the end. We are going to miss you, Michael.'

'I taught Trevor everything I know. I think he will be an excellent man. He knows *Daisy May*'s sails, her masts and her rigging, so I believe I'm leaving you in good hands. I'm going to miss the four of you, but I know you will miss me the most when you are in a gale, and I'm in a warm bed with a beautiful hot water bottle. And I know you will miss me the most when you want to have a nice warm bath, and you can't have it or when you are holding on to the mast with your fingernails! But I'll tell you this; I will always be with you because I will miss you and I will miss *Daisy May*. She has been my mother, and she will always stay a part of me.'

He turned and walked out of the wheelhouse. When he saw Trevor, he put both his arms around him. We don't know what he said to him, but they both seemed to be as one, as brothers. They walked together to the gangplank. Michael turned and looked at us, waved his hand and disappeared down the gangplank.

I walked up to Dominic and Philip. 'So, how are you two vagabonds?'

Philip replied, 'A lot happier now we're back on *Daisy May*'.

I looked at them both. They were still fit and ready for action, but when I looked at their faces closely I could see they were so much older. The war had taken its toll on them. I sensed Lesley behind me. She gently rested her head on my arm. I asked them, 'Where is Reno, what has happened to him? I know that he didn't return from one of your little holidays.'

The look on Dominic's face told me, with pain in his voice he said: 'He was an idiot; he was the best idiot I have ever known'.

Lesley's voice broke in to protect me from breaking the secrecy act.

'When the Lancaster bombers went into Germany and bombed the ordinance factories, railways, shipping yards and many other military installations, aerial photography could only show them so much so we were sent in to verify that these installations were indeed destroyed. We were working with the French underground network. The Germans didn't know we were there. We had completed our assignment and were on our way back to the submarine. The French were hiding us in a small village near the coast. Reno, being Reno was bartering with a man in a house for four bottles of wine. Before we knew what was happening there were Germans in the street, they were looking for the underground network. One or two of the Germans were firing their weapons at anything that moved. Reno noticed a young girl, about six years of age, in the courtyard, she was frozen with fear'.

Lesley's voice quivered at the memory that was with her and would never leave. 'Reno ran out of the doorway, grabbed the little girl and ran back to the doorway. As he was pushing the little girl through the open door a bullet hit him in the back.' She stopped talking for a moment and then raised her voice. 'He gave us that stupid little grin—he had saved the little girl—and then he collapsed down, dead in the doorway.

The Germans would never have known he was an Italian in the British Army fighting for what he believed. He is buried in the little churchyard in the village. The little girl and her mother place flowers on his grave, the inscription on his gravestone simply says *Reno, my Hero.* Philip said they couldn't put any more words as he was under the securities act and was not there! The French got us out and back to the submarine. Our mission had been completed.'

Dominic spoke in a low voice. 'He was my friend, the best friend a man ever had, we had big plans for the future, now I know the idiot is bartering with St. Peter for the best spots in Heaven, and I know he will get them with that silly grin all over his face.'

Tears started to flow. They were not just for Reno but all the others he had lost in the war. He walked over to the baulkworks and looked out over the harbour. Philip walked over and stood next to him. Lesley walked up behind Dominic, put her arms around his shoulders, and pressed her head against his. I don't know what she said to them. She was no longer Commander Lesley Johnson, she was just Lesley, with all the female feelings, emotions and compassion for those she loved and respected. I went back into the wheelhouse and left them together.

So my crew now were Jacko, my partner; Ted, my coxswain; Les, my cook; Trevor, my sail-maker and deckhands Lesley, Margaret, Philip and Dominic. Reno had not made it through the war. Jarrett, when he gets back to Australia will take over his father's position in the company. I think his mother is in for a shock. Terry is in his rightful place, looking after the estate. There's also Malcolm and Tommy, but I wanted one more.

'Permission to come on board, sir.'

'Mervyn, you certainly have my permission.'

Lesley raced forward and flung her arms around his neck.

'Mervyn, come and meet Les.' She led him away to the galley.

Just on daylight the next morning the tide was with us and we were ready to set sail again. Les brought me in coffee.

'Looks like I've lost my coffee cup for good, doesn't it Les?'

He didn't answer me; he had that sad, lost look in his eyes.

'What's wrong, Les?'

'Will we ever see Michael again, Skipper?' Michael had been with us for so long there was a profound sense of loss.

'I don't know Les. The cargo may bring us back to Devon, but I don't know what the future has in store for us. It's in the hands of the gods.'

Les hunched his shoulders and looked down at the deck.

'Yes, Skipper, everything is in the hands of the gods.'

He turned and walked back to his galley.

Jacko, Ted and Lesley walked into the wheelhouse.

'Good morning to you all! The tide is right, and all our paperwork is in order, so the time has come. Prepare to cast off. Set the flying jib, fore upper topsail and spinnaker on the mizzen mast. Philip, prepare the engine to start, but don't start it. I want to leave this port as if we had never been here.'

I saw Les on the stern. He had been the father to many sons, mending their aches and pains and listening to their sorrows and plans for their lives.

Daisy May was starting to glide down the Channel silently. She passed the ferry and where the *Mayflower* had left from all those years ago. We watched the houses on either side of the Channel, climbing higher and higher on the cliffs. As we passed the fort I saw a man with hunched shoulders with a hat on his head. He was smoking a cigar and alongside him stood Jackie Evans. The man took his hat off and waved it. I saluted him and then walked slowly to the stern.

There was a moderate wind from our starboard side. I shouted out, 'Mr Coe set all her sails.'

Daisy May's bow gently rose, and she tipped to the waves as she leaned over slightly. There was nothing to obstruct her; her hull was clean; there were no barnacles or weeds to hold her back. She was free, and she looked beautiful. Jacko was at the wheel, and I stood alongside him. I had my arm around Lesley, holding her tightly to my side. Cat was sitting on Colin's jacket on the bench; his pipe rested still on the windowsill. I watched the rays of the sun glittering on the new varnish on her decks. It seemed to illuminate her white sails. What more could a man ask for? I have it all.

Then I heard his voice in my head, *'You have made it Boy. You have made Daisy May come alive!'* Cat stood up and stared at me. I thought to myself, *'Yes, Colin's here.'*

Jacko turned around and grinned at me. 'He's always been here!'

'Jacko, you are a very spooky man!'

Whisky jumped up onto the bench and sat down alongside Cat and Cat rested his head on her neck. Jacko did one of his little chants and did that little dance he always does and held three fingers in the air.

www.ingramcontent.com/pod-product-compliance
Lightning Source LLC
Chambersburg PA
CBHW071454110726
47908CB00003B/609